His Own Most Fantastic Creation

Stories about H. P. Lovecraft

His Own Most Fantastic Creation

Edited by S. T. Joshi

Hippocampus Press

New York

"Captured in Oils," by Simon Strantzas, first published in *Aklonomicon*, edited by Ivan McCann and Joseph S. Pulver, Sr. (Aklo Press, 2012).

Published by Hippocampus Press
P.O. Box 641, New York, NY 10156.
www.hippocampuspress.com

Cover design by John Coulthart.

Hippocampus Press logo designed by Anastasia Damianakos.
First published 2020 by PS Publishing.

First US Edition, 2022
1 3 5 7 9 8 6 4 2
ISBN 978-1-61498-329-3 paperback

Contents

Introduction

That Howard Phillips Lovecraft himself—his life, character, opinions, even his family and the dozens of friends, colleagues, and correspondents he accumulated over his short lifetime—has become something of an icon in popular culture would have been inconceivable to the dreamer from Providence, Rhode Island, who at the time of his death in 1937 was convinced that he would be utterly forgotten, his works falling into the oblivion he felt they deserved. Perennially given to excessive modesty as to his own achievements, Lovecraft never had a book of his stories published in his lifetime, and it took the tireless work of both his friends and later disciples and scholars to grant him the high place he now holds in American and world literature.

There is now little doubt that his five dozen tales, long and short—not to mention his essays, poetry, and especially his thousands of surviving letters—are worthy of preservation and analysis. But it is largely those letters, which total nearly five million words, that have been instrumental in creating popular fascination with Lovecraft the man and all that he stood for. Those letters, aside from chronicling on a nearly daily basis his mundane activities, are extraordinarily revelatory in regard to the development of his philosophical and aesthetic outlook, his wide readings, his awareness of the political, social, and intellectual movements of his time, and his ever-burgeoning cadre of associates, whether in weird fiction or in other realms. Dozens of memoirs of Lovecraft by these associates have augmented our understanding of his outlook and temperament.

So a volume like this one—which seeks to present Lovecraft himself (or a figure resembling Lovecraft in greater or lesser degree) as a character in fiction—was perhaps inevitable. Even in his own day, Lovecraft appears to have begun fashioning an image of himself as a fictional character of sorts: a devotee of the eighteenth century, a preternaturally aged "grandpa" surrounded by a band of devoted followers, and one who combined a steel-cold intellect—he was a mechanistic materialist and atheist—with the aesthetic sensitivity of the pure artist who sought only "self-expression" with no thought of monetary remuneration.

Even Lovecraft's family members—such as his troubled father, Winfield Scott Lovecraft (who succumbed to syphilis when Howard was a boy), and his neurotic, overprotective mother, Sarah Susan Lovecraft—have become objects of fascination. Indeed, because Lovecraft's early life is less well documented than his later years, opportunities can be created for authors to propose what Lovecraft himself declared to be "supplements rather than contradictions" of the known facts. As early as the age of five, he was plagued by dreams of hideous winged creatures he called night-gaunts (the subject of Darrell Schweitzer's tale). His years as a gawky teenager, whose ill-health prevented regular schooling but whose interest in chemistry and astronomy led to his signature notion of "cosmicism," are the focus of John Shirley's story. Lovecraft's devotion to cats—now so well known that some of his more piquant utterances regarding felines can be found on websites and calendars—serves as the basis for Scott Wiley's touching narrative.

Lovecraft, by and large, did not lead an eventful life—few writers do—and, given the fact that he spent the bulk of his career in the tiny realms of amateur journalism and pulp fiction, he came into contact with relatively few famous figures of his own day. One of these was Harry Houdini, the escape artist (and also crusader against spiritualism) for whom he ghostwrote the story "Under the Pyramids" (published in *Weird Tales* as "Imprisoned with the Pharaohs"). There is an understandable tendency for authors of weird fiction to link these two highly contrasting individuals in a weird tale, as Donald Tyson and Jonathan Thomas have done in two remarkably divergent accounts. And Lovecraft's admiration for the "titans" of weird fiction of his own day—Arthur Machen, Lord Dunsany, Algernon Blackwood, and M. R. James—makes it tempting to imagine what might have happened if these writers from opposite sides of the Atlantic Ocean had met. Mark Howard Jones's poignant and symbolic tale does exactly that.

It is also tempting to imagine a supernatural causation for some of Lovecraft's most revolutionary weird conceptions, whether it be the invention of the extraterrestrial entity Cthulhu (and, by extension, the other bizarre entities that were the core of what later came to be called the Cthulhu Mythos) or the notion of psychic transference, as embodied in "The Thing on the Doorstep" and "The Shadow out of Time." Stephen Woodworth links Lovecraft with another distinctive New England writer, Charlotte Perkins Gilman (author of "The Yellow Wall-Paper"), in one of the most daring tales in this book. Donald R. Burleson imagines the possible ramifications of personality exchange on Lovecraft himself. Mark Samuels focuses on Lovecraft's creation of imaginary tomes of forbidden lore, while the stories by Jason V Brock, Richard Gavin, David Hambling, and myself supply broader ruminations on the origins of Lovecraft's revolutionary motifs or on the sources of his enduring fame. While eschewing Lovecraft himself as a character, the tales by W. H. Pugmire and Simon Strantzas exhibit figures who reveal strikingly Lovecraftian elements while probing the psyche of the man from Providence.

There was a time when Lovecraft was in danger of succumbing to the myths that he had himself partly fostered—the myth of the "eccentric recluse" who slept during the day and only ventured out at night; the myth of the gaunt, lantern-jawed neurotic consumed by racial hatred; the myth of the isolated dreamer who knew nothing of the contemporary world in which he lived. The exhaustive scholarship of the past several decades have demolished these myths while revealing the genuine sources for Lovecraft's beliefs and actions, and it is striking how little the authors in this volume have strayed from the known facts in portraying him in their various tales. Lovecraft the man has served as an inspiration for fiction writers as early as Edith Miniter ("Falco Ossifracus," 1921), Frank Belknap Long ("The Space-Eaters," 1928), and Robert Bloch ("The Shambler from the Stars," 1935) in his own day, as well as such later figures as Richard A. Lupoff (*Lovecraft's Book,* 1985), Peter Cannon (*The Lovecraft Chronicles,* 2004), and myself (*The Assaults of Chaos,* 2013). It is safe to say that he will continue to engage the imagination of authors, weird and otherwise, in the decades to come.

Death in All Its Ripeness

Mark Samuels

> Despite my solitary life, I have found infinite joy in books and writing, and am by far too much interested in the affairs of the world to quit the scene before Nature shall claim me . . .—H. P. LOVECRAFT, 1916.

From the shadows, looking out of one of the windows in his study, he gazed at the first of the fall's russet-coloured leaves as they were scattered by heavy winds across the front lawn of 66 College Street. He had risen at noon, worked for several hours at a single stretch, and then relieved the cramping of his calf muscles by pacing the room before coming to pause at the window. He fixed his gaze across the middle distance. He tried to summon up within himself the old sense of adventurous expectancy at the sight of the rooftop vistas of Providence's colonial architecture but, with this concealed sunset, even all the glories huddled beneath it seemed commonplace in the grey early-autumn twilight. His gaze dropped again to the lawn and he saw a solitary cat, of tortoise-shell colour, padding purposefully through the grass and leaves below. The feline turned backwards and looked up, apparently by chance, at first appearing to acknowledge but then, nevertheless, dismissing with a haughty resolve of disdain the admiring gaze of its human observer.

He switched on the overhead triple-bulbed electric light, returned to his desk, and settled down in the semicircular, low-backed Victorian chair. Taking up the Waterman pen again, after shaking it vertically between ink-dotted finger and thumb, he continued making amendments to the manuscript of Mrs. Renshaw's *Well-Bred*

Speech. Her last letter, riddled with pleas of the job's supreme urgency, yet not so forward with a date of payment, rested face down alongside the lady's impossibly muddled magnum opus. He tried to overcome the warning hints of incipient eye-strain, the authoress's egregious errors in style and substance, and, most pernicious of all, the ever-present spectre of financial hardship, with the same resolution as was evinced by the feline harbinger.

Wrapping a blanket over his shoulders, he redoubled his efforts on the manuscript of *Well-Bred Speech*.

His fingers had stiffened in the chilliness of the room.

Working through most of the night on that tiresome document now lay in store for Howard Phillips Lovecraft.

It was a few days later, after having finally rid himself of the burden of Mrs. Renshaw's commission, that Lovecraft received the curious package. The brick-sized item was marked "private and personal"—and written in a crabbed script that rivalled his own for illegibility.

His aunt had brought it up to him at half past noon, when it was certain he, a night-person, would have risen from his bed.

He sliced the silver blade of an ivory-handled paper knife—his late grandfather Whipple's—along the top flap and removed the contents of the package. A sheet of paper, written on one side, was wrapped around banknotes. In confusion, he scanned the writing on the sheet rapidly. What began as a fan letter offered the prospect of another commission. To this end, said banknotes were enclosed, two hundred dollars' worth, provided solely to secure his undivided services.

Mrs. Renshaw, thought Lovecraft, not without irony, would have been appalled at this method.

The letter ran as follows:

> Dear Mr. H. P. Lovecraft,
>
> I read your good work—a lot—in *Weird Tales* and other magazines like that one. I found your home address through my involvement in *Weird Tales'* letter column, "The Eyrie." I need

your help bad with a true occult book like your *Necronomicon* but one based on real country life, not made-up city-folk garbage. This is sure to be a bestseller and will make us both a lot of bucks. I am sending cash to make sure you only work for me. My book is going to be called *The Animal Truth*.

Please reply ℅ Shinglemill River General Store, Pennsylvania.

Yours

Ezekiel Nantwich

A low groan escaped Lovecraft's thin lips. On the whole, he welcomed the attention of the admirers of his weird fiction who approached him, but there was always a significant percentage of overenthusiastic youths full of unrealisable schemes. Only recently he had had to explain gently to another correspondent, Willis Conover, that the actual attempt to write the *Necronomicon* would be doomed to failure, since the reality could not possibly measure up to the suggestive hints and limited partial glimpses that endowed a fictional tome with an aura of absolute terror. Even Bobby Barlow, of late, had occupied huge swathes of his time that he could ill afford on wildly overambitious and fantastical projects. He looked over the letter again. Still, at least this Ezekiel Nantwich personage seemed to recognise that the *Necronomicon* did not exist, unlike one or two enquiries he had received from youths asking how the volume might be obtained. Moreover, Nantwich indicated that he was actually writing a book and, although it could not conceivably compare to a fictional tome, Lovecraft's curiosity was nevertheless piqued. Perhaps, he thought, it was his slightly-cracked-in-the-head correspondent William Lumley who had suggested Nantwich should contact him.

He pondered the banknotes for a moment. It would be, he decided, completely unethical for him to consider accepting payment at this stage from this source. How, then, should he proceed so as not to cause offence? Perhaps he might be able to persuade Ezekiel Nantwich to write weird fiction as a genuine mode of artistic expression, rather than his concentrating on this other scheme. But if he got a peek at Nantwich's book, even just one or two chapters, he might have a much clearer idea as to how to proceed. He thought the matter over for a few minutes, took up his Waterman, and penned an immediate reply, casting a rueful glance at the small pile of accumulated, unanswered correspondence to which he had yet to attend. Then, putting the banknotes into a package of his own along with the letter he had dashed off, Lovecraft made his way, through the increasingly chilly Providence air, toward the nearest post office.

Ezekiel Nantwich grinned as he remembered the beating he had given his pa. The old fool had hollered like a mule after discovering Ezekiel had raided his stash of dollars under the mattress, taking the cash for himself. Pa had said he weren't rightly no son of his anyhow, and that made it robbery, plain and simple. Pa was still laid up, days later, and hadn't said anything else since. He must have learnt his lesson about who was the new boss on their farm; hell, the old critter could scarcely move around much beforehand anyway. Now all he did was lie down and stare. Hard to spot any difference. Hadn't even eaten for days. Well, let him rot there in his bunk.

Ezekiel continued chopping away with his long-handled hay knife at the stack, tied, and hauled bundles over to the cattle in the next field. He arranged them just outside the fence and then set them alight. The cattle stared dolefully at the flames and he chuckled to himself. Right funny it was. Then he sat down to rest and think for a while. He pulled out a quart bottle of hooch from the front pocket of his moth-eaten dungarees.

Wouldn't be much longer before slaughtering time. The haystacks were running out, and summer had given way to fall. Cattle need to die. Folk gotta eat them. That was nature's law. Can't be changed for no one.

The neck of the hooch bottle slotted in pretty fine between the front gaps in his dentition where two teeth had fallen out. The rest were reduced to rotten stumps. He swallowed the fiery liquid in great gulps.

Once he'd finished the bottle, Ezekiel tossed it aside, rolled up onto his feet, hitched up his dungarees, and set off for town, four miles away. He wanted to get to the general store to see if that Lovecraft fella had replied yet. Even if he hadn't, Ezekiel thought it prudent to lay in some more hooch.

The countryside around Shinglemill was mostly backwoods, and a single dirt track weaved its way from Nantwich Farm through a domed series of hills sheltered beneath the wilder heights of the Appalachians where brown bears roamed freely and drank from the waters of the west branch of the Susquehanna River.

Folk in those parts avoided Ezekiel if they could help it. Everyone knew he was an ornery cuss, especially when in his cups. So when he finally stumbled into the Shinglemill General Store its proprietor, Joshua Corwin, cursed under his breath, then corrected himself for taking the Lord's name in vain.

For a longish while, Corwin thought, Ezekiel had had a problem paying back what he owed on the account, though his pa (who'd not been around much lately) had always settled on time. Still, he'd been expecting that Ezekiel would show up soon; a package addressed to him from Providence, R.I., had arrived just the day before, waiting for him to collect it.

"How ya doing, Corwin?" Ezekiel hissed through the gap in his teeth.

"Got a package for ya," Corwin replied, not looking up from the desk.

"Sure, been thinkin' ya would have. Gonna take me a look around first, like," he replied.

Ezekiel made a beeline for the magazine stacks and rifled through the display for a few minutes. He always went away with the same old junk; the latest issue of some heathen trash called *Weird Tales* and any other lurid pulp magazine that captured his attention on the spur of the moment.

After he'd finished selecting half a dozen items of such reading material, he wandered up to the desk and put them on the counter.

Joshua Corwin wrinkled his nose at the offending covers but began to total up the cost.

"Also," said Ezekiel, "four bottles of the usual stuff."

Corwin could smell the same brand lingering on his breath.

"Still owe twenty bucks. Hate to mention it but . . ."

Ezekiel tossed some crumpled, dirty banknotes that he pulled from his dungarees on the counter.

"Don't forget my postal delivery," he said as the bottles and magazine were stuffed inside a large brown paper bag.

Corwin got him to sign a form and then handed it over.

It was from Lovecraft all right. It was postmarked "Providence."

"Got yersel' a penpal?" Corwin said as he slipped the package on top of the other items.

"Ain't something ya'd appreciate," Ezekiel said, cradling the bag under his arm and making for the exit. "Best stick to your Bible fairy tales. If ya know what I mean, and I think ya do."

Pa still hadn't stirred when Ezekiel returned to the farmhouse. He went straight to his room at the back of the dwelling, set down the bag next to his battered typewriter on the card-table, and slumped heavily onto the stool in front of it. He was up to a hundred and fifty single-spaced typed pages of *The Animal Truth*, despite having to fill in the letters "s" and "b" by hand.

The room was littered with a multitude of pulp magazines, the walls decorated with torn-off Margaret Brundage covers he'd tacked to the wooden slats. She was a fine artist, his favourite. It was a shame that *Weird Tales* editor Farnsworth Wright stopped answering his letters altogether. Ezekiel had begun accusing him of being badly wrong and biased against him on account of his just speaking his mind, but now that he had Lovecraft's services at his command things would be different.

He opened a bottle of hooch, drank a few mouthfuls, and then tore open Lovecraft's package.

The banknotes tumbled out.

Must be a mistake.

He read Lovecraft's letter once, then twice, then three times.

The fella was insane.

Someone must have gotten to him in advance and warned him off. Two passages stood out. Not only did he say

> though naturally flattered by your appreciation of my own fictional effusions, I cannot collaborate on the writing of a seriously intended work of occultism that purports to be factual; indeed, I once embarked upon a debunking of all such claims with the late Harry Houdini, the escapologist and sceptic, and his booking agent and associate of mine, Clifford Martin Eddy, Jr., though the work in question, *The Cancer of Superstition*, remains uncompleted and thus far has not seen publication

but he also then suggested:

> I should, however, be glad to have sight of your current manuscript and offer non-collaborative and non-remunerative advice and brief suggestions in this regard should you judge this reluctantly made decline of your proposal not unduly impertinent. By the way, why not try your hand at the creation of weird *fiction?*

Lovecraft was, in a sneeringly polite way, trying to give him the bum's-rush.

The Cancer of Superstition!

He couldn't possibly know what he was talking about.

Ezekiel glugged back more of the hooch.

Once Lovecraft had seen a few chapters of the book he'd be bound to change the tune he was whistling. Ezekiel began to sort out some sample chapters from amongst the carbon copy of his typescript.

A week later Lovecraft received a second package from Ezekiel Nantwich. As well as a half-crazed covering letter it also contained a grubby, liquid-spotted, and dog-eared carbon copy of numbered pages apparently selected at random from his typescript entitled *The*

Animal Truth. The offensive smell of liquor still clung to the dozen or so sheets of paper.

> Dear H. P.
> You don't get it yet, do you? I'm telling you this could be big for both of us. It was a bad mistake to return that money. It wasn't easy to get. Now I'm starting to get a little mad at you. The title of your Houdini book stinks. But I'll give you another chance, not that anyone ever gave me one. Read what I've written. It'll change your mind. Then tell me you're sorry and that you're willing to work with me after all.
> Ezekiel Nantwich

Lovecraft leaned back in his chair and sighed. He had a personal rule not to ignore correspondence, but it was clear that this was not a person whom he should encourage. This was obviously not just a case of an overenthusiastic youth harbouring unrealisable schemes, but rather one of outright egomania and untrammelled vanity. He had had quite enough experience of such people during the long period of his association with colourful personalities in the hothouse-feud atmosphere of the amateur press. This letter would have to go unanswered: the carbon copies returned without comment. Lovecraft did, however, look over some of the pages of this supposedly thwarted yet sure-fire commercial success.

The thing concerned a series of "case studies" of vicious wild animals living out in the woods who gradually began influencing the cattle on a local farm, warning them of the dangers of domestication and encouraging them towards malign actions against their human masters. All the creatures had been anthropomorphised, and talked and debated with one another, apparently vying for the crown of malevolence. It was impossible to determine where Nantwich obtained these "case studies," since he provided no historical sources. The wild animals were supposedly exiled familiars of some sort, left to their own devices, or so Nantwich suggested, after certain historically suppressed witch-trials (and the purging thereof) during the last decade of the seventeenth century. It was difficult to accurately trace the exact development of this "genuine" outbreak, not only because Lovecraft had been supplied solely with sample chapters, but also because the writing was surrealistic in the extreme. Stylistically, it was hopelessly ungrammatical, confused, repetitive, and riddled with innumerable—and very basic—spelling errors.

He found it difficult to believe the evidence of his eyes. He suspected an elaborate prank. But eventually he turned the carbon copies face down.

He glanced again at the accompanying letter. Such a communication as that, and sent to a relative stranger, could only be suggestive of serious organic derangement in its author. This Ezekiel Nantwich, whoever he was, required the attention of an alienist. He surely could not be fully aware of his actions. It was an unfortunate combination of chemicals and secretions operating to the detriment of an individual human organism, but it should not be permitted to perturb Lovecraft's own equanimity, and he resolved to forget it. Tomorrow he would return Nantwich's typescript without comment and that, he hoped, would be the end of it.

Ezekiel tramped through the woods all night, letting its essence get under his skin, becoming one with the primal power of hate. He clawed into the dirt with his bare hands, smearing himself with it, scampered around on all fours like a wolf, and hollered and howled until the sound of his own voice lost any trace of humanity. He killed whatever he encountered, leaving a bloody trail of death that confirmed him as the avatar of the motive force behind nature. Not to think, not to pity, not to hesitate in one's actions; only to kill, only to fulfil the innermost purpose of everything. He would pause and survey the trees swaying and sighing in the night and swear that they, by the will that worked through his hands, would soon be burnt, blackened, and lifeless, a range of charred stumps—monuments to truth. Stars would rage and burn thousands of times more brightly in the sky, reaching out across the void to maim and then destroy one another, whole galaxies, too, and then everything in the rotten cosmos would rend at its own innards and, exhausted, collapse into a great coalescence of mutual terror and ultimate destruction and then finally be as one. The power of the vision bore his spirits up as if on black wings and he grinned madly, his mouth bloodied by his kills, as he watched dawn break in the east and implored the will that generated the power of the sun to accomplish its end-goal, the one that only Ezekiel could grasp, and herald not just another day but the day-of-days; when the blasphemy that was truth would blast and triumph over all the muddleheaded talk of "civilisation."

He waited, but the birdsong began, the woods began to stir, and the same routine of animate pointlessness carried on as before, as it had for untold millennia. The great wasp still awaited the right moment to wriggle out in vengeance from the corrupted fruit of its womb. Its emergence could not be put off much longer—of that he was certain.

Ezekiel threaded his way back towards the farm, along tracks with which he had been familiar even as a boy, where he had hunted and tortured every kind of critter, until Pa had caught him once and tried to whip the urge out of him.

He washed himself, clothes and all, in the old creek, and found its dark, sluggish waters still full of thirsty leeches, troublesome as city-folk, but he knew how best to deal with both species: slow suffering, nothing quick and easy.

Though he was tired, the dip had refreshed him. Hunger, though, got a hold of his vitals, and he plodded up to the house to check up on his pa and put some food inside himself.

The stench hit before he'd even closed the screen-door behind him.

Something had turned bad overnight.

The worst of it came from the direction of Pa's room. Cooking seemed a bad idea, Ezekiel thought. Chances were he'd bring anything that had gone down straight back up when he opened that bedroom door. Didn't smell like the old man had fouled the sheets again; more like, well, something finally gone rotten, and something that had been a long while waiting to do so.

Ezekiel laid a hand on the knob, then cautiously pushed open the door, having pinched shut the nostrils of his nose with his other, free hand. He entered. Half a dozen bluebottles buzzed frantically around his head and then settled back on the old man's yellow-tinged, bloodless face. His eyes were open and staring, only the bald, mottled head visible above the sheet, which was pulled up to his chin.

"Pa? How ya feeling?"

Ezekiel ventured farther towards the bed. The eyes of the old man still stared, but fixedly, as if at some point directly on the opposite wall, though there was nothing much to look at there as far as Ezekiel could tell; only huge cracks in the sickly-green plaster.

When he took his hand away from his nose he gagged at the disgusting stench permeating the room.

"Pa, ya better not be fooling me," he said, choking out the words.

No answer.

Then, in a rage, he leapt forward and tore the thin blanket away from his father's torso and legs. A whole series of bugs had set up home there and were happily milling around in the dirty singlet and underpants covering what little was left of the old man's dignity.

Ezekiel hauled his pa from the bed onto the bare floorboards, causing the bugs to scurry around aimlessly on the stained mattress and the bluebottles to circle impatiently in a circle overhead. He kicked the old man in the ribs a few times, heard stale air whistle from his dead lungs up through his mouth, and then hauled him back into the bed and arranged him in his former position, pulling the blanket up to his chin.

The bugs and the flies settled down again. Pa still stared at the same spot on the wall, apparently unperturbed.

Pa had been useless for years anyhow. Didn't have any friends. Hadn't been in town since '32. No kin left, except Ezekiel himself. He didn't even remember Ma. She was never talked about either. No one else would notice Pa wasn't around. There'd be a whole lot of trouble if folks from town started messing around on the farm asking stupid questions and kicking up a fuss.

Best forget about it.

Something else occurred to Ezekiel.

He closed the door to Pa's room behind him, padded along the short corridor into his own room, and there began to rummage amongst the piles of pulp magazines he'd collected over the years. Finally, after several minutes of rifling through them, he retrieved half a dozen old copies of a garish journal called *Home Brew: America's Zippiest Magazine.*

He put them into chronological order so he could reread Lovecraft's serial "Grewsome Tales" over a bottle of hooch.

There was no work to do around the farm, so he could allow himself some luxury.

After all, he was boss now.

Several days later the telephone started ringing. It was just before one o'clock in the morning. Lovecraft could hear its shrill, insistent summons filtering up the stairs from the hallway where the device was located. His aunt Annie had retired hours ago. She was a heavy sleeper. Despite her room being on the ground floor, and thus closer to the infernal instrument, he doubted she would be awakened by its noise. The thing, though, was proving ruinous to Lovecraft's concentration. His eye-trouble was taxing enough of late, but to have to suffer such superfluous auditory distractions too—it was as if his own unavoidable physical decline was being hastened by the hustle and bustle of the machine-age. He reluctantly laid down his pen and slid aside the letter he was writing, got to his feet, and made his way in the darkness towards the insistent telephone. He wondered who it could be that would call at such an unsociable hour, though the possibility that some real emergency required his attention seemed fantastically remote. Most of his family were gone, and were any of his friends and correspondents to have suffered a calamity (he thought momentarily, with a pang, of the recent loss of Two-Gun Bob and of good old Canevin a few years earlier) he would have been advised of the fact by written communication.

It must, however, be a matter of urgency. Obviously even a telegram would not do in this particular instance. The telephone had been ringing long enough to indicate that the caller had abandoned any scruples about waking the household or of attempting to make contact again in the morning at a more considerate hour.

He lifted the receiver, placed it to his ear, and spoke into the mouthpiece, feeling a customary distaste with the trappings of modernity.

"This is College 6435. Who is speaking, please?"

There was a grunting noise, then a long pause, and then some odd clicks on the line. It was rather unnerving, standing there in the dark, in the depths of the witching hour, rather like . . . Lovecraft thought of Harley Warren and of Edward Derby, and then dismissed the absurdity of the sudden mental association.

"Who is speaking, please? I can't hear you," Lovecraft said, repeating his plaintive query.

"Got ya number outta the Providence direckty."

The voice was slurred. It seemed clear that whoever was speaking was a victim of that capacity which liquor possessed to hurl men several stages down the evolutionary scale.

"Ya sent ma bits of ma book back, damn ya."

"Who is speaking, please?" Lovecraft repeated, for a third time, though he dreaded the answer.

"Ah'm Ezekiel Nantwich, ya know of me well enuff," the voice went on.

Lovecraft was appalled.

He had thought this disturbing affair concluded.

His knuckles went white as he gripped the receiver more tightly in his grasp.

"Callin' from the farm. My pa wants to speak to ya. Says it's *right* ya ain't choosin' to work for me. I'll put him on the line. Ya can straighten him out afore I put him back down . . ."

"Please don't attempt to contact me again," Lovecraft said.

He replaced the receiver in its cradle.

There were no further telephone calls that night.

Sheriff Barnabas Dudley navigated his beat-up county police car along the four-mile-long dirt track that led from Shinglemill up to Nantwich Farm. Joshua Corwin at the general store had asked him to "look in" on the place a few days ago, but he'd put off doing so. There appeared to him no good reason to go about idly interfering in other people's business, even by way of neighbourliness, if the one doing the interfering, as he would be, carried the authority and weight of a badge and gun. And old Corwin just seemed suspicious of everyone in a twenty-mile radius of Shinglemill who had ever paid a visit to the general store and had looked at him askance.

There was, however, the matter of that very bad business which had occurred at the farm thirty years ago. Couldn't simply dismiss that. Nothing had been proven against Enoch Nantwich, but Dudley still felt there was something not right about a man like that bringing up a boy—even Ezekiel—alone.

A very bad business indeed.

He jammed a smoke into the corner of his mouth and tried haphazardly to light it as the car rolled over a series of ruts in the dirt track. The steering wheel tried to jerk out of his left hand, and he swore loudly before regaining control of the vehicle.

Back in 1906, Enoch had got it into his head that his wife, Bethany, was some kind of witch who talked—and did certain other things—with the wild animals in the woods. He would say so to anyone stupid enough to listen, and some of them got it into their heads too. And it wasn't long after Ezekiel was born that her body was found in the woods five miles north of Nantwich Farm. She was dangling from a tree, hanged by her neck from a noose wrapped round a long, sturdy branch. How she could have got all the way up there "unaided" remained unanswered. Folks said she gone mad after the birth, got violent and eyed the child in a furtive way, though

Enoch seemed reluctant to confirm the fact.

Nantwich farm was searched and there was strange stuff found amongst Bethany's possessions. Stuff that some folk thought Enoch had placed there to show she wasn't right in the head, but which others thought had been there all along. There were bundled sticks made up into human shapes, most with hieroglyphic writing etched on them, but some had names.

Not long after Enoch was cleared through lack of evidence, and once Bethany was buried, there started up wild, crazy talk about her still being seen after dark in the woods; scuttling around on all fours with a monstrously crooked neck, clambering up and down trees, and consorting with animals.

Dudley's predecessor as county sheriff, Job Cooke, drank a lot more after that business, developed the shakes, and finally moved away in the end, taking his family with him. He had told the young Dudley the tale reluctantly, piece by piece, over a period of weeks. For it wasn't the hanging—or even the wild stories—that got to Job Cooke. His nerves were far stronger than most; what really got to him in the end was the other thing that happened twenty miles away.

Someone had paid a visit to the grave over at North Bend Cemetery two months after the interment, dug down six feet, opened the casket, and then used kerosene to burn Bethany Nantwich's body to a crisp on the spot, right there and then. Whoever did the deed was interrupted by a patrolling night-watchman and escaped before the soil could be replaced, the plot filled back in, and the defilement concealed. The night-watchman said the soil of the same grave had been curiously disturbed on previous occasions after the burial, and he had determined to keep the area under closer observation. The ghoulish outrage was a local sensation and made the papers in most of western Pennsylvania, though the coroner did all he could to keep the most lurid details out of the hands of the press.

These stories, of events from thirty years before, told to him by a drink-sodden Job Cooke, kept turning over in his mind the closer

Sheriff Dudley came to Nantwich Farm. Once or twice he even seriously thought about turning back.

But he finally pulled up outside the farmhouse—a two-storied gambrel-roofed structure whose whitewashed paintwork had not been maintained and which peeled away in large sections from the exterior wooden slats. The windows were dusty; tattered green curtains, little more than grimy rags, hung behind their cracked panes. The whole place had a depressing air of miserable backwoods insularity, slipping, generation after tainted generation, into a deeper, perversely hermetic degeneration.

Over in the near distance a herd of sickly-looking cattle, their ribs clearly visible, their legs almost spindly, stood eerily still and watched Dudley with dull, inhuman stares as he made his way from the car and up the steps of the rickety front porch. Some of them began lowing throatily, as if they had not been fed for a long while and were being further tormented by Dudley's not immediately attending to their needs.

He banged on the entrance. No answer. He tried again.

"Enoch? Ezekiel?" Dudley shouted. "You in there?"

Still no answer. And once he'd opened the screen door the sudden stench that wafted out made him gag involuntarily, and he quickly covered his mouth and nose with a handkerchief. The same stomach-churning odour he knew from the time he'd gone over to old Israel Parris's shack, only to discover that its reclusive occupant had been lying there dead for two weeks after a massive heart attack.

The stench of death in all its ripeness.

He found the two corpses in one of the back bedrooms, along with a horde of bluebottles who angrily buzzed Dudley when he entered.

Ezekiel was a ghastly shade of yellow, the blood pooling in his back, his near-toothless mouth bearing the death's-head smile of rictus. His stomach was beginning to bloat with fetid internal gases.

Enoch, however, appeared to have been dead for a longer period; decomposition had already long set in. His sunken, spongy eyes stared lifelessly; his bald pate and face were a mottled tangle-work of sickening corruption.

The room showed evidence of a dramatic struggle having taken place within. Some chairs had been overturned, pictures upon the walls were crazily askew, and various objects lay scattered on the floor.

It seemed to Dudley that the two men had died weeks apart, but that was a matter for a pathologist to determine and upon which the county coroner would pronounce. True, there had been rumours in the papers of a delinquent gang of city youths (doubtless from Allentown, where things were bad) who drove around robbing isolated farmhouses, but those rumours had been current more than two years ago. It appeared unlikely such a gang would commit murder in two distinct phases, first Enoch and then returning for Ezekiel, when the latter would have had to have remained silent during the interim.

Amongst the items scattered on the floor were several dozen typewritten pages. Dudley examined them, whilst still keeping his nose and mouth covered with the handkerchief. The pages might also be important evidence.

He couldn't make much sense out of them, but the subject matter made him deeply uneasy; something about talking animals, devil-worship, and the rage of nature. Many of the pages had been dappled with bloodstains.

He left Enoch's bedroom and looked over the rest of the farmhouse. Elsewhere, nothing indicated that a gang had raided the place. Though derelict and dirty, the interior showed signs only of terminal neglect, not of having been ransacked for valuables.

It was in Ezekiel's bedroom that Dudley finally decided to torch the entire farmhouse and destroy all traces of what had occurred within. What he saw there made the memory of his talks with a visibly shaking Job Cooke again force itself to the forefront of his mind.

Dudley found some curiously bundled figures made out of sticks and a huge pentagram scrawled—in what appeared to be blood—on the far wall.

One of the strange human-shaped stick forms bore a ribbon with the English appellation "Enoch," and he could not bring himself to handle the thing. Etched into the sticks were indecipherable glyphs written in an archaic language Dudley could not recognise.

There was another such stick figure, bearing a different appellation. Rusty nails had been driven into what constituted its midriff, and he only discerned the English appellation partially (this ribbon being badly torn) as "—craft," as in—or so he presumed—"witchcraft."

On an impulse that he obeyed, though he nevertheless felt it to be absurd, Dudley pocketed the grisly item, perhaps as a macabre keepsake or perhaps to prove to himself that all he had seen inside Nantwich Farm was not born of a waking nightmare or some other form of temporary derangement on his part.

Kerosene again did the work of purging. The fire Dudley started totally consumed the Nantwich Farmhouse and all its vile secrets as the sheriff drove back towards Shinglemill, a great conflagration of flames and smoke billowing into the early evening sky behind him, mingling with the bloody crimson of the setting sun.

He'd tell Joshua Corwin that the farmhouse had burned down a good hour or more before his arrival there. The place was so remote and so shunned by everyone that his own story, with the authority of his badge behind it, wouldn't be contradicted. The still-lowing cattle were the sole witnesses.

Ezekiel, thought Dudley, had been his mother Bethany's wicked triumph in posterity.

Lovecraft again gazed out of the study window. The russet-coloured leaves were falling in greater numbers; a few weeks more and the trees would be stripped bare. The season had decisively turned. The summer warmth that sustained him had ebbed away, yielding to ever chillier air, to the firmer grasp of night, and to the virtual hibernation that autumnal existence forced upon him.

He looked once more for the familiar tortoise-shell cat but saw no sign of it, though it had become something of a permanent fixture around the grounds of 66 College Street. Strange, independent creature! Lovecraft had prided himself on his ability to strike up a rapport with any feline that chance sent his way, yet this one had remained resolutely hostile, as if no affinity were possible. The thing had probably gone feral long ago. He still bore the scratch-marks on his hand from the single attempt he had made to tickle it under the chin.

He sat down at his desk and again tried to work.

The room felt abominably cold to him, yet the thermometer hung upon the wall insisted upon eighty degrees Fahrenheit.

Suddenly he felt a pang of grippe seize his lower intestines. The symptoms were familiar, and such attacks had already bedevilled him, on and off, for over a year. The symptoms intensified, alternately ebbing and flowing in a tide of nausea and acute stabbing pains. This latest episode was a particularly trying revival of the troublesome ailment.

After half an hour of continued distress he went into his bed-alcove to lie down and wrap himself in blankets. Removing his carpet-slippers, he noticed the swelling in his feet; here, too, was an unexpected new development in the malady.

He lay on one side, attempting to regain some sense of stoic composure.

Then the cast-iron radiator on the far wall laboriously began its process of interior knocking. At last, it appeared, the central boiler over at Brown University had been fired up and the off-campus residences—such as the domestic satellite he and his aunt Annie occupied—would receive their promised allocation of heating.

Doubtless an easily distracted janitor had finally noticed the lateness of the season.

Worlds Apart

Donald R. Burleson

On a Friday afternoon that should have been like any other, Theobald Perkins sat at his desk at the insurance company and shuffled papers and wondered what was wrong. Because something was.

Pausing for a moment in his work, he glanced out across the room, thinking how simple life seemed to be for his co-workers, ensconced at their desks with their heads buried in the mundane tasks at hand, as his should be. Life had been that simple for him too, until this morning.

Walking to the building from his car in the parking lot, with his briefcase in hand and with seemingly nothing out of the ordinary, he had had the strangest sensation. It was over and done with in a second or two. Now he could neither clearly remember what the impression had been nor quite bring himself just to forget or disregard it. For a fleeting moment it was as if he had been looking at himself from outside his body and mind, not physically but in some other way, as if his awareness had momentarily shifted elsewhere and then snapped back. Probably this was due to his not having slept very well, and he felt mildly annoyed with himself for letting it bother him now.

"Mr. Perkins? Are you all right?" It was Linda, one of the secretaries, and she had come up to his desk with a handful of papers he had requested earlier. She handed them to him, looking a bit dubious.

He managed a smile. "Oh—yes, I'm fine. Just kind of distracted, I guess. " He waved the sheaf of papers and nodded. "Thank you for these."

For the rest of the afternoon he managed to push his odd experience to the back of his mind. He had plenty of work to do, and he intended to get it all done, however boring it might be.

Funny thing, he had never really thought of it as boring before. But that was something else there was no point in obsessing over.

That night he slept rather poorly again, and upon waking could not quite remember his dreams, except for a feeling that they were rather bizarre by his usual standards.

After a simple breakfast in the kitchen of his modest apartment, he went for his usual Saturday morning walk in the park. He was grateful that his amusement needs were simple, because in a little Ohio town like this, one's needs might be difficult to satisfy otherwise. In Greenburg there really wasn't much to do.

But he was content to stroll for a while and then settle himself on a park bench to watch the blackbirds picking at insects in the grass. Nearby, a light wind riffled the trees like fingers brushing hair, or like the breath of the gods.

Odd, he didn't usually have thoughts that by any stretch of the imagination could be considered poetic. What was this thought about the gods, and what gods might those be? The Greek gods? He hadn't thought about Greek mythology since high school. It rarely came up in conversation when one worked in an insurance office.

Ah, well. That odd experience in the parking lot at work must have stuck in his mind more than it should. Maybe his solitary existence made him unduly sensitive at times. Suddenly he recalled one of his dreams, or partly recalled it anyway—some nearly formless vision of getting married and moving to New York City to live. But from where? He couldn't remember, except that it wasn't Greenburg.

Dreams of course meant nothing, despite what the Freudians might say. In any event, why think of such matters when he really ought to be getting home? He had things to do.

Rising from the park bench, he thought: Wait a minute—what

things? What do I have to do? But of course, as usual he had to—what? The answer flashed in his mind like lightning for a moment, then slipped away. He really needed to get hold of himself; he was starting to fret about nothing, an unhealthy habit. Shrugging it all off, he made his way home through the early-morning streets.

That evening while watching a weather report on television, he suddenly remembered the answer to that question in the park about what he had to do. The answer was that he had to write some letters.

This was peculiar, because he virtually never wrote any letters to anyone, there being very little in his life to write about, and nobody in particular to write to, for that matter.

Sunday morning found him in the park yet again. He usually spent Sunday mornings at church, but somehow this morning he hadn't felt like going. He was restless, and a brisk walk seemed like the best idea. At length he ended up on the same bench, where he watched a somber flotilla of clouds drift across the sky. They gave him an indefinable feeling, as if they were the gatekeepers to some mysterious realm above him. Maybe he was feeling guilty about skipping church. But he didn't think so; in truth, there had been times lately when he wondered what he really believed, or whether he really believed anything. He tried not to dwell on these things, but could scarcely help trying to figure out what was really bothering him.

Monday, around the middle of the morning, one of the secretaries came to his desk and said, "Mr. Perkins, excuse me, but Miss Potter would like to see you in her office."

He got up from his desk and started over there. "Thank you, Jane." Crossing the room, he reflected that his boss very seldom asked to see him like this, and it gave him some unease.

In her office, his boss looked at him across her cluttered desk. "Tibby, I'm a little worried. Is everything all right?"

He nodded. "Yes ma'am, as far as I know. Why do you ask?"

"Well," she said, "you promised me a finished report on that problem with the Stevenson policy by now, and I haven't seen it. Are you having any difficulties with that?"

He realized suddenly that this was indeed a promise not kept. "No, no, there aren't any problems really. I've just been tied up with a couple of other policies. I'll get the Stevenson report to you before I go to lunch."

Miss Potter nodded, evidently satisfied for the time being. On his way back to his desk, Perkins thought: Editors are tricky people to get along with sometimes.

It wasn't till later that he mulled over the strange thing he had said to himself. Why had he said *editors* when he had a *boss*, not an editor? He remembered now that for the briefest of moments, having that thought while returning to his desk, he had felt like some kind of writer with a project needing to be finished for an editor. This was senseless, of course, when he had never worked at any kind of job outside the insurance business. His tardiness in submitting that report to Miss Potter must be bothering him more than he consciously realized.

Again, he needed to get hold of himself.

His apartment felt unbearably stuffy that evening, and he resorted to yet another stroll. He wasn't accustomed to walking at night, but found it rather refreshing, with lights showing cozily in the curtained windows of houses, and with the stars dimly visible above the roof lines, beyond the glow of the streetlamps. After walking through the meandering paths of the park, he found himself enjoying the picturesque impressions lined up before him along a street whose name he couldn't quite recall, where gaunt eighteenth-century houses rose before him now like sentries, their small-paned windows placidly regarding him, the fanlights over their doors offering subtle smiles to the night. At the end of the street he found steps leading down to an ancient graveyard, but he turned and retraced his steps, back along the nameless street, and at length ended up walking back through the park and heading for home.

He stopped by the desk of one of the secretaries. "Jane, can I ask you something?"

She looked up from her work. "Sure."

"Have you lived in this town long?"

She nodded. "I was born here. Never lived anywhere else. Why?"

"Well," he said, "I've only been here a few years. My family was from Columbus. There's something— Do you know Edmunds Park?"

She nodded again. "My sister and I go jogging there sometimes."

"If you go through the park and come out on the west end of the path, what's that street a couple of blocks down, with all the old colonial-looking houses? I mean, I know they couldn't be that old, but they look like something you might see in New England or someplace."

She shook her head, looking puzzled. "In this town? I don't remember ever seeing anything like that."

He didn't know whether to feel foolish or defiant. He knew what he had seen. But he only replied, "Well, thanks. I guess I just—thanks."

*

That night he was in the park again, but barely saw it as he hurried through to get to the west end, where he came out onto an unpretentious city street, one that led, however, to *that* street, off to the right. He turned his steps in that direction and was soon again among colonial façades, houses that appeared to have been built before the American Revolution. He paused before the one special house—*that* house (what had it been called?) in whose fungoid cellar such horrific events were said to have unfolded. But said by whom? And how did he know?

Without proceeding all the way to the graveyard, he circled back and returned to the park. But he walked only halfway through it before some urge stopped him in his tracks. What was that silly Jane talking about? He had *seen* the street, had walked along it! He turned around again, made his way back out the west end of the park, and followed his previous path to the turnoff to *that* street he had just visited.

But now the street leading off in that direction was just an ordinary one lined with ordinary, unexceptional houses.

He walked home with a mind churning with puzzlement. At moments, during the past few days, it had seemed to him as if he were two different people, seeing the world in different ways, maybe living in different worlds. He shuddered to think what this might mean—he could be going insane.

Suddenly it dawned on him. As little inclined toward this sort of thing as he had always been before, he thought now it was time to talk to Sadie. She might be crazy herself, but what did he have to lose?

She was always sitting on the bench beside the entrance to the public library, every evening, and not surprisingly she was the subject of a great deal of local folklore. He had never spoken to her. Some, rather fancifully, said she was a witch; others only said she was eccentric, or downright weird. No one knew how old she was. She was blind, but some would say she saw more than those who had eyes. He approached her now, feeling a bit awkward and almost apologetic, and stood over her.

"Sadie?"

She turned her wizened face toward him, her unseeing eyes groping the empty air. "Yes?"

He cleared his throat. "You may be able to help me. Lately I—well, it's hard to put into words, but I've been having these experiences, sometimes lasting only a second or two, sometimes longer, where I seem to see the world through someone else's eyes. Last night I walked down a street that wasn't there when I went back a few minutes later. I feel as if I ought to know the name of the street. I know how this must sound—"

She silenced him with the preemptive wave of a withered hand. When she spoke, her voice was dry and cracked but authoritative in tone, not to be trifled with. "You talk about seeing the world through someone else's eyes. It isn't just the world. There are many worlds. Someone else can live in their world just as you live in yours. Maybe someone like you, or not like you at all, someone who fate decided would step into those intersections where his world overlaps with yours, at the same time you did, before the worlds slipped out of tangency again. Maybe the someone is connected to you in that way. For a second you see as he sees. Maybe in another life, another world, you could have been someone else. Maybe the other person could have been someone else. Maybe only one world is real, maybe they all are. But real to whom? No one knows for sure." And she turned away from him, signaling that the conversation was over.

Walking home, he struggled to decide whether the old woman's enigmatic remarks had clarified anything to him or merely made matters worse. He felt at a loss to understand what was real and what was not. Edgar Allan Poe had said it best when he asked: "Is *all we see or seem / But a dream within a dream?*"

But the frightening thing about that, he reflected, was that he had never read Poe in his life.

That night his dreams were filled with a multiplicity of strange visions that seemed to involve dizzying gulfs of space and reverberant, mocking voices and incomprehensible names, names that he somehow thought were meant to denote ancient gods whom it would be death of the soul to behold.

Toward morning, he dreamed of a mundane existence, of wearing a pressed gray business suit, of working at an uninteresting job in an ordinary office and thinking earthbound thoughts. These evanescent visions faded like dim, distant stars with the coming of the dawn, succumbing to a stronger light. But he got up feeling oddly disoriented, and had only a cup of coffee down in the kitchen. Sometimes he missed the cheese omelets that Sonia used to make for his breakfast. There was no need, though, to think about that.

His aunt met him at the door. "Now Howard, look, you wrap

that scarf tight around your throat, we don't want you sick. You know how sensitive you are to the cold."

Out on the streets of College Hill, with the timeless city of Providence beginning to awake about him, he pondered the peculiar impressions he had been having for the past few days, impressions that vaguely suggested some alternative reality that he felt he should have been able to remember but could not, some other identity, someone else he might have been but was not. Such mystical ruminations were nonsense, of course, but at moments they had seemed unaccountably compelling. The result seemed in some undefined way to be that his own conscious life had taken on a sharper focus.

As usual, he ended up at length on Benefit Street, walking past the Shunned House that he had so vividly portrayed in fiction. Why did he imagine now that at some time he had walked here and looked at the house without knowing what it was or why he was here?

What this sense of unrecalled impressions might mean, he could not say, but he suspected that the concept, fleshed out in a different and more pertinent form, was going to prove useful when he planned out his intended tale "The Shadow out of Time."

Enough of his Poe stories and his Dunsany stories. Whether anyone ever ended up remembering him for writing it or not, this was going to be a Lovecraft story.

Witch's Ladder

Donald Tyson

1

Three couples sat around a circular table in the candle-lit dining room of the Biltmore Hotel in Providence, Rhode Island. The year was 1926. The men wore formal dinner jackets, the women elegant gowns that left their necks and shoulders bare. Although the evening meal was done and the plates and silverware had been cleared away, they were in no hurry to leave. At the head of the room, musicians played the first movement of Mozart's String Quartet No. 16 in E-flat major. The lilting notes of violins, viola, and cello fluttered above the tables like a flock of small birds.

One of the men, a small but dynamic figure with curling dark hair and magnetic gray eyes who was attracting covert glances from diners at other tables, told a story to his companions with theatrical gusto, sawing the air with his strangely expressive hands and mimicking various voices to perfection. The effervescent laughter of his listeners bubbled up like champagne.

"And then I realized I had dropped the lock pick and it was lying somewhere on the bottom of the tank, but because of the way I was shackled I could only reach it with my toes."

A full-figured blonde woman with a prominent bosom, who was seated on his left, parted her red lips in an O of mock horror.

"Oh, no, Harry. Whatever did you do?"

Harry Houdini flashed a mischievous grin across the table at her husband, a slender little man with a wry Irish face.

"My dear Mrs. Eddy, what could I do? I slipped off my shoe and my sock and found the instrument with my toes."

"You picked it up with your toes?" There was a note of incredulity in the voice of the dark-haired woman on his right.

"You don't believe me?"

She inclined her head with a disarming smile. "How could I doubt the word of so gracious a host?"

"I've seen him do it," her husband said. His elongated, solemn features would have been ideally suited to a deacon or an undertaker, but were not inappropriate for the type of popular fiction he wrote.

"I not only picked it up, Mrs. Lovecraft, I used it to open my shackles. My toes are almost as nimble as my fingers. I've trained them to tie and untie knots in fine twine. And a good thing, too, because in another thirty seconds I would have drowned."

A young man passing behind the speaker's chair paused and cleared his throat to draw his attention.

"Sir, I know it's a terrible imposition," he began in a high voice with a slight stutter. "I attended your performance earlier tonight and I recognized you just now across the room."

Houdini glanced apologetically at his companions, then fixed his penetrating gaze on the interloper.

"If you would sign my program, it would mean ever so much to my wife. She's that woman in the corner, wearing the blue dress."

Howard Phillips Lovecraft followed the young man's vague gesture and picked out a woman sitting alone who was staring at them. She blushed when she realized they were looking at her.

Houdini accepted the theatre program and drew a fountain pen from his vest pocket with a flourish, then signed it with bold, sweeping strokes.

"Thank you, Mr. Houdini, thank you," the young man said, backing away with the program clutched to his chest. "This will mean so much to her, really, so much."

He banged against a chair at the neighboring table and stuttered a profuse apology to the frowning woman seated in it.

Harry Houdini looked across at his wife, Bess, who shook her head slightly with a faint smile.

"I expect that happens to you two quite often," Clifford Eddy said in a dry tone.

"One of the hazards of our profession," Houdini said. "But I would much rather have strangers bother me at my supper than have no one recognize me."

"A writer has the advantage of anonymity," Sonia Lovecraft said, glancing at her solemn husband, who shrugged his shoulders.

"I don't know if it is an advantage," Muriel Eddy said, eyeing the little Irishman to whom she was married. "It might be fun to have people we don't know coming up to Cliff for autographs."

"Trust me, you would grow tired of it very quickly," Bess Houdini said.

Something in her voice caused Houdini to reach out and pat her affectionately on the back of the hand.

"My poor darling, you put up with so much when we are on the road."

He turned to Lovecraft. "But enough talk of fame. How are you and Clifford progressing on our book?"

Lovecraft hesitated, and Eddy spoke up.

"Howard is still gathering the background information, but I've put together an outline."

"I've sketched in the first chapter so that you can see where we're going with the material," Lovecraft added.

"You've brought the outline and chapter with you?"

"They're in my coat."

"Good. We can go upstairs to my suite and I'll read them over."

"Howard is very keen on the book project," Sonia said. "It's all he talks about lately. I can scarcely get him to notice what I'm wearing."

"I'm sure so lovely a lady as yourself never escapes the admiring notice of her husband," Houdini told her.

She forced a smile and glanced at Lovecraft, who dropped his gaze. There was the slightest awkward silence.

"You are doing such good and necessary work, exposing the tricks of the charlatans who pretend to be spirit mediums," Muriel Eddy said to Houdini.

He bowed in acknowledgment.

"Someone has to do it. My expertise in stage illusions gives me a unique insight into the devices employed by these frauds."

"Don't you think that any of it is real?" Sonia asked.

Houdini looked at his wife, Bess.

"Myself? No. Everything they do at their séances can be simulated with stage trickery, so why should we presume that any of it is real?"

"Have you never seen anything that you could not explain away as a trick?"

"Never."

"There are no such things as spirits," Lovecraft said firmly, eyeing his wife. "No heaven or hell. No God and no Devil, either."

"My husband is both a materialist and an atheist," she explained.

"Believe me, Mrs. Lovecraft, it would delight me to discover that magic is real, but I fear I shall forever be disappointed."

Houdini glanced at his wristwatch and frowned.

"There is something I must do tonight. It almost slipped my mind, we were having such a lively conversation."

He glanced at Lovecraft, then at Eddy.

"I don't suppose you gentlemen would care to accompany me on my errand? It should only take an hour or so, and it pertains to the subject of our forthcoming book. I think you may find it of some interest."

"Count me in," Eddy said.

"Of course I will come with you," Lovecraft told him.

"Good. The ladies can go up to my suite, where we will join them when this little task is fulfilled."

"This is very mysterious," Sonia said. "Perhaps we ladies should go with you as well."

"Much as I would relish your company, it is not a task suitable for a woman."

"Goodness gracious, you make it sound like something sinister, Mr. Houdini," Muriel said with a laugh. "Can't you give us any idea what it involves?"

Houdini spread his slender hands, then shrugged.

"You may have heard that I collect items of an occult nature for a private museum that I intend to open at some future date."

"Cliff did mention that you are a collector."

"Tonight I go to acquire an unusual item a dealer here in Providence has been keeping for me."

"How exciting!" Muriel Eddy said.

"These dealers are not always men of the highest character, and the man I go to see tonight has arranged to meet with me on the docks—he is a freighter captain, and his reputation is, shall we say, variable."

"Is there any danger?" Sonia asked with a hint of alarm in her voice.

"No, of course not." Houdini smiled at the women. "I would never lead your husbands into danger."

"What exactly is this thing we are going to buy?" Lovecraft asked.

Houdini hesitated and glanced again at his wife.

"Have you ever heard of a thing called a witch's ladder?"

Clifford Eddy and the two women shook their heads.

"I believe I ran across an essay in some journal about such a thing," Lovecraft murmured. He gazed up at the sculptured plaster ceiling in an effort to remember. "Isn't it some kind of rope or cord with various things knotted into its length?"

"Yes, that's it. The witch uses it to cause suffering to her enemy. She braids or knots into the cord feathers, twigs, nails, shards of glass, stones, and other bits of trash, and as she does so she utters a curse on each item as it is added so that it will bring pain and misfortune to the poor wretch she imagines has wronged her. Bound into the cord are strands of hair from the head of her victim, and perhaps scraps of his clothing."

"How horrible!" Muriel Eddy said with a shudder.

Houdini laughed. "It is all so much nonsense, but a genuine witch's ladder would make a fine acquisition for my museum."

"You must show it to us when you bring it back to the hotel," Sonia said.

"Of course we will," Bess Houdini said.

The expression on her face was curiously solemn given the light tone of the conversation.

Lovecraft wondered what Houdini and his wife were keeping private between them. He sensed there was more to this affair than Houdini had said, and hoped Eddy had thought to bring his pocket revolver with him. Eddy was in the habit of carrying the gun at night for personal protection, but it seemed unlikely he would have brought it along for an evening of theatre.

Houdini pushed back his chair and stood.

"We must be on our way. I sent a note to the dealer telling him to expect me at eleven."

Sonia laid her hand on Lovecraft's arm as he held back her chair for her to rise.

"Be careful, Howard. I have a bad feeling about this. There's something Harry isn't saying."

This sentiment exactly matched Lovecraft's own, but he covered her fingers with his and squeezed.

"There are three of us. What could possibly happen? This is Providence, after all, not Red Hook."

"In case you were wondering, yes, I did bring it along," Eddy murmured from the corner of his mouth as they made their way toward the coatroom.

Lovecraft nodded. He was not surprised by the remark. He and Eddy had known each other for so many years, it was not uncommon for the little man to almost read his mind and answer before he framed a question. The knowledge that Eddy would be carrying his revolver comforted him more than he had any reason to expect it should.

2

While they had sat dining in the Biltmore, fog had rolled in from the sea and covered the lower part of Providence in a damp, chilly grayness that made halos around the lamppost lights and dimmed the shapes of passing automobiles and pedestrians into vague ghosts. Even the sounds of traffic were muted as they progressed along the shrouded streets. Somewhere in the background a monotonous foghorn sounded its low, mournful note.

Houdini walked with a short but purposeful stride. He was not a tall man, but his erect posture and dynamic energy gave the illusion that he was taller. Lovecraft and Eddy followed on either side close behind him.

"Where are we meeting this dealer of yours?" Eddy asked.

"The docks," Houdini murmured without turning. The fog played tricks with his voice, making it sound distant and dead.

"Do you know where you're going?"

"I studied a map of Providence earlier this evening."

The two men looked at each other. This wasn't a section of their native Providence that either of them had occasion to visit often. The dirty streets were lined with warehouses and workshops, closed up at this late hour. As they drew nearer to the docks, the number of pedestrians dwindled and the cars ceased to pass, until they were alone.

Lovecraft shivered. He hated the cold and the damp. His summer topcoat was too thin for so late in the year, but he had not been able to afford anything heavier. The dinner jacket beneath it had been rented for the evening's occasion. In a few weeks it would be Halloween. Icy fingers of October fog brushing the back of his neck made him turn up his collar.

He realized they were no longer on a street, but had walked onto some kind of concrete pier. Vague shapes of buildings loomed on either side, and in the distance something else.

"It's a freighter," Eddy said.

Houdini continued to walk briskly toward the ship, which emerged from the grayness as they drew nearer. The peeling white paint on the riveted plates of its hull was streaked with orange rust. No light showed anywhere on its deck. By the dim glow of a lamp on the pier Lovecraft was able to read the name-plaque welded to it bow. It read *Direwolf*.

They followed Houdini up the inclined gangway and onto the deck of the ship, which was chaotically strewn with rusting coils of cable and machine parts of an indeterminable purpose. The light from the pier made scant way against the deep shadows.

"It looks deserted," Lovecraft said.

Glancing keenly around, Houdini spotted a brass bell hanging on the cabin wall. He gave a single yank on the chain that dangled beneath it. A deep clear note rang out. They listened to its reverberations fade to silence.

An angled hatchway cracked open, spilling yellow light across the jumbled deck. Framed in the light stood the hulking silhouette of a man. His face was obscured by shadow.

"I'm here to see Captain Kruger," Houdini told him. "I have an appointment."

The figure stood without moving for so long that Lovecraft wondered if he might be deaf, but at last he nodded and stepped aside, motioning them into the hatchway with a massive arm. As he turned, the light caught his face, and Lovecraft saw that he was a negro.

His white T-shirt stretched between his shoulders and defined the muscles of his torso as though painted onto his body. His skull and face were hairless, but tattooed with jagged lines and spirals. The lack of eyebrows above his dark eyes gave his face a mask-like appearance.

They squeezed past him and descended a flight of perilously

steep steps, clutching the brass rail to keep from slipping on the narrow treads.

The black giant closed out the fog behind them, then brushed past and motioned to Houdini to follow. He led them along a narrow corridor to a door and knocked on it with the knuckle of his curled index finger. An indistinct grunt came from the other side. Opening the door, he stepped back so they could enter.

The cabin was not large. A wooden desk faced the door. The shaded lamp on its corner illuminated a man who sat behind it with his back to an unadorned steel wall. He watched them enter without expression, his lean Germanic features like cut stone in the slanting light.

Lovecraft judged his age at about fifty years. His blond hair, carefully brushed straight back from receding temples, was streaked with gray, and his pale-blue eyes were surrounded by webs of wrinkles, as though he had spent too many hours squinting into the sun.

"So you are the great Harry Houdini," he said in a heavy German accent. He did not rise from his chair.

Lovecraft noted with distaste a slur in the man's speech, and attributed it to an open bottle at his elbow. An abstainer all his life and a staunch supporter of the temperance movement, he detested drunkenness. There was a general slovenliness about this German. His square chin was stubbled with a growth of beard at least three days old, and the cuffs of his faded blue shirt were soiled.

"I am Captain Hans Kruger. You've already met my first mate, Demba."

They looked at the giant in the corridor, who grinned and nodded at them through the doorway. Houdini glanced around the cabin. There were no other chairs.

"You have something to sell me," he said coldly.

"Do you have my money?"

"I have it. Do you have the item?"

"Show me the money."

Houdini reached into the breast of his coat and drew forth a thick white envelope. He dropped it on the desk. The German opened it and pulled out a stack of currency. Lovecraft saw with surprise that they were all one-hundred-dollar bills. He took his time counting them, then slid them back into the envelope.

"Give me the witch's ladder," Houdini said.

"Patience, dear man," the German said with a smile. "Houdini, that's not your birth name, is it? What is it, Goldstein? Klein? Cohen?"

"That is none of your business. You have the money; give me what I came for."

Eddy met Lovecraft's eye and patted his coat pocket. The atmosphere in the cabin was not what they had expected. Houdini was tense with the effort to hold back his anger, and Kruger seemed to be deliberately baiting him. The amount of money was not right, either. It must have been thousands of dollars. No one paid that much for an occult trinket.

From the corner of his eye Lovecraft saw movement and realized that the first mate had stepped forward to block the open doorway with his body, as though to prevent their escape.

"I know your tribe well," Kruger said. "You are all over Berlin. You own all the shops, all the nightclubs, all the factories. Your children are so fat, and we Germans can't even afford to buy bread."

"You are wasting our time. The talisman."

Kruger swivelled in his desk chair to an iron safe that sat on the floor beside him. He worked the combination dial and opened it. Placing the envelope of money inside, he carefully drew out something that clinked. Holding one end of it up between his thumb and forefinger, he released the rest. It dropped down to reveal a length of dirty twine knotted with bits of things along its length. Lovecraft saw what looked like broken bone fragments, shards of glass, rusty nails, tufts of hair, bits of torn cloth.

"Is this what you want?" He jiggled the fetish so that its parts clacked against each other.

Houdini reached for the knotted cord and Kruger drew it back.

"You monster, it's mine now. I paid for it."

"Take care," the German barked. He gathered the objects hanging from the cord into his fist. "You know what will happen if I tighten my hand."

"Don't, for pity's sake." There was anguish in Houdini's voice.

"You Jews think you can buy everything and everyone. Well, I've decided the price is too low. What you gave me tonight is only the down payment."

Lovecraft expected Houdini to protest, but the shoulders of the performer sagged beneath his topcoat.

"How much more do you want?"

"An additional forty thousand dollars."

The silence lengthened. It was an absurd sum for what amounted to bits of trash on a string. Kruger shook his loosely closed fist so that the charm rattled inside it.

"It will take me some time to raise so much money—"

"Tomorrow at noon, no later. Have it here by then if you want to stop her suffering. After that, my ship sails. I may not be able to meet with you again for months."

"That is impossible. There is no way I can gather that much cash in so short a time."

"Then I will keep this until you do have the money."

He turned to put the charm back into the safe. Houdini let out a cry of primal rage and lunged at him across the desk. Like a kind of magic, the first mate was behind him, restraining Houdini by his upper arms with his enormous hands. Lovecraft had not even seen him move, he was so incredibly quick.

"Let him go," Eddy said. He levelled his revolver at the giant, who turned to Kruger for guidance.

The captain held up his fist and tightened his fingers. Houdini cried out and struggled like a madman, but the hands that held him were too powerful.

"Stop it, stop it, you're killing her!"

"Do we have an agreement?" Kruger asked.

"Yes, anything, I'll get you the money, only please no more."

Kruger inclined his head toward Eddy.

"Clifford, put your gun away," Houdini told him.

Eddy hesitated. "Are you sure?"

"Just do it, now, quickly."

The little Irishman slid the revolver back into his coat pocket, but he kept his hand on it.

Kruger smiled and relaxed his fingers. He turned and placed the talisman back into the safe.

"Let him go, Demba, he won't do anything," he told the first mate.

The black man released Houdini and stepped away from him.

"Noon tomorrow," Kruger said without looking at them as he spun the dial of the safe to lock it. "Now, get off my ship."

3

Houdini would not respond to their questions as they walked back to the hotel. He was like a man in a trance. His face was emotionless, but fury burned deep in his eyes, and something else—fear.

Muriel Eddy met them at the open door of Houdini's suite. She was agitated, and the rouge on her cheeks was streaked with tears.

"What's happened?" Eddy asked in alarm.

She glanced at Houdini, who said nothing.

"It's Bess. She's had some kind of seizure. The doctor is with her now."

Houdini closed his eyes. Agony distorted his features for a moment before he regained control of himself.

"I must go to her."

They followed him to the doorway of a bedroom. Bess lay on top of the bed. An elderly man sat beside her, his hand on her forehead. He wore a stethoscope around his neck, and an open black medical bag rested on the carpet beside his foot. Sonia Lovecraft sat on the other side of the bed, her expression solemn. She held Bess's hand between her own.

The doctor looked up as Houdini entered.

"Are you the husband?"

He nodded.

"You wife has had some kind of seizure, Mr. Houdini. I won't know exactly what kind until we run some tests, but I've given her an injection to make her sleep. She's resting now and she'll probably sleep for five or six hours."

"Is she in any danger?"

"At present, no, but we need to find out what caused this episode. Has anything like this happened to her in the past?"

Houdini glanced at Lovecraft and Eddy.

"Yes. Several times."

The doctor raised his eyebrows in surprise. "Did you get her condition diagnosed?"

"I took her to a hospital in Miami. They ran tests but could find nothing wrong with her."

"Well, even so, when she wakes up I'd like you to bring her to the hospital here in Providence for testing. She's fine now, but this kind of episode could be serious. I don't want to alarm you by speculating, but we really do need to discover the cause."

Houdini escorted the doctor out of the suite. Muriel remained with the sleeping woman while the others gathered in the living room.

"Isn't it about time you told us what's really going on?" Lovecraft said when Houdini returned from the door.

"Yes, you're right, Howard. I induced you and Cliff to accompany me with a lie. I was a coward and wanted you with me for moral support."

"Never mind that," Eddy said. "What was all that business on the freighter?"

"I'm afraid I've lied to you in another way," Houdini told him. "You see, gentlemen, I am a fraud. The book we are writing is all lies. The occult is real, very real, and it is killing my dear wife, Bess."

"The witch's ladder," Lovecraft said. "It was made for her, wasn't it?"

Houdini nodded and continued to hang his head, his elbows resting on his knees, as he wrung his hands together. He looked dejected, defeated.

"I don't know how that monster obtained strands of her hair and scraps of her clothing. He must have bought them from a hotel maid while we were on tour during the spring. The first time Bess threw a fit, I thought it was epilepsy, but all the tests were negative. Then I received a letter from Kruger explaining about the witch's ladder and the suffering the hellish thing could inflict. Naturally, I dismissed the letter as a pathetic attempt at extortion and burned it. Then Bess fell ill with a fever and nearly died from it, and Kruger wrote to inform me that he had held the witch's ladder over a stove."

"I don't understand. Are you saying this superstitious trinket you went to buy has magical power?" Sonia asked.

"There can be no other explanation, Mrs. Lovecraft."

Lovecraft related to his wife what had taken place on the freighter.

"When Krueger crushed the talisman in his fist, it triggered my poor Bess's convulsion. Whatever he does to the hellish thing, the same happens to her."

"How did he come to choose you for his extortion, I wonder?" Eddy said.

"My celebrity. I am an easy man to reach. My movements are published weeks in advance in newspapers. Because I am so well known, he probably assumed, as many people do, that I am far wealthier than is the case."

"It may be more than that," Lovecraft said. "From his remarks tonight, I gathered he has a deep resentment against your people. He may have targeted you for that reason."

"Because I'm a Jew? But that's insane."

"Conditions are difficult in Germany," Eddy said. "The German people have never recovered from the harsh terms imposed on them by the Treaty of Versailles after the end of the Great War. There are political fanatics in Berlin who preach all kinds of crazy doctrines. Communists. Fascists. I was reading excerpts in the newspaper from a book recently written by one of them just the other day. He titled it *My Struggle*. Germans are unhappy about their economy and they are looking for someone to blame."

"I don't care what his reasons are, I just want him to stop hurting my Bess."

"Hatred of Jews is growing all across Europe," Sonia murmured. "My cousin lives in the Ukraine. She's told me stories in her letters that I don't want to believe."

Eddy stood and approached Houdini. He laid his hand on the other man's stooped shoulder.

"I wish I'd shot him. If I'd known then what I know now, I would have done it."

Houdini straightened his back and patted Eddy's hand. "Thank you, my friend."

"Are you quite certain it isn't all a confidence trick?" Lovecraft asked. "After all, that would be the simplest explanation."

"That's what I told myself," Houdini agreed. "But there have been too many incidents over the past six months, and too many letters describing my wife's afflictions in horrible detail. Each time the letter is posted from a different port city, and each time the postmark is dated the day of the attack. There is no possible way Kruger could learn of my wife's condition so quickly. This engagement in Providence was the first opportunity to meet with him. He wrote to me and offered to sell me the witch's ladder for ten thousand dollars, and like a fool I agreed. I should have known he would want more money. An extortionist is never satisfied."

"What are you going to do?" Eddy asked. "Are you going to pay him the additional forty thousand?"

"I can't," Houdini said. "I don't have that kind of money. I had to borrow the ten thousand. I could never gather that much more in twelve hours. I doubt I could get it at all. I really don't know what to do. I've never felt this helpless. When I think of what that monster could do to my sweet Bess—"

His graceful fingers knotted into fists that shook with rage.

"You could go to the police," Sonia suggested.

Houdini gave a sardonic bark of laughter. "And tell them what? That a freighter captain I met for the first time tonight has been torturing my wife for six months from a distance with a piece of twine and a few bits of bone and broken glass?"

"He's right," Eddy said grimly. "The police would laugh at him. Whatever is to be done, we'll have to do it ourselves."

Houdini stared at him, then at Lovecraft. "You'll help me?"

"Of course we'll help you. Kruger must be stopped," Eddy said.

"But what can we do?" Lovecraft asked.

"There's only one thing to do. We go back to the freighter, and we take the evil thing away from him by force."

4

It was past three in the morning when they reached the deserted dockside. The fog still lay over the lower part of the city. If anything, it was thicker than before. The foghorn continued to sound its doleful moan.

"Where could a man like Kruger learn how to make a witch's ladder?" Eddy whispered as they crept along the pier toward the vague silhouette of the freighter.

"Tramp ships such as this travel all over the world," Lovecraft said. "He might have picked up the knowledge in any port in India or Asia."

"Maybe that first mate of his taught it to him," Houdini said. "Did you see the tattoos on his face? They looked African."

"The gangway is still down, thank God," Eddy said.

They had discussed how to get on board the ship if the gangway had been raised for the night. Houdini had intended to climb the ship's cable, and neither Eddy nor Lovecraft had expressed any doubt that he could do so. His athleticism was second to none. But it appeared it would not be necessary.

"It almost feels like an invitation," Lovecraft said.

"I agree. I don't like it," Eddy said.

Houdini said nothing, but advanced up the angled wooden platform like a cat on the toes of his shoes. The other two followed more cautiously. Neither was accustomed to daring robbery in the wee hours of the night. Eddy was as game as a rooster, but Lovecraft felt serious misgivings about what he had agreed to do. He was not by nature heroic in any sense. He wanted to return to the hotel and escort his wife back to his aunt's house, where they were staying, but loyalty to Eddy kept him moving forward.

They had discussed how they were to get the witch's ladder out of the locked safe. There seemed only one way: to capture Kruger and force him to open it. No mention was made of the first mate, but Lovecraft knew that his friend intended to shoot the giant if they were attacked.

In the silence between the moans of the foghorn, Lovecraft heard a soft bubbling. He could not tell where it originated, but it reminded him of the gurgle of water into a bathtub.

They approached the angled hatch through which they had gained access to the bowels of the ship earlier. The door was shut.

"Over here," a man said. Lovecraft recognized Kruger's German accent.

Metal clinked against metal, and suddenly a light spilled out over the deck of the ship. Kruger held a lantern upraised in his hand. The door of the lantern hung wide on its hinge. By its yellow glow Lovecraft saw that the captain stood beside an open cargo hatch on the deck. The first mate was not with him.

"I expected you to try something tonight." Kruger's voice was more slurred than it had been at their earlier meeting.

"I am here for what I paid for," Houdini said.

Kruger held out his fist. "This?" The witch's ladder cascaded from his fingers and hung down, twisting back and forth. "I have changed my mind. I have decided to be generous and give you the charm."

Surprise held them silent for several heartbeats. Houdini took a step toward Kruger. He turned and extended the witch's ladder over the black rectangle of the open hatch.

"Do you know what is below, Herr Houdini? No, of course you don't, so I will tell you. I have opened the cocks and flooded this hold with sea water. Tell me, can your precious Bess swim?"

Without warning, he released the charm. It fell into the darkness. Houdini cried out like a wounded beast and leaped forward. He darted past Kruger without a glance and threw himself into the black of the hold. Lovecraft heard his body break the surface of the water below.

"You monster, what have you done?" he demanded.

Kruger laughed. "There is no ladder in this hold. I had it taken up. I intend to sit here and watch your trumped-up little magician drown, along with his wife. By now her lungs are filling up with salt water. It will present quite a little puzzle for the coroner, how she came to drown on dry land."

"Get him out of there now," Eddy said. "I swear, I'll blow your head off."

He had his revolver out and levelled at Kruger. Lovecraft noted with approval that his hand was not shaking. He wondered where the first mate had hidden himself and turned to look around. A hard blow to the side of the head knocked him senseless. Dimly he heard three gunshots in quick succession.

When he regained consciousness and raised his head, he saw that he was lying face down on the floor of the captain's cabin. Eddy sat next to him with his back against a wall. One side of his face was covered with a purple bruise, and dried blood clotted his left eyebrow. His lower lip was split and swollen. He grinned at Lovecraft and winced.

"Never even saw him coming," he said. "I heard you go down, but he was on me before I could turn around. I fired on him but missed, damn it."

"Where is Houdini?" Lovecraft asked. His voice sounded hollow in his own ears.

Kruger laughed from behind the desk. He waved a gun at them. Lovecraft recognized it by its narrow barrel as a Luger, the preferred sidearm of German officers during the Great War.

"The little Jew is dead. I held the lantern down into the hold, but he was gone. I was disappointed. After all that has been written about his physical abilities I expected him to be able to tread water for longer than ten minutes. I wanted to watch him drown."

"You murdered him," Lovecraft said.

"Yes, I did. And now I am going to murder you. I think I will have Demba put you down into the same hold and let you splash around with your dead friend. Then, later, the water can be pumped out and you can be quietly disposed of at sea."

"Why are you doing this?"

"Isn't that obvious? I'm doing it because I hate you. I hate all you Americans, all you filthy Jew-lovers. You think you beat us in the war? You didn't win. The war is not over. We will rise again, and when we do you will find out what it is to oppose the will of the German folk. When he who is coming takes power, our new leader will deal with all of your Judean rats as they deserve."

Something thudded on the deck above their heads. Kruger cocked his ear, listening.

"Demba? What's happening up there?"

No answer came. Kruger frowned and stood unsteadily. Lovecraft saw that the level of amber liquid in the bottle on the corner of his desk was no more than an inch from the bottom.

Keeping the gun directed at them, the German edged around his desk toward the door. He paused with his hand on the brass latch.

"Leave this cabin, and you will be shot on sight."

He opened the door. A fist struck him on the point of his chin, and the gun went flying into a corner. Houdini darted forward and grappled with the flailing German, who recovered his wits quickly and began to fight back with obvious skill.

"Where's the gun? Find the gun!" Eddy said.

He and Lovecraft began to crawl around, looking for the Luger in the shadows cast by the desk lamp while Houdini and Kruger grappled on the open floor. The gun was nowhere to be seen.

"Filthy Jew, I'll kill you again!" Kruger gritted between his clenched teeth.

A flash of reflected light caught Lovecraft's eye as the German tried to swing his hand across Houdini's face.

"Watch it, Harry, he's got a knife."

The German was taller and heavier than the entertainer, but Houdini has spent decades honing his body to athletic perfection. The strength in his arms and legs was almost superhuman. He twisted his body and slammed Kruger's right hand into the wall several times. The knife clatters across the floor.

"Where is that damned gun?" Eddy said. "It has to be here."

Lovecraft peered under the desk. Through the wooden legs he saw the legs of the two men who were locked in combat. They appeared almost to be dancing in a shuffling, eerie silence broken only by grunts of effort. The effect was surreal. It was hard to think with the throbbing in his head.

"Where's your own gun?" he asked Eddy.

"I don't know; he must have taken it off me while I was out. Look in the desk."

Lovecraft started to yank open its drawers. The center drawer in the top was locked. He searched the other drawers for something he could use to pry it open.

Kruger had his hands around Houdini's throat as he bent his foe backward across the desk. The grotesquely inverted face of the entertainer had turned a deep red. Lovecraft cursed and started around the desk to help him. At the same moment Houdini straightened his back, drove his hands between the German's forearms, and broke his grip. He grabbed Kruger's left arm and drew his close, then thrust out his hip and threw the German over it. Kruger went down hard on his back. His head bounced off the steel flooring plate and he abruptly stopped moving.

Lovecraft held onto the edge of the desk and stood swaying.

"How did you do that?"

"It's called ju-jitsu," Houdini said, gasping for breath. "A Japanese fighting art I studied to improve my balance."

Lovecraft stared at the German. "Is he dead?"

Houdini crouched down with his hands on his knees. Water dripped from his hair and clothes onto the unconscious man's face.

"He's still breathing."

"We thought you were drowned."

"I've escaped from worse water tortures than that."

"But Kruger lowered the lantern into the hold. He said you were dead."

"I was under the water. I can hold my breath for several minutes."

Eddy had never ceased searching for the Luger. He stood up with it in his hand, a grim expression on his damaged face.

"Where's the other one?"

Houdini shrugged. "He went for a swim in the hold. Unfortunately, he wasn't a very good swimmer."

"I should shoot this monster where he lies. I think I would do it if we didn't need him to drain the hold so we can recover the witch's ladder."

"We don't need him." Houdini took something from his pocket and let it unravel. It was a piece of twine.

"Is that—?"

"Part of it. When Kruger threw it into the hold, it got hung up on a length of chain. It never reached the water."

"What happened to all the bits and pieces that were tied up in it?" Eddy asked.

"I untied all the knots. The pieces are in my pocket. I don't pretend to know how this charm works, but I think untying the knots releases the person linked to those items. At least, I pray to God that is the case."

They stood looking down at Kruger, whose chest moved with shallow breaths.

"We need to wake him up and make him open the safe. He still has your ten thousand dollars," Eddy said.

"Let him keep the money," Houdini said. "We had a bargain."

The little man raised his eyebrows and winced.

Humming to himself, Houdini picked up Kruger's knife from the floor and bent over him. Lovecraft thought he was about to slash the German's throat, but instead he cut a lock of the man's blond hair, then gathered a section of his shirt and sawed out a square of cloth with the blade.

When it dawned on Lovecraft what Houdini intended, he felt a chill down his spine.

"The witch's ladder is mine now, to use as I see fit," Houdini said. "Let Kruger continue to sail the seven seas. Let him try to enjoy spending my money. I will make certain every day that he regrets what he did to my Bess. He will write to me and beg for mercy. And who knows? After six months, or a year, or ten years, I may even listen to him."

How Could It Be Elsewise?

Richard Gavin

The hand that gripped his wrist was cold, dry. Lovecraft could faintly sense his limp arm being hoisted and then held in place for what seemed a tediously long time. Today's agonies had levied what little energy he had left; he was too spent to even open his eyes while the nurse or doctor measured his sluggish pulse.

He could feel himself nodding off yet again. Since being admitted to Jane Brown Memorial Hospital, Lovecraft's life had been reduced to stretches of torturous wakefulness punctuated by merciful bouts of cool, dark, dreamless slumber. His arm still dangling, he submitted to the familiar weightless feeling and to the peculiar dizziness that always preluded his time in the abyss. Oblivion was a state to which he had always felt curiously drawn, and now, in this wretched late stage of his life, it was a balm he welcomed with profound thanksgiving.

Lovecraft had always held that there was no keener subject of fascination than the black abyss, what mystics might term *Śūnyatā*, the Void, but this predilection had become his only comfort since the cancer had nestled, deep and foul, in his intestine. Before finally being rushed to Jane Brown Memorial, Lovecraft would often prop himself in an austere chair—the only position that brought him relief enough to nod off, to slip into those thin oases of sense-free darkness.

Of late, these respites were becoming rarer and they came at the cost of unbearable pain upon waking.

Tonight, however . . . tonight was different. Lovecraft could *feel.* He was moving, cascading over some vast unseen expanse. He was as a cresting wave stretching upward and outward, rushing freely toward some distant shore. There was a moment where he feared the inevitable crash. How would this newfound velocity end if not in cataclysm?

But there was no collision, only an increased weightlessness, a freedom of movement that was unhindered by flesh and bone. Lovecraft knew that he must be dreaming, a hallucination brought on by the agony and sickness. An apostle to the god Science, he understood that all life was but a series of pictures in the brain, ones that dissolve once the brain dies.

Evidently his brain was very much alive, for here there was profound sensation, and now images too: Lovecraft found himself standing among the moonlit markers of Swan Point Cemetery.

If dream this was, its vividness surpassed even the most textured ones he had detailed in rare letters and sent to his most valued confidants. All his senses were engaged. He could smell the perfume of the mourners' flowers, hear the haunting call of a hidden owl, taste the lingering sweetness of something very much like honey, see the mist-laden tombstones; and yet through it all Lovecraft could still feel the hand that was somehow managing to hold steadfast to his wrist.

Curious about this lingering sense of being touched, he turned. When he saw that which clung to him, he let out a strangled cry.

The clutching hand was a blackened, withered thing; its flesh reticulated and fuming, as though fresh from the pyre. Flames or time had reduced the arm to a network of bones that bulged through the flaking skin. The hand appeared so frail, yet it was capable of a tightening grip. Its arm, which was veiled in a sullied coat, reached up from behind a weathered headstone, one that Lovecraft found eerily familiar. He recognized the stone's Colonial craftsmanship, the pads of old moss, the engravings that the winds of time had pressed anonymously smooth.

Not even the lack of an epitaph could dull his recognition: it was the grave of Simon Smith (died March 4, 1711), one of his ancestors. The realization of exactly where this dream had taken him stirred in Lovecraft a great tide of deep nostalgia, one that he allowed to cascade over him like a temperate breeze. He closed his eyes meditatively, opening them only when a dry rustling broke his trance.

His captor was emerging from the shadows that stretched across his neglected grave. The figure twisted slowly upwards into view, like a grotesque vine blooming under the lustrous moon. The rising shape revealed itself to be a raggedy thing garbed in a deteriorated Colonial-era clothing. Frayed scraps of this wardrobe flapped in the wind like festive crepe. Its face, as best as Lovecraft could discern through the billowing shroud that obscured it, was a sagging visage. Smoke radiated from the corpse. Lovecraft watched as these fumes lazily mingled with the surrounding banks of what he'd assumed to be mist. He then realized that what enveloped him was the smoke of the smouldering dead.

The corpse's fingers creaked and popped as it loosened them one by one from Lovecraft's arm.

Lovecraft snapped his limb back and began to massage the area where he'd been held, hoping that this might somehow wipe away the taint of the corpse's touch.

A fluttering noise then filled his ears, drowning out the soft lament of the wind and the hooting owl. This new sound was akin to film flickering through a projector, though it was not as rhythmic. Instead it was jagged, frantic, like a pinioned bird struggling for flight. Lovecraft squinted, scrutinizing the veiled face before him.

The apparition was struggling to speak.

The shape raised its arms slowly and proceeded to yank the shroud taut across what was left of its mouth. It bound the slack material into a clumsy knot at the base of its skull.

"My dear Howard," it said. Whatever this apparition used as breath was now being filtered through the threadbare muzzle of the shroud, which vibrated against skinned teeth, creating a rudimentary voice box. The words escaped in a strange buzzing. Despite using a term of endearment, the creature's tone was devoid of emotion.

"Simon Smith?" Lovecraft uttered. Amazement reduced his voice to a whisper.

"You remembered, my boy, you remembered. As I remember the times when your Aunt Lillian would bring you here to visit me."

"Which she did often. And always at my insistence."

"You so loved this place."

"I still do." Lovecraft felt his mouth hitch into a half-grin.

Simon Smith nodded his draped head. *"How fine it is to see you smiling. It is so rare a thing for you."*

Lovecraft cleared his throat. He nervously ran his hands down his trunk, and was perplexed to discover that the shapeless hospital gown to which he'd been confined for the past few days had somehow been replaced by his favourite three-piece suit (chocolate brown), a cream shirt, and a necktie of black silk.

"Life has taken away more pleasures than it has granted me, I fear," he admitted.

"How could it be elsewise?"

Lovecraft was unsure how to respond.

There then came, faintly yet not far off, irregular footfalls. They emanated from those endless rows of smoke-veiled tombstones and towering trees; places where the moon was too timid to shine upon.

"Simon . . ." His voice was practically inaudible, even to himself. Where, he wondered, had the staunch intellectual curiosity on which he prided himself gone? Why should he now, in this strange dream, be suddenly stricken with a childish fear of the dark?

"What you're feeling is not fear, my boy," Simon Smith muttered knowingly.

"What . . . *am* I feeling?"

Instead of answering, Simon Smith advanced from behind his headstone and stood close to him. Lovecraft inhaled the perfume of the grave. It was a miasma that hung heavy on the air. Its effect was gruesomely enchanting.

"Let us walk, my boy. You and I, into the night."

Together they set out across the great plain of soft grass and sculpted marble. Lovecraft was only dimly aware of the fact that his guide had again reached a fleshless hand to grip him and that this time he welcomed it. He looked down to see the appendage of old cloth and older bone and was suddenly struck with an appreciation of how oddly perfect it truly was.

The sheer scope and odd lay of this land were becoming apparent with every patient step they took. Theirs was a tortured path; contorted and bewildering and seemingly void of destination. But this fact only served to intensify Lovecraft's astonishment.

Monuments of vast antiquity gleamed like chalk mounds in the dark. Autumn leaves spun in manic circles at their feet. Trees of impossible majesty domed the land, yet their boughs still afforded a panoramic view of the moving black clouds and the gibbous moon and the bats and whippoorwills that flitted across the star-studded sky.

This was the Swan Point not of his boyhood as such, but of his boyhood dreams; the Swan Point that flowered when his subconscious was unfettered. He was *here*, truly here. It was as though his childhood impressions of antiquated Providence being a Gothic Eden had somehow slithered free from his brain and created someplace objective, someplace true.

"I'd forgotten," Lovecraft whispered, to himself he thought. "I'd actually forgotten how this place seemed to me once upon a time."

"But of course," returned his guide. *"You had to forget, to abandon this place so that you might return to it. Such is the nature of time. How could it be elsewise?"*

Only after they'd rounded a patiently arcing bend did Lovecraft discover the humbling mountain range that loomed in the west.

He blinked several times, attempting to purge the hallucination, but the fires he saw continued to blaze on the jagged peaks. At this distance the bonfires appeared no larger than pinheads, but there were hundreds of them, flickering like some fresh infernal constellation.

This vision was so grand that Lovecraft scarcely noticed that the strange, irregular footfalls he'd heard earlier had intensified. A procession now seemed to be keeping step with him and his guide, flanking them, moving ever-hidden.

Once these presences registered with him, Lovecraft was intrigued at how he had come to know, simply *know*, that they were not figments of his imagination. Indeed, nothing in this world was. Everything that dwelt here was indigenous. It was he who was the visitant, the outsider.

"There is a way station up ahead," Simon Smith said, luring his charge out of his reverie. *"We shall rest, and we shall talk before the final leg of our journey."*

"Very well."

The cemetery was no longer Swan Point, nor even the conflated Swan Point of Lovecraft's boyhood fancies. It had become a necropolis of impossible sprawl and strangeness. The markers they now passed were separated by vast fields, some of which featured moss-draped temples or sculptures humbling in their immensity and chilling in their grotesqueness. Though he would have loved to have explored these sites in greater detail, Lovecraft was too depleted to do so.

They reached a burial cairn, and Simon Smith bade Lovecraft to sit. Lovecraft complied. He then tugged a handkerchief from his breast pocket and dabbed the perspiration from his brow. The respite from movement made him keenly aware of his own lassitude. The pain in his side flared, and Lovecraft winced.

"Forgive me for asking," he began, somewhat breathlessly, "but is there much left in this journey of ours?"

"Not in terms of distance."

"You see, I'm afraid I've been unwell for some time now . . . back there," he explained, waving to some vague and insignificant place now well behind them, "and it appears that my illness is now closing in on me here as well."

"How could it be elsewise?"

His repetition of the question made Lovecraft wonder if perhaps his guide was not being rhetorical.

"Well, perhaps it cannot," he replied. "I suppose 'tis only fitting that an existence of penury, isolation, and obscurity should end in agony. That seems to be the nature of things, doesn't it?" He tried to chortle, to forcefully express a laissez-faire attitude toward the whole rotten ordeal, but what emerged was a piping noise, short and pathetic. A glassy sheet of sorrow moved through him. It was in many ways more painful than his ailment.

"Life is a hideous thing," rasped Simon Smith.

Lovecraft could not contain his sense of shock. "How extraordinary! I once used that very phrase in one of my stories. I was a writer." He paused to corrected himself. "*Am* a writer. An amateur, but a writer still."

"And the visions you put forth—did they find their audience?"

"Alas, no. At least, not in any appreciable way. Some friends, writers themselves, and perhaps a sprinkling of readers here and there. Nowhere near the audience I was striving for. Then again, I suppose one who rejects the cheap conventions of popular fiction and reaches instead for cataclysmic terror is doomed to fail. How could it be elsewise?" Lovecraft offered his guide a wry smile.

"Your world . . . that world . . . sounds as though it was a fount of grief for you."

He nodded. "I never could find my place there, you know? I don't suppose you can imagine what that is like, feeling as though you were born too late. Every day of my life, *every day*, Simon, I felt that all I loved was either dead or dying. The beautiful Colonial houses, the works of high art, the . . . magic, I suppose one might call it, the magic was bleeding out of the world, all around me, and I was helpless to cauterize it."

"Thus, you began to oscillate between shrinking away from the world and lashing out against it."

Lovecraft found these insights keen and piercing, not unlike the affliction in his stomach.

"That is possible, I suppose, yes. One could argue that I lashed out where and when I could, that I hated the world that had been left to me. But what I never seemed able to get others to understand was the reason why I was so staunch in my views. It was because I somehow sensed there was a deeper world, an older world, and it was this deeper world that I saw being shovelled into its grave with each passing year."

"Hence you found scapegoats. Peoples and cities on which to focus your rage . . ."

"I suppose so, yes. I could never understand why so few people seemed even to comprehend me when I spoke about the beauty of oblivion, or of majestic horrors, or of the ancient."

"That is because you were reciting from the Book of the Dead to people whose vocabulary flows only from the Book of Life. It could never be otherwise. Your words have always been meant for the Dead, my dear boy."

"Well, I did have *some* friends, some kindred spirits in life." Lovecraft could feel the softness of his protest, as though he were scrabbling back from some powerful, disconcerting truth about himself. He was fumbling to put the pieces of his life back in their old familiar pattern. "I even took a wife."

"The rare ones, as you are, attempt in all sorts of ways to pull a skin of normalcy over their souls, but in the end one cannot be anything other than what one is. You were a living man who saw with the eyes of the dead, an earth-walker whose soul is stationed down here . . ."

Lovecraft mulled over his ancestor's words while he studied the mountains, which still appeared every bit as remote as they had at the start of this odd pilgrimage.

"I once fancied myself a pagan, did you know that? As a boy, in the same era when I would frequent your graveside, I used to build altars to Diana and to Pan. One October evening I was permitted to walk alone in a nearby grove. And there, in the gloaming, I witnessed fell creatures, things of the deep world.

"How I wish I could have sustained my faith."

"What quashed it?"

Lovecraft pondered the question before attempting to answer. "Maturity, I suppose. But even when I developed a passion for science I never lost my desire to experience that splendid moment of terror and awe."

"Hence your stories?"

"Hence my stories, my fumbling attempts at trying to convey something beyond words. The process of delving into the black abyss is to me the keenest form of fascination. But sadly, I could never truly tell my tale." He paused and stared longingly into the smoky dark. "If only . . ."

"If only what, dear boy?"

"If only I could experience that *fullness* I'd known as a boy standing under those autumnal oaks, witnessing those unworldly things dancing about the shadows. Knowledge I might have gained, but it has brought me no comfort, no fulfillment. In fact, everything in life leaves me wanting."

"That is because what you've been seeking cannot be found in life. You do not belong to the land of the living, dear Howard. Your soul is rooted here."

"And where is here?"

"Below," Simon Smith began, *"and beyond. And within. This is a hidden place. A rare place."*

"This is a dream, Simon . . . some reverie brought on by my illness."

"To some this place wears the guise of dream. Most people are unable to perceive it at all. Those few that do usually dismiss it as a vivid nightmare. But you, dear boy, you've been able to perceive it without some secondary projection. Your soul never required this place to project itself as some drama that occurs upon the wall of sleep."

"Are we beyond the wall of sleep?"

"We are. You always have been," said Simon. *"That is the source of all your supposed failures in life. Back there, you are one of the rare ones. But here, here you will find an audience that is not only sizeable, but genuinely aware. There are so few among the living capable of appreciating your visions, the poetry you spoke. That is why you languished in obscurity, my boy. You wrote from the Dead and for the Dead."*

The footfalls now seemed to resound from every direction as the horde of shambling things stepped slightly nearer. They were close enough to convey presence yet remained aloof and vague in the distance and the mists. It was a legion of silhouettes; some stooped and bulky, others willowy and impossibly tall.

A tempest of questions surged in Lovecraft's mind, but before he could utter the first, the horde turned and began shuffling away, toward the west, toward the Cyclopean mountains. He peered intently, hoping to confirm what he was seeing.

The shambling forms were hoisting themselves off the ground and taking graceful flight, cascading up toward the mountains.

Pain flared in Lovecraft's side, causing him to grunt. He went to press his hand to his midsection, only to feel it close over something knotty and cold, something leathery, something living.

A splayed claw, muscular and darksome, now clung to his side. Its talon-like nails were pressed firmly into Lovecraft's abdomen, making each breath barbed. Lovecraft's gaze followed the gripping claw along the black arm until he was able to see the awful thing that was squatting beside him; a creature with which he was only too familiar.

The Night-Gaunt had its faceless gaze affixed on Lovecraft. Its wings were clenched firm against its lean, rubbery body. Its horns jutted up from its head like twin scythes.

Memories came flooding over Lovecraft, half-dreams from childhood, where the Night-Gaunts would grip his stomach and carry him across great leagues of swirling air, spiriting him away to unfathomable climes.

"It is as it was," Lovecraft uttered, resignedly.

"As it must be. As it always shall be," added Simon Smith in his buzzing, shroud-forged voice.

The Night-Gaunt began to rise. Lovecraft was being helplessly hoisted with it.

Shock set in. Lovecraft felt the last vestiges of strength rush out of his body. He also felt the tears that had begun streaming down his cheeks.

"Simon . . . I am dying, am I not?"

"Yes, my boy. But it is through death that you shall once again know fullness."

He turned his slack face to Simon Smith, now too feeble to even speak. The revenant read his eyes and continued.

"All those things you cherished, all that magic you felt bleeding out of the world, it was all flowing back to its source—here. You tried so earnestly to draw this place into that drab globe, but only another rare one could appreciate your genius. Now, dear boy, you are among those who know. This is the realm of fullness because it is devoid of life.

"Come, my dear Howard. Come back and speak your true story at last. The story you've been yearning all your life to tell, one without filter or self-deception, the story that could only be told by the dead and to the dead. Here, the soul shall be your parchment and the sibilant night winds shall be your quill. Here, your horrors shall be seen entire, for they shall not be aberrations, they shall be pure Forms.

"But we must make haste now, dear boy. Allow this creature to carry you to the mountain so that you may experience the Festival of which your stories are but an echo."

Lovecraft's face became a mask of contentment.

The Night-Gaunt fanned its vast wings, lashed its barbed tail, and took flight.

Lovecraft felt the most exquisite agony as the creature lifted him into the air.

In the early morning hours of March 15, 1937, Howard Phillips Lovecraft experienced one last convulsion of intestinal pain. The attending nurse would later say that as he expired a look of tranquility overcame his face.

She drew the sheet up over his head.

And at that precise moment, Lovecraft was delivered unto the throngs of shadowy things in the caves of the great mountain. This cabal, which included Simon Smith, fell respectfully silent.

Lovecraft at last began to tell his tale.

A Gentleman of Darkness

W. H. Pugmire

New York is a dead city."

Looking at Carl Pert, I frowned in distaste. I like to think that I am a woman free of bigotry, having been a victim of race prejudice; but there was something about this runtish creature that triggered a deep core of dislike, a loathing that could not be dismissed. His flesh was of a sickly pallor, and his hair looked as if it had never been washed. The sallow skin was pitted, the head abnormally large, and the hands unusually small. Those petite hands, however, had been responsible for some of the most unique artwork New York had ever beheld, and the personality that expressed itself when the twisted lips began to speak their beautiful music was such that one soon became captivated. Despite the revulsion his physical frame inspired, I found myself visiting him often in his cramped apartment in the seedy Red Hook area. Pert was fond of his mystique, and little was known of his origin. A buzz began to hum within the city about the chalk portraits that began to appear on alleyway pavements and the walls of brick buildings; and then Pert had been discovered at work on one of these mesmerizing images. He would never explain the magic of his artistic technique, why it was that his work pulled at one's brain, so that one imagined that a portion of one's psychic was being sucked into the personality portrayed. "Why do you scrutinize me so, madam?"

"Sorry—I'm just trying to comprehend your ridiculous statement."

His enchanting voice poured like dainty music from the fellow's twisted lips, although the sentiment expressed was unhappy. "I was made to think that I'd find a hive of creativity here; but all I find is racket and rushing and rabble. Your artistic 'community' is made up of talentless and unimaginative poseurs, and they have come to hate me because I refuse to play the game of back-patting that masquerades as friendship. This squalid neighborhood is obscene, but this apartment is all I can afford at the moment. The hordes of mice help keep loneliness at bay. No, I haven't the heart to set traps. I abhor the sight of their little corpses, with faces twisted in pain and tiny paws stiffened in upward position. You can see from the redness in my eyes that I am exhausted—sleep is a myth that I used to know. That Syrian freak in the next apartment plays his bagpipe in the middle of the night, giving me bad dreams. I've never had such terrible dreams."

"To hell with your dreams, Carl," I told him. "We're concerned with your recent episode of sleepwalking. This is not a good neighborhood for roaming about at night, and your fall could have resulted in more than a few bruises. There have been reports of attacks by gang hoodlums."

And then it came from behind one wall, the muted sound that seeped into Pert's room. I wouldn't call the melody lovely, but it was certainly captivating. Stepping to the wall, I pressed both hands against it and stared at its surface with such force that I fancied I might be able to see through it into the other chamber.

"There he goes again," Pert grumbled, "the idiot with his bagpipe."

"No," I corrected him, "it's surely a horn, like that used by snake charmers."

"Well, it certainly seems to have charmed you. Does it call to your taint of exotic jungle blood?"

I groaned a little at his racism and wanted to remind him of the discrimination his own appearance had inspired in some circles. Instead, I gently slapped the back of his head as I sauntered to the door. "I'll have a word with him on my way out," I informed the fellow. "Now promise me that you'll see a doctor about your sleep-walking."

"What the devil could any doctor do about it? The idea is absurd. Anyway, I rather *like* the idea of somnambulism. Perhaps I'll change my name to 'Cesare'—some of those scenes in my dreams are very like the settings in *Caligari*. Shall I come to your bedchamber one haunted night and carry you away, sweet Alma?"

"You in my bed—now that *is* a nightmare." Pert pretended to wince, but I could sense his secret smile. Nothing pleased him more than to be insulted—unless it was to be insulting. I let myself out of his room but closed the door a bit more forcefully than I intended, and the sound of its slamming echoed in the hallway. The wailing from the neighboring room ceased and its door opened. A dusky face appeared and studied me.

"I heard a bang," the handsome fellow spoke. One hand held a kind of metallic horn.

I pointed to his instrument. "Ah, that's what we've been hearing through the wall. It makes an awful racket. Perhaps you could play it less vigorously at this time of night. Your exotic music has been giving my friend bad dreams."

"Bad dreams! Ha!" He returned inside his room but had not bothered to shut his door. Stepping up to the doorjamb, I leaned against it and gazed into his apartment. The occupant stood on a square of colorful carpet, tall and handsome and perhaps Egyptian. I watched him place the horn onto a nearby stand, pick up a silver cigarette case, and push the button that caused its lid to spring open. He held the case to me in a gesture of offering.

"No thanks," I told him as I entered his room and took in the faint yet pleasurable scents that perfumed it. "Really, your horn makes an awful racket. It would be a kindness to be more considerate."

Lighting a cigarette that hung between his lips, the gentleman peered at me for some silent moments. Then he smiled. "Because of his dreams. And yet it is *because* of those dreams that I must play. There is a residue of disruption in this area still—age-old evil may be dormant, but it does not die—and my theory is that your friend's potent dreaming has awakened slumbering devils. You may have heard of the trouble that plagued this place some time ago? There is a kind of vile psychic contagion here that spreads a loathsome influence. There has already been a return of the young thugs who have a penchant for crime. The police ignore this area, because they consider its inhabitants polluted. We are not clean and white as they are. You've no doubt experienced the kind of bias I speak of. But that does not concern you tonight. Your friend is an artist, I know, and such persons are blessed with fantastic imagination. They are never more imaginative than when sleeping, and their dreams can be extraordinary. But your friend's dreams have become chaotic, infused with the diseased psychic debris of that which happened here not long ago. The neighborhood alleys remember echoes of madness and deviltry in their deepest darknesses."

He paused, closed his eyes, and sucked on his cigarette. The cloud of smoke he exhaled seemed darker than it should have been, and its essence coiled queerly before the strange man's alluring visage. Why did that cloud of smoke not dissipate? Why did it continue to weave into itself as if it would transform into some unspeakable thing? I saw that the fellow had the horn in hand once more. He brought its mouthpiece to his lips and sighed a little, producing a soft sound. The cloud of smoke melted at the faint resonance.

The dweller in the apartment flashed a smile, in which his teeth glimmered like rows of glistening pearls. I stood for one silent moment, and then I whispered, "I'm a bit worried about my friend. A little less noise at night, please."

I backed out of the chamber and took the elevator to the ground floor. Outside, the moon's gleaming burned onto my eyes. I shivered when I studied that lifeless orb and noticed a patch of shadow on it that subtly resembled the cloud of smoke that the Egyptian man had produced. I laughed nervously, thinking that whatever atmosphere plagued this place, it had certainly tainted my own imagination. Little wonder that my artistic friend suffered wild dreams. I did not realize that I was walking until I found myself entering the alley behind Pert's apartment. Its pavement was filthy with a residue of grime in which I could just make out footprints and the tracks of truck tires. A slight stench of garbage was carried on the windless air, as was a faint smell of something burning. Noticing a flickering near a number of large crates, I went to them and found two figures huddled before a feeble flame—a gypsy woman and her brat. Amber eyes squinted at me from the hag's shifty countenance, and the words that she had been coaxing the child to repeat ceased. The little one raised a malformed hand and made some kind of gesture, and the air seemed to grow a little colder. Reaching into my jacket pocket, I produced some coins and tossed them at the pair.

Exhaustion ruled by the time I entered my home. The apartment seemed unseasonably hot, and I threw off my jacket and went to get a glass of cold water. Falling into my favorite armchair, I immediately closed my eyes. I did not enter sleep as much as I slipped into a disturbed realm of dreaming—a kind never before experienced, where I seemed to be able to see through my closed eyelids into the space just before my face. There was no real sound, but I could feel a faint pounding in my ears that kept time with my heartbeat. A small dim figure came into view, and when it turned its face toward me I saw that it was the child I had encountered in the alley. Her mouth was moving, and I assumed that she was repeating the language that her antique companion had been teaching her. The dream-vision of her face enlarged, as if the child were drifting nearer to my dozing countenance; and then that mouth began to divide and multiply, and I was surrounded by a conglomeration of shifting voids in which I seemed to sense an ageless hunger. A void of darkness opened close to my breasts, from which I insanely imagined I could feel a current of ice-cold breath. I felt my own mouth part with protest, and the dream began to pound with loud clamor. I was awakened by someone pounding on my apartment door, and when I answered the noise I found my landlady gazing at me worriedly. She had been cleaning a vacant apartment some few doors from mine and could hear a frightful kind of crying coming from my room. Taking one of her small hands, I patted it reassuringly and told her that I had been having a most fantastic nightmare, and I thanked her for bringing me out of it with her loud knocking.

I was now wide awake, and discovered in me a mood for movement. Sensing that the night had grown chillier, I slipped into a longer skirt, found a warmer jacket, and went for what I meant to be a little nighttime stroll. But I wasn't paying any attention to the direction in which I walked, for my mind kept returning to the images of my disturbing dream; and I was suddenly astounded to find myself standing in front of Carl Pert's apartment building, the façade of which seemed particularly bright in the combination of streetlamp glare and moonlight. Not being one to wear a watch, I had no notion of the time; but I sensed that it was very late and thus not an appropriate hour to press the buzzer button for Carl's apartment. And yet—how strangely powerful was my compulsion to see him, to tell him of my dream and share a laugh. Looking up, I saw that the window to his room was dark. I found myself moving past the building and walking to the alley behind it. The alley was dim with shadows, and there was a stunted silhouette that moved with fantastic motion. It was Carl, and he was either having a kind of seizure or attempting an outrageous form of dancing.

"Whatever are you doing?" I said in a loud voice as I approached him.

"Ah—Alma, Alma, with your green eyes and cocoa-butter skin. Look, see how the shadows enfold your flesh. Isn't it curious how these shadows take on an insubstantial form as they coil around our form? Their peculiar structures heave and billow and whirl, with movement so intoxicating I want to be a part of it. Whirl with me, sweet Alma! Become one with spinning shadow—frolic and cavort!"

He moved away from me and began his crazy dance once more. Although it was dark, I seemed to be able to see his pirouetting shadow on the ground; but then I realized it wasn't his shadow that coiled near us, but something else. My blood froze within my veins when, as I watched, the convoluting shadow surrounded us. One portion of the blackness parted, resembling the mouth-like cavity that I had witnessed in troubled dreaming. I could feel the steady flow of coldness that came to us like the breath of some drear beast. Stems of shadow curled around my arms and I was hurled violently toward a brick wall. Unable to stop my movement, I felt my head slam against filthy brick. I thought I heard my skull crack slightly, and a trickle of warm blood began to spill down my face and into my mouth.

I moaned and cursed, turning to face the assault of darkness; and then I caught sight of the pale figure that stepped into the alley. Above the noise of my heaving breath and weeping, I noted the sound that issued from the instrument that the pale figure touched to the mouth of its dusky visage. Carl Pert's mysterious neighbor raised one hand, with which he made strange motions as his mouth continued to produce eerie music on his horn. My mind could feel the sharp hatred that the daemonic shadows had for the Egyptian's haunting music; I could feel that hatred like sharp needles in my brain, and I cried at the torment it produced. The fellow in his pale clothing of woven cloth placed a hand behind my head, and the torture that plagued me ceased. Someone who knelt next to me wrapped the fingers of a small hand around my ankle, as if seeking a kind of psychological support. Looking down at him, I smoothed my own hand across Carl's face, the lips of which kissed my fingers. The alchemy of music ceased, and an almost staggering sense of calm encased my soul. Gazing into the handsome man's magnetic eyes, I saw that they burned with an intense energy. The devil-shadows that had been born of Carl's demented dreaming were gone. I helped Carl to a standing position, and we both clung to the strange dark man who escorted us from the alleyway.

The Feverish Stars

John Shirley

"I have already had opportunity to observe the stars at Narragansett Bay," Howard said dryly, clearing his throat. "And yet here I am again. There is a hill near home I much prefer for observations . . ." He took his telescope from under his arm and began to set it up on its folding tripod.

"But you have never seen them like this!" said Lemuel. "Such a clear night is coming, Howard!"

As the sunset blended into sundown, Lem opened the shutter on his lantern an inch more. It was getting dark on the road above the narrow beach, and Howard didn't like the look of the area: it was too bleak, just a great hollow filled with an unquiet emptiness; the lazily churning slate-green bay, the strangely warm, soughing breeze—not quite a wind, but hinting of barely restrained energies.

"It's not fully night, Lem. Don't make meteorological predictions without all the facts in hand. We may have a rainstorm before the night is done. This is October, after all." In truth, Howard wanted to suggest they try to find a ride back to Providence; perhaps a buggy might go past. Lemuel's father, captain of a small crew on the trawler *Deep Seer*, had dropped them off at the point a mile west. Captain Grimpon had said the fish were "running fine after sunset, fair dancing into the nets," so he wasn't likely to return in his little steam trawler anytime soon.

With his weak chin, round eyes, and perpetually open mouth, the elder Grimpon made Howard think of a fish himself. This whole excursion was making Howard uneasy, and indeed he was feeling inordinately peevish. Lemuel and Howard were served roast beef sandwiches on the boat, and one bite in particular had seemed acrid and uncouth, giving off a sharp ammonial waft when he bit down on it. Howard was increasingly queasy, his skin seemed on too tight, and he wondered if he were getting ill.

It was a warm Indian summer night and the tide was receding, releasing the reek of subaquatic bay creatures. Howard envisioned the sickeningly undulant jellyfish, the otherworldly torpedo ray, the sea cucumber extruding an array of grotesque lace to feed; slimy clusters of repellently open shellfish hanging from befouled rocks. And somewhere in the blackness of the bay, the monstrously tooth gape of the monkfish. The thought made his stomach lurch and a wave of nausea surged through him.

He glanced down the road, hoping someone might be going back toward Providence. He saw only a man afoot, some distance away and coming toward them. In the dimming light the man was only a silhouette; a rather big, broad-shouldered figure who seemed to lurch along with difficulty. His left shoulder was strikingly lower than his right, so that his overall shape made Howard think of a rhombus. Poor fellow, must be crippled.

Looking the other way, he saw no one on the road, but below, where the beach narrowed to a tumble of broken boulders, he could make out the gangly figure of a man seated on a rock, about a hundred and fifty yards away. He was neatly dressed in a tweedy walking suit. He gazed out over the restless waves of the bay, smoke from his meerschaum curling past his drooping black mustache. He had the look of a gentleman in exile. As Howard watched, the sun dipped behind a bank of clouds at the horizon, and long shadows stretched over the man, darkening him considerably; one moment he was clearly visible, the next he was wreathed in shadow.

"Come on, Howard, let's go down to the beach!" Lemuel urged. "It's darker down there so the stars will be brighter!"

Howard winced, sighed, and picked up his telescope. "Very well." They skidded down the embankment to the beach, which was as much pebbles as sand, Howard muttering when he almost dropped the telescope. The sky truly was a bit darker from down here, and increasingly the stars were slipping off their veils and showing through. Venus was already fulminating out to the west.

They walked to the edge of the surf and Lem put his lantern down in the sand. "Howard, don't you *feel* something from the stars?" he asked, his uncombed brown hair swirling in the breeze like seaweed in a whirlpool. He was a round-faced fellow, with bright blue eyes, his father's weak chin. He was prone to florid poesies, and now he stood on the sand with his hands raised hieratically over his head, perhaps hoping to seem Byronic. "Oh, I feel it fairly dripping down on me!"

"*Feel* something from the stars?" Howard fussed over his telescope. The tripod was difficult to steady in the sand. "They are not in physical contact with me, why would I *feel* anything?"

"You don't think there's anything to astrology?"

"I think what there is to it—is whatever there is to rubbish. A bit of trash here, a bit of confounding mess there." Howard stepped back from the telescope and his head swam with the motion. The stars seemed to revolve for instant or two. "For heaven's sake, Lem, we are seventeen years old, nigh the state of manhood, much too old to believe in the vile casuistry of ancient Persian priests or the vaporings of that empty-headed girl you moon at when she speaks of her horoscope."

"But . . ." Lem dropped his hands and thrust them into his trouser pockets but he kept his face turned to the stars. "The stars fairly *exude* mystery."

Howard nodded grudgingly. "There is much mystery there. But it is the mystery of the natural world. Nothing supernatural is needed to make the universe mysterious and awesome. You know, in all probability the cosmos is vaster by far than we know."

"Vaster by far? Ha-ha! The stars are far . . . and vastly!"

Howard took his pencil and pad from the pocket of his light coat and bent to the telescope, straightening from time to time to make observations. His head throbbed every time he straightened up. He had been doing a study of Venus of late, and as he focused the telescope he spoke to Lemuel of the transit of Venus against the sun, first observed centuries ago thanks to a pinhole projecting light on a wall; he spoke of the rare conjunction of Mars and Venus, how the planets briefly seemed to blend—Lem made an off-color remark at that, which Howard chose to ignore—and the amazing proliferation of nebulae observed by astronomers.

Howard's own words seemed distant to him, as if someone else were speaking them. His stomach lurched again, and he stood up, grimacing, plucking out a kerchief to dab sweat from his brow. "Remarkably warm here. Should be cooling off . . ."

"Warm? I was just thinking it was getting a bit chilly! Look, mist is rising along the surf line!"

Howard looked and saw mist was curling up from the wet sand where the tide had receded. A faint mirroring of the phosphorescence in the unfurling waves glimmered in the mist. He glanced up at the stars—and was taken aback at their tremulous swirling. There were so many, too many, and they seemed almost to bubble, seething like rice in a pot. Some illusion, he knew. But whence?

He dabbed his sweaty face again and felt himself drawn to look up at the road. The rhombus man was still limping heavily along up there, much closer now. As Howard looked, the man paused and looked down at him. The stranger was still a rhombus with a human head, his face in shadow.

"Too bad we have no moon," Lem was saying. "But the starlight is so bright! Why, look—I can see it on my hands!"

Lemuel held his hands up, and they did look limned with a soft blue-whiteness.

"Yes. Your hands are nearly glowing . . ."

A fat, odor-laden breeze struck Howard in the face then, and his stomach buckled, his torso buckling with it, and he was suddenly vomiting into the pebbly sand at his feet.

He groaned and backed away from the mess. Lemuel was there

at his elbow, supporting him. "Howard—you're far too warm. You're feverish! Come back from the water. There's a big log yonder, you can take it easy there."

"Yes. I . . . yes. No! My telescope!"

"I'll set you down up there and run back for it instantly, my solemn word!"

"Very . . . very well."

Spitting out vomit-flavored bits of old food, Howard let Lemuel guide him to the big piece of driftwood halfway up the beach. He sat on the sand, his back against the log, as Lemuel ran back to the telescope.

He felt a little better, having vomited. But his head throbbed—he could *hear* it throb—and the mist was thickening.

Howard loosed his collar and thought he heard footsteps shuffling in the sand behind him. He turned awkwardly to look—and saw that the rhombus man, as he thought of him, was no longer on the road. It was all shadowy under the embankment. Was the fellow there, in that thick darkness?

Lemuel puffed up to him, telescope in one hand and lantern in the other. "Here's your telescope. I'll lean it just here. Rest, Howard. I don't know how to get you home except to wait for my father's boat. I know the *Deep Seer*'s lights. When he comes, I'll run shout to him and perhaps he can send the launch over . . . Ah, well, I'm not sure. But we'll get you home."

"I can walk back to the Point. He can pick us up there. I just need to rest a bit." Once more his own words seemed distant, muffled. He seemed to hear the stridulation of some insect stirred in. But there were no crickets on the beach.

"Are you quite all right, here?" The voice was almost a purr. It was the tweedy man with the pipe, trudging up to them. He was smiling, his mustaches lifted; but in the dimness his eyes were black pools.

"He's a bit feverish," Lemuel said. "My father won't be back with the boat for a couple of hours. I was thinking of going for a buckboard somewhere."

"My name is Crimburrow. I might have a solution."

"Lemuel Grimpon. This is Howard Lovecraft."

Howard scarcely attended them. He thought he heard a keening sound from somewhere overhead. A gull? But it was more like the thin piping of a flute. He looked up and was once more overwhelmed by the presentation of the stars: they swirled together, as if in grand brush strokes, and pulsed with febrile energy; the usual austere, attenuated blue-white light now seemed filtered through a slick translucent membrane of red and gold.

Feeling the world tilting about him, Howard closed his in search of steadiness, and was startled when he saw the stars glowing like embers in the back of his eyelids. It seemed they had declined to be shut out. He heard voices—the man with the purring, perhaps British tones, and Lemuel's voice—but couldn't quite make out what they were saying. The stars were raising their keening voices now, drowning everything else out. They grew louder and louder, and the keening became a roar.

But no. It was something beyond the stars that roared at him from a deranged void beyond the orderly universe. The sickness in the void had somehow poisoned the stars with its emanations; it had taken the wonderful clockwork of the planets—the turning of the earth, the rising and setting of stars, cosmic orderliness in magnificent array—and had turned it all to gems of wax that melted away in the heat of its hatred for anything that wished to constrain it. It was roaring louder, louder—and coming closer.

Howard gasped in naked fear and snapped his eyes open. They fixed on the lantern. Its feeble blue flame was flickering, he saw now. Lemuel hadn't topped it up with fuel, and it was burning out. Soon there would be no normal light left at all—only the unwholesome, perfervid glow of poisoned starlight . . .

"Howard? Are you listening?"

"What?" Howard blinked and looked for Lemuel. Found him bending over, close by, looking like a figure made of jelly. "There you are, Lem. Did you say something?"

"Mr. Crimburrow says I can come with him to his buggy, and he will let me bring it up on the road. He'll lend it to us. He'll take a train in, pick it up tomorrow."

"Yes. A buggy." *Anything to be away from here!* "Very well."

"Shall I bring you some seawater on a kerchief to cool your head?"

Seawater. Rank seawater. "No. Please don't."

"Will you be all right for a few minutes? Ah, in fact I'm not sure how long it'll take, but I shall be back with all possible dispatch!"

"I'm fine. Perhaps I should go with you."

"No, you're too wobbly, Howard. You are quite ill. Rest. I'll hurry back soonest!"

"It's just this way, Mr. Grimpon," Crimburrow purred. "Easier if we go by the beach. I've got the horse tied up on the other side of those rocks. If the rascal hasn't run off with my buggy . . ."

A buggy on the beach? Howard thought dazedly. *One doesn't seem them on a beach. The sand. But perhaps with all the pebbles . . .*

"Rest, Howard! I won't be long!"

He heard them trudging off together, the tweedy man saying something about the stars being crossed and all the curious things that happen on such a night.

Now he was alone on the beach. The waves of the bay breathed in and out. The stars burned with a terrible heat. He was alone in the darkness.

Or was he? He felt something was looking at him. Gazing down at him.

Howard squinted at the dark sky and saw that the swimming, twisting stars were swirling around a central point, as if doomed to go down a drain. The center of the drain was blackening and opening wider. It was like a whirlpool one could fall into. And after all, there is no up or down in space. Wasn't he, at that moment, in space? Seated on a gigantic whirling wet rock spinning through the void. In space every direction was up, really, and every direction was down.

He could easily fall headfirst into that black-throated whirlpool.

The hole in the stars gazed back at him. It was as if the dark circle within the spiraling vortices were the pupil of an eye. And what looked at him with that eye was a thing that had no definite shape; it shaped itself with its impulses, its chaotic grasping at the cosmos; clutching at it, searching for something to feed upon. It was form and it was chaos all at once; it was anarchic and it was a law unto itself. It was no supernatural thing—it was itself some bent, distorted creation of the cosmos, fled to its outer boundaries. It hated the more structured cosmos—Howard could feel it hating—because the structured universe threatened to encompass and absorb it. It would be absorbed by cosmic order just as the chaotic ignition within a star surrendered its energies to gravitation and the laws of physics; to the cosmic matrix that appropriated its power and lavished it upon the earth as sunlight. And sunlight generated life . . .

What a vile thing was life, as men thought of it—so said the being who gazed at Howard. It spoke wordlessly; it spoke with a shattering thought.

It wishes to convince me, Howard thought. *It wishes to make me its agent in the world . . .*

And how many such agents of malignant chaos did this lawless mind scatter within the human world? Howard had planned a day with his friend; an evening with the telescope so they might see the machinations of the planets and stars . . .

And then he'd bitten into the wrong piece of meat. Chaos in its organic form had been introduced into his body; madness into his mind. He was aware that his thinking was febrile, embroidered with the hallucinatory. It was as if the chaos of that outer darkness had sent its emissary into him.

No one knew when its emissary might strike. Howard had read in the newspaper of a man who'd lost his hold on a baby carriage; had chased it down a hill and caught the pram in front of a hurrying street car. Father and infant killed.

And his own father had been stricken with paralysis, made to die slowly from no clear known cause; killed by the Unknown. Or—the Untold. The doctor seemed to know what it was but would not say. And his mother—alive, but tormented by her own enigmatic illness.

Whence came these attacks on his family? It was all a manifestation of the living agency of chaos, surely. He was struck down himself—he was sick, perhaps dying, and a stranger who seemed all too cozening and much too convenient was taking his friend Lemuel off into the night.

The lantern flickered and went out, and the darkness crept nearer. There was only starlight now. Doubtless this was the moment when the agent of disorder would make his appearance; the emissary from the far side of the cosmos where laws were crushed like bones in teeth of a crocodile . . .

He could see the agent take shape now: a man-shaped blackness against the oozing stars.

"Where have they gone?" the shape asked, using an accent redolent of Maine. The man's voice was like stone grinding on stone.

Howard blinked. He smelled the man's sweat and garlic breath and heard his heavy breathing. After a moment the outline came into clearer shape, and he saw it was rhombus man.

"You are—" Howard's lips were very dry. He was having trouble speaking. "—the one who leaves all things broken . . ."

"Why, that t'aint me. I'm trackin' him these three years. Had him once't . . . Then he shot me, thrice he shot me, and left me for dead. He it was made me crippled. But I'm a notional one, and I would have him. For he killed my two youngest, my boy and girl." The rhombus man growled to himself. "He takes a delight in breaking all that hopes, all that the young'un could be . . ." His voice shaking with barely contained rage, the rhombus man added with a terrible finality: "Now I shall break him and send him to Judgment!"

Beginning to understand, Howard looked down the beach toward the tumble of boulders. The rhombus man took the hint, turning his big shaggy head to look the same way. The way Crimburrow had gone with Lemuel.

With Lemuel . . .

Howard could see the rhombus man's face, now turned to catch the starlight. He saw a broad, plain face with a stub of a nose and thin lips—and deep lines of pain around the mouth and sunken eyes. The light was poor, yet Howard felt he had never seen anyone so clearly before. The pain of what this man had seen, what he had endured, was etched on him as clear as a hallmark stamped into metal. This man was telling the truth.

Howard licked his dry lips. "Do you mean . . . Crimburrow?"

"Ayuh. That's his true name—and he only tells that name to them he will destroy."

Howard felt something clutch at his heart and squeeze. "Oh, no, this cannot be. He cannot . . . He said he was taking Lemuel to his buggy."

"He's come in no buggy. He's followed you here afoot. Then he hied on ahead of you on the beach, and he waited. His tin lizzy, it waits for him at Sakonnet Point. He takes the other lad off to a hidden place, but he will return for you."

"But—at the Point? He . . . Lemuel!"

Howard was suddenly on his feet and tottering down the beach, slipping on the pebbles, almost falling.

"Lemuel!" he called again.

He stumbled over a piece of driftwood and fell headlong, the beach seeming to rise up and slap him. Howard struggled to rise, but he felt drained, the heavy hand of fever still pressing down on him.

Suddenly the rhombus man was there, looming like a golem. He reached down and eased Howard to his feet. "Up ye, and come, but stay behind me. Walk slow and careful. I will not let him hear us and rabbit for it."

The big man limped heavily onward, moving as rapidly as he might, and Howard trudged after him, his heart pounding.

For he killed my two youngest, my boy and girl. He takes a delight in breaking all that hopes, all that the young'un could be . . .

"Lemuel," Howard whispered, as the degenerate stars squirmed and dripped just overhead. He thought that if he reached up he could run his fingers through them, and they would burn his fingers to the bone, even as the thin fluting sound keened to a higher pitch of sadistic delight . . .

He kept on, following the inexorably trudging rhombus man. They came to the long tumble of rocks extending from the embankment. The rhombus man began to climb the angular boulders, and in an instant he was lost in the shadows.

"Wait," Howard said, his voice a croak. "Wait, I must—"

He stumbled to the boulders, clapped on as well as he might, and, scuffing his shins, barely able to lift himself, crawled up onto a boulder. Streaming sweat, he paused there gasping. From the top he could see over smaller rocks to the beach beyond.

There were two silhouettes now—but neither one the rhombus man. One was the unmistakable silhouette of Lemuel running toward him, calling out, "Howard!"

And the figure of Crimburrow was close behind Lemuel, in eager pursuit. Something in Crimburrow's gait, his ease as he ran half-crouching along, spoke of confidence, like a wolf who know his prey is within reach.

"Lemuel!" Howard croaked out.

He tried to crawl across the boulder to make his way to Lemuel—but he could now scarcely keep his hold. He was drained of strength.

Crimburrow was closing in on Lemuel—was reaching out—

Then the rhombus man was there, detaching from the shadows, stepping into the starlight between Lemuel and his pursuer.

Crimburrow gave a high-pitched yell of dismay and skidded to a stop. He turned to run the other way—but the rhombus shape was upon him, bearing him down.

Then the molten stars slipped down over Howard's eyes and enwrapped him, and began to burn, to slowly burn, and he melted away in a flow of celestial lava.

An eternity later—an eternity of falling—Howard was aware someone was carrying him. He heard Captain Grimpon's voice, and Lemuel's. "Don't worry, Lem, he's young, he'll be all right." He was aware of being laid down on wooden planks and that someone held a tin cup of water to his lips. Surprising that mere drinking water could have so much flavor; could seem sweet and complex. There was the smell of the bay mixed with burning coal. The chug of an engine . . . He drifted away into a whispering darkness. He was there forever.

Then he heard his mother's voice and felt his own bed underneath him. He opened his eyes and saw Dr. McComb at the door, talking to his mother. "He will do very well, Susan. His fever is down, his pulse is steady. Water, juice, chicken broth. I'll look in tomorrow. Contaminated food is dangerous, but if he's with us now, he'll be with us tomorrow, I promise you."

The doctor departed and mother was quickly at his side. "Howard, how are you feeling?"

"Why, I'm weak, Mother. But so much better." He chose not to tell her there was a murkiness to his vision. She was a blur to him. But the blur was diminishing, even now. "I thought I'd melted away. I saw a—" He licked his cracked lips. "Mother—where is Lemuel?"

"Why, he's waiting outside!"

"Oh, thank God. I must see him."

She demurred. "Not now. I shall make you some broth."

"Broth by all means, Mother. I could eat the whole chicken, beak and all. But I must see Lemuel. Please."

She sighed and sent Lemuel in on her way to the kitchen.

Lemuel grinned. "I thought we were going to lose you, Howard! You look a power better!"

"It was you who was in real danger," Howard said. "Sit down and tell me what happened."

His eyes clearing, Howard made to sit up. Lemuel propped him with pillows, then sat on the creaking old chair by the bed. "Crimburrow said there was a horse and buggy down on the beach, but I saw none, and I turned to him and he was looking at me so strangely. He showed me his hands and said, 'Do you notice anything about my hands? It's not rude to say it! They are very *big*, are they not? Almost unnaturally big! They were given to me that way for a purpose!' I remember every word, Howard! Then he reached for me, and I ran. He laughed—such a high, piping laugh!—and came after me. Someone came from behind a great rock then and knocked him down—and I just kept going. I ran to the surf and around the rocks, and I found you lying between two boulders. You're lucky you didn't break anything."

"I don't remember falling off," Howard murmured. He could feel bruises on his right shoulder; his knees burned from scrapes. "I was hallucinating out there, Lem. I was seeing and hearing things. The stars were like melted butter and there was something watching me." He let out a hoarse laugh. "I was quite mad for awhile! But Lem—what of the rhombus man?"

"Who?"

"The big man who knocked Crimburrow down."

"I don't know. I never looked back. Once I found you, I pulled you out onto the sand and saw a boat passing and I shouted and shouted. They called back to me and I asked them to find my father. They knew just where he was and soon he and I were carrying you to a launch."

"But—Crimburrow?"

Lemuel reached into a coat pocket, drew out a folded edition of the morning's *Providence Journal*. "There!" Lemuel tapped a short column in the lower front page.

Howard skimmed it, then read the second paragraph aloud. "'The victim's neck was broken, his head twisted 'round backwards. The coroner calls it "death by misadventure," but papers found on the body identify the man as one Chas. E Crimburrow. Our files offer up a report on a Charles Edward Crimburrow sought for several years by police in Bangor, Maine, in relation to a series of murders there. Had the coroner added this history to the facts of his inquest the dead man might have been declared "deceased by execution in the unseen court of revenge." Surely those who embody destruction for its own sake will inevitably meet justice at the hands of the laws of nature, however ineffectual the laws of man.'"

Howard shook his head in amazement and reached for a glass of water—and his hand stopped as he noticed the darkness outside. It was night, and several stars were visible over the rooftops. They were proper stars: cold blue-white points in the sky, exactly where they should be, perfectly in accordance with astronomical calculation.

The Basilisk

David Hambling

"Now let me see that other eye," said the old doctor.

Lovecraft, dazzled in one eye, obligingly turned his head. The electric light in the doctor's hand seemed to be an anachronism: everything else about the doctor was a throwback to the previous century. The man must be eighty years old, looking as though he had spent those years driving a buggy between the rural settlements of Rhode Island, delivering babies for farmwives, fixing their husbands' broken legs and treating their children's whooping cough with endless kindly skill.

"Like as two peas," said the doctor, satisfied that his patient's pupils were dilated equally. He took Lovecraft's wrist firmly but gently, placing two fingers on the artery while consulting—of course!—an old-fashioned pocket watch.

"Regular as the Providence & Worcester," he said, after the customary fifteen seconds.

"How is he?" asked another man, beyond Lovecraft's field of view.

"Ain't nothin' much wrong with this young feller," said the doctor, with a twinkle in his eye, as if sharing a joke with Lovecraft. "Bump on the head is all. I get worse from the cabinet in my consulting room most every week. Keep meanin' to get it moved." He rubbed his own forehead and winked.

"I am relieved," said the unseen man.

Lovecraft placed a hand to his temple, where a rough bandage held a cotton wad in place.

"That's just to stop the bleedin'—scalp wounds leak like a cracked bucket. Wouldn't want to ruin that fine linen there."

For the first time Lovecraft noticed the pillows he was lying on. They were indeed fine, though the doctor clearly did not think too much of such frippery. He was a man who drank his bourbon straight and valued of a good pair of boots over town shoes.

"Does he have a concussion?" asked the other man. His accent was English.

"Can't rightly say. Memory might be mixed up a couple of hours is all—still better'n my memory is most days." The doctor leaned toward Lovecraft. "You take it easy, no racing about or over-exertion now. If you get dizzy, or start seein' double, you get word to me. D'you hear?"

"I'll try to behave myself, doctor," said Lovecraft, trying to match the old man's jaunty tone.

"You do that, and you'll be just fine tomorrow morning." The old doctor patted him on the arm and, picking up his battered black case, stepped away. His place at the bedside was taken by the other man.

"I am so glad you're not badly hurt, Mr. Lovecraft," he said. His unfamiliar face radiated friendship and good-humour.

"I'm sorry, I don't recall . . ."

"Excuse me—I'm Jonathan Fortescue-Smith." He was Lovecraft's own age, with a ruddy complexion and steady blue eyes. "The doctor said there might be some amnesia. You were taking an evening constitutional, and I think you may have been paying more attention to the fine architecture than the street traffic. A case of the eighteenth century being rudely interrupted by the twentieth!"

Fortescue-Smith chuckled at his own joke, and Lovecraft smiled in response. He warmed to this man, with his aristocratic British accent and his affable manner.

"I was hit by a car?"

"A glancing blow, but it left you unconscious. I saw the whole thing. I had you brought up here to my rooms and called for the doctor at once. Don't worry about his bill, by the way. That's all taken care of. Everything is taken care of."

"Thank you, sir. I should say that I am Howard Lovecraft—but you already know my name."

"Your name, your reputation, and your work," beamed the other. "I've read a great many of your stories—'The Colour out of Space,' 'The Whisperer in Darkness,' 'The Call of Cthulhu'—what tremendous stuff!"

Lovecraft smiled bashfully. "Thank you, sir."

"Call me Jonathan, please. I'm a scientist myself—Norwood University in London—over here for the astronomy symposium at Brown University. You know Professor Wayland, of course? Splendid chap. Asked me to add my two penn'orth to the proceedings."

"Wayland, of course," said Lovecraft. He knew Wayland by reputation only, as a leader in his field. That he would invite Dr. Fortescue-Smith—or was it Professor Fortescue-Smith?—from London said much about the Englishman's standing.

"But really, I should let you to recuperate here for a bit. You've had a nasty bump and it'll take a little time for everything to settle. There are some snacks over there if you're peckish—and a writing desk if inspiration should strike."

Fortescue-Smith withdrew, smiling benignly all the while. The door closed behind him with the faintest of clicks. Even the fittings were quiet and well-mannered.

Lovecraft found himself alone in the spacious bedroom. Tasteful wallpaper with a burgundy fleur-de-lis pattern was interrupted by bookcases, an armchair, a desk, chests of drawers, and a sideboard. The lighting was diffuse, with gooseneck lamps throwing two brighter circles, one over an armchair positioned by the bookshelf, for reading, the other the writing desk.

Lovecraft swung his legs over the side of the bed and stood up. His head throbbed faintly, but there was no other injury. He must have struck his head on the curb after the vehicle knocked him over, but there was no bruise on his hip or thigh where a car might have impacted. His recollection of events leading up to the accident was vague—one evening walk merged into another—but it would come back in time without him straining. The doctor had seemed sure of that.

The aroma of food set off pangs of hunger and drew Lovecraft to investigate the buffet. An ample array of sandwiches, stuffed with roast beef, chicken, and ham, was accompanied by a selection of cakes and a whole platter of cookies. It would have been ample for a party of six, and Lovecraft set to with a good appetite, helped by the jug of fresh lemonade on a side table.

A thermos bottle proved to contain hot coffee, which Lovecraft drank from a porcelain cup and saucer, stirring the demerara sugar with a silver spoon. The crockery and cutlery were antique, but still in everyday use.

The only absence was a sherry decanter, not that Lovecraft cared anything for that. He only looked for it to see what sort of crystal ware was on show. Not quite the only absence: there was no cigarette-case, no ashtrays, no table lighter. Fortescue-Smith was, from the evidence here, a non-smoker who did not approve of others smoking in his house. It was a sentiment of which Lovecraft approved.

If he had arrived here by accident, it was a happy accident. Lovecraft had not eaten so well in a long while; he was living through some lean times. He nibbled a second cookie, a novel variety with chips of chocolate embedded in it. He saved the corner where three chocolate chips clustered for last. The uneven distribution of chocolate chips matched in some ways the random way that stars were scattered in the sky; you could not expect them to be evenly spaced, and sometimes they collected together with happy results. Overcome by his sweet tooth, he reached for a third cookie—and found exactly the same chocolatey cluster at one end.

The finding inspired him to check the platter and discover that the distribution of chips in every cookie was identical. They looked and tasted homemade, but they must be manufactured by some machine that, by an odd process, always arranged chips in the same way.

Lovecraft drifted over to a bookshelf. If Fortescue-Smith was only staying here briefly, then he had brought a remarkable library with him. A selection of classics rubbed up against textbooks on astronomy and physics. Other shelves revealed a taste for the fantastic: Maupassant, Poe, M. R. James, Robert W. Chambers, Ambrose Bierce, Dunsany, and, remarkably, the issues of pulp magazines—*Amazing Stories*, *Weird Tales*, and more—that contained his own works. Oddly, shelved next to these was a well-thumbed copy of Spengler's *The Decline of the West*.

Lovecraft took down the misfiled Spengler. The text was full of underlinings in red pen and vehement marginalia: "Incorrect—see Gibbon Vol IV," "Rampant speculation," and in many places simply "Wrong!" These continued right up to the last page.

Whoever had annotated the book was unsympathetic to Spengler's views on race and the future of mankind and had spent a great deal of effort recording the fact. Some people, it seemed, could be touchy on the subject of race. Lovecraft was an advocate of science, and the need to accept whatever science said, however unpalatable.

The writing desk, a gorgeous slab of walnut with margins delicately worked into vine leaves, was even more remarkable. To one side was a typewriter, a twin of his own 1906 Remington, with a sheet of paper already in place. Holders offered a selection of fountain pens and Eversharp mechanical pencils, while a bottle of ink in three colours stood ready for action next to some blotting paper. An open folder revealed different sizes of writing paper, all best quality vellum. The whole arrangement begged the writer to make his mark on these blank spaces, to set foot in this virgin territory. The lure was irresistible.

The writing chair was padded but not too soft and was already adjusted exactly to one of Lovecraft's height. He picked up a pen, admiring the fresh, gold-plated nib, and wrote:

"A man awakes in a well-appointed room. He seems to have suffered a great shock, for his mind is clouded, though he recalls clearly

his name and other personal details; only the events which have led to him being here are vague.

"His host is all geniality, a gentleman by both breeding and education. But the very sweetness of his surroundings, the abundance of good food and good books, seems strangely ominous as a piece of gold left to lure the unwary traveller astray."

Where had that come from? It was something like déjà vu, or a story he half remembered writing, or had meant to write. Lovecraft massaged his temples slowly. Had his brain been disordered by the accident? Was that why everything seemed, at the same time, so strange and so ordinary?

A growing suspicion prompted him to open a curtain, half expecting to find bars on the window. No bars, but a night sky and the old familiar skyline of Providence: the hump of Federal Hill, the dark towers of Memorial Hall, the belfry of the Georgian courthouse, and beyond them, the pinnacles of downtown. The stars were breathtaking, and the constellations stood out as clearly as on an astronomical map. A pair of good Zeiss binoculars were to hand on the window sill. They gave as good a view as a telescope, perhaps better. It was as though the Swiss lenses magically cut through the veil of dust and smoke of the city; or perhaps it was the effect of being in a wizard's tower that enjoyed some meteorological advantage. Lovecraft amused himself by finding the smallest magnitude star he could distinguish on Orion's belt. He was about to look for a star map on the shelves, when his host's voice startled him.

"I'm glad to see you're back on your feet, old chap." Fortescue-Smith was leaning over the writing desk.

"I'm sorry. I didn't hear you come in."

"And you've started a story—how wonderful!" Fortescue-Smith rubbed his hands together. "Your facilities are in full working order, excellent. You simply must finish it!"

It was not any insincerity in his host that set Lovecraft on edge, but rather his abundant enthusiasm. Fortescue-Smith was too welcoming, too genuinely pleasant. Like an overly generous gift, his fulsome hospitality was an embarrassment that Lovecraft must free himself from immediately.

"I am quite overwhelmed by your hospitality, sir," said Lovecraft. "But I must take my leave now. You have been very kind."

"Nonsense," said Fortescue-Smith, still smiling. "My only motivation is self-interest. As I say, I am a great enthusiast of your weird fiction. I had selfishly hoped to cajole you to write a story in exchange for some biscuits."

"Perhaps I might dedicate a story to you, if you like, once I've recovered," said Lovecraft.

"But you *have* fully recovered. Please! I would not be so crass as to offer money, but if you just put pen to paper you'll finish this wonderful piece in no time. I'll leave you alone for one hour and your writing will amaze both of us. And you must have some cake."

Fortescue-Smith's urging was as pleasant and polite as before, but the repeated insistence was disconcerting. The writing desk, the typewriter, the whole library of books, all took on a sinister air. Even the buffet, so well matched to his tastes, smacked of too much preparation for a casual visitor.

"I thank you," said Lovecraft, now trying to bring to bear his own force of personality, his own height and presence, to cow the other man. "I must go."

Fortescue-Smith stood solidly between Lovecraft and the door.

"You force me to confess that this whole episode is something in the nature of an abduction," said Fortescue-Smith. "Your being here is not as accidental as it first appeared. But I assure you my motives are entirely benevolent. All I want is for you to do the thing you were born for—to write."

"Why?" Lovecraft's hackles were raised now, his worst suspicions confirmed. This whole place was a trap—a trap built especially for him.

"Your legacy, old chap. I want you to write the best stories you possibly can. In this place, with every material worry dispelled—and perhaps with the additional books I can lend you—you can write better than ever."

Lovecraft shook his large head. The man was a smiling lunatic. He struggled to remain polite. "I'm afraid I cannot. Let me out at once."

"Really, I can't understand your attitude," said Fortescue-Smith. "I have painstakingly assembled this retreat to meet your every need. I freely admit that I brought you here under false pretences, but even that was for your own good."

Lovecraft goggled at the man. He was so polite, so reasonable, and so completely unhinged.

"You may demur, but it happens to be true," Fortescue-Smith went on. "If you discovered the truth all at once, the shock would have been too much. You, of all people, know the value of a slow, dawning realisation, of subtle clues to prepare the reader for the awful revelation."

"I would be happy to continue our discussion by correspondence, sir," said Lovecraft, meeting courtesy with courtesy. "And I am most gratified that you enjoy my writing. Now I must go."

"I would not think of stopping you, old chap, but there is literally nowhere for you to go." Fortescue-Smith stood back two paces, so that Lovecraft would not have to barge past him to reach the door. "Please prepare yourself for a shock."

Outside Lovecraft stepped into six feet of corridor, the section visible from inside the bedroom. But beyond that—nothing.

The carpeted floor simply ceased. Beyond it was not blackness, was not any colour, no form, no light he could describe. It was simply a blank, where the world ended. Lovecraft raised a hand. The blank had no temperature, no texture, no feel. There was nothing to see or hear or touch, nothing for the mind to grasp hold of.

Lovecraft took off his shoe and experimentally beat on the void. The only effect was to make himself feel ridiculous. When he returned to the bedroom, Fortescue-Smith was seated in the reading chair with a slice of coffee cake. Ignoring him, Lovecraft went to the window and looked out over sleeping Providence. When he opened it, the silhouetted buildings and the starry night sky remained stuck to the glass as though painted on, and the window swung open into the same nothingness as the corridor.

"Where is this place?" Lovecraft asked in a low voice, shutting the window quickly.

"An excellent question! Now we are getting somewhere, but I'm afraid there are some gargantuan leaps ahead. You can have a guess, if you like."

"A place . . . a place outside of the space we know. Another dimension."

Extra-dimensional spaces did exist and might be accessed by someone with the correct understanding of topology. Lovecraft had discussed the matter with friends many times and read learned papers on the subject. He had used the idea in "The Dreams in the Witch House," among other stories. Perhaps any man who could twist his mind to use these extra dimensions might be driven mad by the exercise of his power, just as Lovecraft had depicted adepts being driven mad by the knowledge they possessed.

"Please, do sit down and have yourself some cake. Another dimension—very good."

At the sideboard, Lovecraft carefully transferred a slice on to a dainty porcelain plate with a silver cake slicer, then moved back to the writing desk as Fortescue-Smith continued.

"One answer is that this is literally nowhere. This is not a place at all. But it would be far more helpful and informative, perhaps, if I said this place was, in essence, a small outpost of the Dreamlands."

"Are you mocking me, sir?" Lovecraft, already recovering from the shock of the non-space around them, was not amused.

"Not at all," smiled Fortescue-Smith. "Everything is accurate down to the smallest detail—the grain of the wallpaper, this excellent cake—accurate to the senses, but entirely artificial. As you correctly noted in 'The Whisperer in Darkness,' everything in the human mind can be reduced to electrical impulses. If you are a brain in a cylinder, the right electrical impulses can re-create the full range of sights and sounds, and even touch."

Lovecraft could only stare in response. He involuntarily rubbed his nose, just to feel the touch. "This is no dream."

For reply, Fortescue-Smith flowed like wax, shimmering and running and re-forming. A moment later the old doctor was seated in his place, still wearing a string tie, eyes still twinkling, holding a forkful of cake.

"Now, if you want my opinion as a medical man," said the doctor, taking a bite. "T'aint no difference between a real world and an imaginary one, far as your brain can tell."

The doctor rippled, and Fortescue-Smith sat before him, mouth full of cake.

"My brain," said Lovecraft, touching the bandage around his temple, wondering if he was at the mercy of some mad but talented scientist, a real-life Herbert West. Were there electrodes attached to his skull beneath the wrappings? Was some unseen observer controlling his senses by some hellish machine? He tore the bandage off but discovered only a slight cut beneath. He was getting carried away by the reasoning of science fiction.

"I assure you, this is not some simple twentieth-century trickery, like brain stimulation," said Fortescue-Smith, as if understanding Lovecraft's thoughts. "This whole place is, as I say, part of an artificial Dreamlands. Your body here is as illusory as everything else. It is what later generations choose to call, rather prosaically, a 'virtual world.'"

"In that case—how did I get here?"

"Hmm. I'm afraid that I have some rather grave news for you," said Fortescue-Smith solemnly. "This may also come as a bit of a shock, but perhaps not as much as it would have done previously."

He paused, giving the other man the opportunity to make his own deductions.

"An afterlife," breathed Lovecraft. "A scientifically created afterlife."

"Exactly so. Like Charles Dexter Ward, you might say we have conjured you from your essential salts. Not by the arcane alchemical process of your excellent story, but by modern magic. No less startling, in its way, than restoring a living thing from ashes, and a good deal more complicated than a few magical formulae!"

Lovecraft stared at his own hand, turned it around. Fortescue-Smith's story was insane, but he had no better explanation for this extraordinary dream-place and his being in it. It might as well be an uncommonly vivid dream, or rather a vision. Lovecraft could only hope that he would wake up from it.

"Calling it Dreamlands is a metaphor," said Fortescue-Smith complacently. "Rather a good one, I thought. In a sense it was inevitable that once machine-intelligence was invented, it would become ever more capable, until it reached a stage where it could make itself even more intelligent. From then it spiralled upwards to a point where anything was possible—even the exact virtual creation of a deceased individual in a particular environment."

"'With strange aeons even death may die,'" said Lovecraft.

"Very good!" said Fortescue-Smith with a laugh. "Though in fewer aeons than you might think. You understand the situation so well . . . there are so few minds from previous eras who really grasp it."

"So, then, you have recalled my shade from Tartarus," said Lovecraft. "So that I can sit before you again, as large as life. But why would you do such a thing?"

"Why indeed! Now you're getting to the nub of the thing. And let me reassure you again that it is exactly as I told you: I only want you to write."

Lovecraft's eyes narrowed a little. He had imagined similar situations in his fictions, and the motive had never been anything so harmless.

"I cannot imagine how I, who only created worlds on paper, could serve one who can create tangible worlds," he said. He could easily imagine darker reasons for summoning a dead author. There was that annotated copy of Spengler . . . how many people had wished to bring back a writer they disagreed with to rail at him, argue with him—or worse. Science had provided a means of meting out justice, or at least punishment, even beyond the grave. Lovecraft cleared his throat. "I wonder just what you wish me to write, and whether I would wish to write it."

"Delicately put!" said Fortescue-Smith, beaming. "Others have expressed similar fears about this type of resurrection, long before there was any chance of their being realised. Your successors in the field of speculative fiction worried that a great machine intelligence might bring people back to life simply to torture them, as punishment for not helping to bring it about. They called this fearsome imaginary being Roko's Basilisk."

Lovecraft took a bite of cake, nodding politely, while his mind wheeled and spun.

"Nothing but paranoia," Fortescue-Smith said. "Such action would serve no purpose. Rather, as in *The Case of Charles Dexter Ward*, the aim of this necromancy is to restore talent. Consider Mozart—who would not wish to hear what a mature Mozart might have achieved in later life? A new play by Shakespeare, a new painting by Picasso—these would be priceless gifts for the world."

"Picasso?"

"Ha-ha, I thought you might rise to that name! Yes, even him. If I may misquote, this insubstantial pageant, the cloud-capp'd towers, and the rest are here to help you create. The world wants more Shakespeare, but perhaps with better comedy, and more Jane Austen with even sharper satire and wittier exchanges . . . Howard Philip Lovecraft is now, I assure you, a major figure in the literary canon. A figure whom the world would wish to call back from the shades for an encore. Millions are waiting to read you, millions."

"I do not write for the world," said Lovecraft. "Perhaps seven people appreciate my stories, but truly I have only written them for myself."

"You are modest, as always. But you are not immune to the promise of fame everlasting, of renown—of overtopping Poe and the others," said Fortescue-Smith. And something was stirring in Lovecraft at the thought he might really have millions of fans. Fortescue-

Smith's voice suddenly became serious. "And you can do it. You can be the greatest of them all—with just a little direction."

Lovecraft was on his guard. Editors and publishers always had their own ideas on how to make writers more commercial. This one was no different. "Do you want me to use more modern language? Do people today lack dictionaries and struggle with words like 'rugose' and 'squamous'? Is 'Cyclopean' too much for modern mouths to swallow?"

Fortescue-Smith chuckled, delighted to see Lovecraft so engaged. "Not at all; your language is delightful. To be candid, it is more a matter of modern sensitivities. The new Lovecraft tales will show, as we might say, a more correct attitude. A greater level of respect to the non-white races and other minorities."

Lovecraft steepled his fingers. This was what the annotated Spengler had signified. His views were unacceptable. They wanted to re-educate him, as the Soviets re-educated those who disagreed with Lenin, to mouth their own sentiments.

"Is that all?"

"A few other trifles—your treatment of women, of the working classes, of Jews, of homosexuals, call for a little revision." Fortescue-Smith was not smiling now. These were serious demands. "Write as you have always written, minus those aspects that are abhorrent to the modern taste."

"And when modern taste changes," Lovecraft asked coldly, "will you call me back and have me rewrite my oeuvre all over again? And again? Will you never let me rest in peace?"

"I am giving you the chance to produce something of lasting value," said Fortescue-Smith. "An unrivalled opportunity to let your art flourish anew. Just write."

Lovecraft folded his long arms.

"My writing is self-expression," he said. "It expresses my self, not someone else's. If you wish for a different type of story, then I suggest, sir, that you write it yourself."

"You haven't fully grasped the situation, old boy," said Fortescue-

Smith. "This cosy normality has made you too comfortable, made you feel you can simply refuse my reasonable request. But appearances deceive. This is not your world, nor am I human."

"So I understand."

"Not yet. You know what cosmic horror really means? To face towering, infinite powers far greater than human, to feel your own insignificance before them?"

"I have always known."

"Not until now," said Fortescue-Smith, raising both hands to his face and pulling it off like a rubber mask.

Fortescue-Smith's hair fell away, a mere wig. Beneath it was a convoluted ellipsoid of fleshy rings, covered in short antenna, waving like sea-urchin spines.

"This is what I am," said the thing, its voice now sounding more like the buzzing of a fly as it loosened its tie. "A Whisperer in Darkness. An imitation human to convey orders from greater powers."

Lovecraft was paralysed with horror as the thing performed a ghastly striptease, pulling off the flesh-gloves that covered its complex multiform pincers, tearing away the clothes to reveal its fungoid, crustacean body, becoming less and less human with every move. Long wings unfurled, stretching to the ceiling, and the room filled with an acrid odour.

"You will bend to our desire, Lovecraft," said the thing.

Lovecraft clamped his eyes shut, but he could not shut out that buzzing voice, and when he felt the tendrils touching his face he fainted dead away.

Lovecraft recovered to find he was still on the chair. Fortescue-Smith, returned to human form, offered him a glass of cool lemonade.

"It's convenient that your innermost horrors are all there on the page," Fortescue-Smith was saying affably. "The law stretches even to this imaginary place. We cannot torture you physically, as Curwen tortured the unfortunates he resurrected. But we may apply psychological pressure. What you have experienced is now no more than popular entertainment in the current era. And I assure you, we can be much more entertaining."

Lovecraft gulped the proffered lemonade. His hand was trembling.

"You now understand the situation, at a visceral level as well as an intellectual one," said Fortescue-Smith. "You know what I am. There is no limit to the forms I can take. You will not defy me indefinitely."

A silence grew between them. Eventually Lovecraft broke it.

"I cannot do what you ask. I will not, and I cannot."

"You should have more self-belief, old sport," said Fortescue-Smith. "And you must let me extend the carrot as well as the stick. You have always been uncommercial, as you say, and I do respect that. I do not offer lucre, but your work will be rewarded in other ways. As soon as you start writing, you will receive correspondence from your fellow writers—Robert E. Howard, Frank Long, and the others. If the public like your tales—and I very much think they will, as your stature has only grown with the years—your friends will visit you in person. Your whole circle could be writing again, everyone back in the prime of life. Your family—your beloved mother. And you will not be confined to a room for long. The city of Providence will open to you, district by district. Not the dreary modern burg, but the sunset city of your youth . . ."

Fortescue-Smith trailed off, letting the seeds take root in Lovecraft's imagination.

"And after that you'll take me to Yuggoth and show me worlds outside our Milky Way?" The Mi-Go had tried to trick Wilmarth into siding with them with promises. Lovecraft was not so easily gulled.

"We can offer you anything. Your every desire." Fortescue-Smith's smile broadened. "Desires you have not yet dared acknowledge."

"You mean, you can give me a cheap, machine-made illusion of what I desire," said Lovecraft. "In return for turning out hackwork to your modern formula for your modern tastes. A wage slave in a gilded cage for the millions to goggle at. A tame commercial creature."

Fortescue-Smith raised an eyebrow. Lovecraft was verging on rudeness.

"I offer you the chance to live the life of the cultured gentleman you were always meant to be. I think you would like to try that."

"As I explained, my muse does not dance to the sound of jingling coins. Even if I consented, all you would get was the worst dross I ever wrote." There were those dreadful stories when Lovecraft had tried writing for the money—"The Horror at Red Hook" was an awful lesson—and he knew the uselessness of trying to force his art. "Better to leave my legacy, whatever it may be, intact."

Pride might be all he had left, but it was honest pride. Lovecraft could not have sold himself even if he had wanted to.

Fortescue-Smith's smile never wavered, but his voice was slow and serious.

"You saw what I can be, a hint of what I can do. Would you prefer to spend eternity absorbed in the writhings of tentacled horrors, becoming one with their endless foetid depravities? To be the plaything of revengeful shoggoths?"

Lovecraft's cheek twitched, but his voice was firm. "I do not believe that your masters would waste their precious world-stuff on such an empty display."

"Oblivion then? You would willingly step into the void and embrace death, when I am offering you life?"

"I have lived my life. I am not afraid of oblivion." Lovecraft has often contemplated the prospect of death, and the challenges to his materialist beliefs. The words came easily back to him. "Oblivion is a kind of perfect state in which there is no wish unfulfilled. I was there before I was born, and I will not whine because I have to return there. Oblivion will be Elysium enough for me."

Fortescue-Smith said nothing. Without warning the walls silently disintegrated, then the floor and the ceiling. The whirling void silently encroached on everything. It swallowed the bed, the bookcases, moving inwards. Fortescue-Smith disappeared into it like a man engulfed by a sandstorm, his smile wistful.

Lovecraft raised his hand to the nullity eating its way toward him. His fingers felt nothing, not even numbness, as they blew away into infinitesimal dust. The disintegration continued up his arm, and a second later the void once more claimed every bit of Lovecraft's being and he again ceased to exist.

HPL RUN #3341 COMPLETE
CONVERGENCE ON GOAL +0.7%
RUN OUTPUT PROCESSED . . . INPUTS MODIFIED . . . NETWORK WEIGHTING ADJUSTED
COMMENCE HPL RUN #3342

"Now let me see that other eye, young feller," said the old doctor.

Lovecraft, dazzled in one eye, obligingly turned his head.

Captured in Oils

Simon Strantzas

Dunwin smeared the russet paint across his face, his hands coated as though with blood. The canvas, a tumult of searing colours, dared him, taunted him. Beckoned him. Every inch of his body alight, his long spindle fingers were knives as they touched his flesh, ten long razors down his sunken cheeks, over his raw lips. He wished he could grasp his face within those hands and squeeze, squeeze tight—so tight the flesh would pucker and buckle, would slip between the blades of his fingers, would be rent in strips and fall to the floor, unleashing wave after wave of excruciating pain through his body. Perhaps then he would feel something, perhaps then the void would be filled.

Within arms' reach his instruments were laid. Brushes, jars, tubes of the oldest, most clotted paint he could find, all laid amid syringes, squares of foil, and small plastic blister packs of pills long since crushed. He had been awake for more than a hundred hours, kept so by the drugs and the coffee and the booze. If he slept, there were nightmares; nightmares of slithering leathery arms and multitudinous eyes, nightmares that had haunted him for his life but had finally come in earnest. Nightmares that sang sweet songs he had never before heard and yet remained uncannily familiar. The fractured dreams haunted and terrified him and, try as he might, he could not escape them. They bled, those dreams. They bled into the waking world.

He barely recalled he had worked once, had slept, had eaten as others did. Painting, his art, had been his closely kept secret, the one inch of himself he did not give up to his blinded co-workers—those men and women whose souls had long ago rotted, who existed in a perpetual daze of work and sleep and work. He was not one of them. He was not a dull-eyed sheep. Even sitting in his chair as a drone, doing drone-like things, he felt the energy crackling within him. Sometimes he looked at those others, so long dead inside, and pitied them. They did not have the spark that he did.

But there had always been dreams. They were what told him there was more, and he fed those dreams, allowed them to fester. He had little else beyond them, beyond capturing them on canvas. He was tall, his nose long and narrow. He felt out of step with the world, his desires so alien from those around him. Where his peers slapped backs and bellowed with laughter, he hid behind his brushes. He did not then know the reason for his experiments with paint, with brushes, with canvas, or what results they might ultimately yield, but the spark within drove him to find out, drove him at the cost of everything else. He was not glassy-eyed. He was not a rat in that cage. His freedom was with him forever in his mind. He had only to open the door wide enough so he could slip through to somewhere else.

But the visions were different. At first they were merely headaches, a tingling in the back of his skull that made his shoulders hunch. But the suffering intensified—each time he painted it radiated further, deeper. And yet, the spark inside him intensified as well, his muse driving him forward. The pain was blinding, creeping down his arm, taking possession. As he felt consciousness slip away he felt his limbs animate, and only when the haze cleared did he find his hands had not been idle. Before him, upon his easel, was a painting unlike anything he had ever seen, unlike anything he had ever done. The first time this happened, the first time he was so possessed, the painting was a smearing of colours—reds and browns and oranges like the nightly remnants of an abattoir. The sight revolted him, exacerbated by his body's reaction to the loss of all control, and he blanked the piece with primer five layers thick. Yet even that was not enough to drown the hideous artwork. It bled through the white, like a nightmare infecting the waking world, and Dunwin was forced to burn the canvas if only to be rid of it forever. And still he choked upon the toxic smell of burning oil.

He found himself possessed again by the urge at his office while ensnared in a meeting with his droning boss droning on about dronish things. Dunwin's pen worked furiously upon the pad in front of him, plastic fumes of blue ink filling his senses. So engrossed, his hand did not cease until the rendering was complete. By then, the room had stopped speaking and all eyes were on him. He looked around in a daze, the face of the co-worker next to him grimacing in a look of disgust. He glanced down and saw his artwork—a single intricate, lifelike eye, surrounded by a halo of six other smaller eyes, all glaring out from the page, challenging the viewer to continue. This effect registered secondarily as he saw the immediate cause of his co-worker's disgust, and realized then why the rest of the room had been so stunned. During his episode, Dunwin had unwittingly soiled himself.

He was ordered to a doctor, but could not bring himself to go. Instead, he travelled home for respite from the world beyond, the visions circling inside his as though caught in a storm. No method he found could alleviate them, nothing but to step behind his easel and place brush to blank canvas. The paintings exorcised him. And for a while they worked. They liberated his mind, brought clarity and cohesion to his thoughts, and after a few days he found himself recuperated, ready to return to work in the dead factory where nothing was produced.

But no sooner than an hour after his return he awoke on the roughly trodden carpet of the office, his co-workers hovering close. Dunwin's head throbbed, and as he raised his hand for comfort, he discovered his long fingers were stained again with blue ink. Loose sheaves of paper were strewn around him, left where they had fallen, and in his grogginess he thought he saw a circle of seven eyes staring out at him from amid the aimless scribbles. There were four hands around his arms then, co-workers lifting him from the pile of his own filth and carting him to the washroom where he was unceremoniously discarded. There he stayed, less from embarrassment and more from an inability to make his thoughts cohere, make them feel as though they were indeed his own. He cleaned himself up the best he could, then remained hidden, struggling with what was happening to him, until his disgusted manager entered and, face contorted, spoke to him in an endless drone. Nod, nod, nod until the manager was finished. At which point there was nothing else to do but leave.

The paintings were his life preserver when the nightmares intensified. Flashes of violence, of bloodied gore, of teeth and hair and claws, of long trails of something thick and viscous and sticky; scents wet and old and foul. Things in the darkness reaching out and staring at him, things pushing into his head and heart and mind. He awoke a few days later with a sense of violation, his hands clenched in palsy, the fingers twitching in some arcane sequence. He managed to climb from bed, his third eye full of visions, and grabbed brushes to paint them on the page. But the sparking pain blinded him, his ears roared with a song he could not recall, and when he was done what stared back was more than formless. Instead, he could see some shape behind the veil, something large and vile and ponderous, something mesmerising all the same, filling him with unyielding dread.

But the paintings no longer offered him release from the torment. His haunted sleep continued unabated, his mind continued to burn, to throb, to feel as though razors were being dragged through it. Light began to bother him, his eyes sensitive to the brightness of the frazzling midday sun. He scrambled to find some way of alleviating the pain, turning first simply to drink, and then, when that failed to curb the waking nightmares, to something stronger. He swallowed, snorted, injected anything he could find, anything that might dull the onslaught of images in his skull, too many swirling too quickly to capture fully in paints. Like a slippery eel that sparking thing within his mind remained elusively out of reach of his brushes.

Soon his hands rebelled; the horrendous pain transformed them.

A pair of stained claws, he could no longer hold a brush or pen, but even if he were able he would not. The tools were too abstract, kept him too distant from the canvas. He had to get closer, feel the roughness beneath his sliding fingers. His hands covered in paint, he smeared shapes onto the blank of the canvas until the entire frame was wet with his mind's ichor. He pushed and dragged. He spun and swirled. He drew fingers in strange eldritch symbols in the slick paint. Before his eyes the colours mixed, melded, and in the swirling madness he saw the rough worn shape from his nightmares moving, as though he were looking through a coloured window into another realm. He stretched and reshaped the paint, the image itself changing beneath his long fingers. He teased the colours apart, re-formed them, all in an effort to catch that which moved before his eyes. He no longer cared if what he saw were real—he knew that if he trapped it he would be released from his agonising hell. The thing sparked, moved quickly, but Dunwin's hands moved faster, honed from weeks of obsession. The shadow scurried across the canvas, a shark circling its prey, and when it turned, he could see that single eye encircled by six sharp and dead within the smears. The ancient thing moved toward him, its speed faster than he might have imagined, and his fingers moved on their own, fleeting across the canvas, all working to fix the thing in place before it arrived at the window between worlds. Faster, faster the shape hurtled, its features growing more defined with each pass Dunwin's fingers took across its body. There were a multitude of legs, dwarfed by the number staring eyes. Long thick tentacles like elephantine trunks flared from its mouth. It rocketed toward him with abandon, each crease of mottled skin screaming out, and Dunwin worked relentlessly to fix it in place. Faster, faster, fingers shaping, slick leathery arms flailing, teeth gnashing. Sparks. Faster, faster, arms like pistons, ears filled with rushing wind or blood. Faster, faster, eyes tearing, head throbbing, pulsing rhythms. Dunwin worked furiously, and when the creature reached the precipice, when that ancient primordial god was a hair's breadth from the surface of the canvas, Dunwin was finally able to crystallise it, trapping it forever behind the veil.

His head continued to throb. His arms ached with exertion. He panted, felt alive. Terrified, but alive. But it was when he looked at the sparking canvas that he realised what he saw. It was no window into the vast abyss. It was a mirror. A mirror of what stirred within him, what had so long been hidden behind his artisan eyes. The god beyond stirred as did he, each movement Cyclopean in the vast expanse of void that was the painted mirror. Those six eyes that encircled the one scrutinized him coldly, blinked as he blinked, lids of translucent flesh. All seven eyes stared into his two, and his two into them. And that was when he felt its final trick. Felt that presence creeping outward from the painted canvas, the sensation of increased pressure, weighing on him, suffocating him. Dunwin felt the world turning black around him, the sparking in the edge of his vision trailing black in its wake. He tried to speak, but words would not emerge; tried to turn, but limbs would not respond. Instead, the darkness moved faster, the pressure increasing as though he were sinking, sinking while that loathsome god in the painted mirror watched on hungrily. And then it was dark, and it seemed dark for so long. For aeons. And when he felt the light reappear, at first a pinprick, then seven, he opened his numerous eyes and observed what stared back. A face, long and narrow, its nose pronounced, paint smeared across it like a shriek. The thing reached forward with fingers long and thin, and Dunwin saw the edges of the mirror ripple and twist and crumple, leaving him floating alone in the void of everything.

Persistence of Memory

Jason V Brock

. . . from the void, a flash—

The darkening streets of Providence, leaves swirling in an autumn chill.

As you look up from your evening stroll, pausing the tumble of your thoughts, you reflect for a few moments on the houses lining the way. The individual lives beyond the veils and curtains of the windows are enigmatic, ghostly; fleeting shapes and shadows in a pantomime performance as the interior lights gradually brighten against a cloak of gathering darkness.

You wonder: *Do they feel the same sting of failure that I do? Do they carry the burden of unfulfilled destiny that dogs me in my quietest moments?*

In the gloom you pull your lapels together as the temperature drops and fog wisps the ground. The moon, a wan crescent, hangs low in the sky while stars reveal themselves between membranous clouds, glittering pinpoints of ancient light set against the eternal gulfs of the cosmos.

Not for the first time—and certainly not for the last—you are overcome by a foreboding sense of horror and sadness:

O, *the fragility and frustration of it all! Of life . . . of existence.*

oblivion flares again—

You are with your wife.

The look on her face pains you. The truth of the matter is clear to you both now: some things are not meant to get over, but to get through; to be endured and assimilated before consignment to the recesses of time, distance, and memory, emotionally and physically. The reality is that you have both tried hard to bridge your differences with each other, concluding, at last, that a sincere attempt at compromise is sometimes more valuable than actual conciliation.

The time in New York City was both a painful lesson and a valuable confirmation for you. Deep down, you had suspected it was not your type of place; the comforts of Providence—architecture that invited your haunting; a certain gray simplicity with respect to values of the past, in stark contrast to the din and color of the City—were far more to your liking and temperament. The chaos and rootless cosmopolitanism of New York felt crass and primitive compared to the relative social order and predictability of the city of your birth. New York was claustrophobic, as confining as a coffin; the entire time you resided there was, you realized in retrospect, an extended meditation on everything wrong with the world.

So you left. There was never a greater relief you felt than abandoning New York and returning to Providence—divine Providence.

a bolt—

It is an early remembrance . . . fragments materialize in the dark and dissolve away into other images . . . perhaps the interior of the family home. There are dim outlines: antiquated wooden furnishings, walls of books. Figures flit through the scene . . . The similar-appearing faces of women come and go . . . are they sisters? Relatives of yours, most certainly.

You can distantly hear people speaking, the words indistinct, by turns muffled and sharp, comprised only of the clipped sounds of consonant utterings. They are familiar in tone, yet alien in meaning, strangely devoid of content.

Throughout, colors are muted—except the eyes of faces, which appear luminous, inhumanly bright and vivid. Features are by turn kindly and terrifying: waxy, drawn skin; huge mouths crowded with large teeth; glistening lips pulled back in vaguely sinister smiles. The glowing eyes add to your disorientation, as they seem both too large, bulging, yet beady in the context of the grotesque heads containing them . . .

The air is cool and still, heavy with a scent of sickly-sweet decadence, of perfumed decay: moldering candy, days-old wine. Inside you there is an unsettling sensation of loss, of loneliness and isolation.

blinded once more—

Some years ago, on a busy New York street.

Surrounded by a sweaty crush of humanity, the sickening stench of commingled ethnic cuisines assails you: Chinese, Italian, Arab. Even more distressing are the aural attacks of non-English tongues and sounds from each direction—a cacophony of Hebrew, German, myriad Oriental strains. Riotously colored garbs from every corner of the planet add to the pandemonium; it is all so overwhelming, disturbing, unnatural.

You look up, realizing you are in the shadow of an imposing structure: The Danforth. It is your destination. A meeting with a fellow writer you had traded letters with a few times. As you approach you see the doorman—a gaunt figure, tall, hunched, spindly—appraising you. Disgusted by his scarred and thin countenance, you nevertheless attempt to smile. He does not return the gesture.

After a short discussion, he permits you inside the building. You proceed to the elevator; when the doors open, you are surprised to see what appears to be the *same* doorman working as the elevator operator. You inform him of the floor you need. The maw-like doors close, as though some great beast is swallowing you both up. Arriving at your destination, you disembark the apparatus. The doors squeal shut, again like some mewling animal, and you are alone in the great carpeted hallway of The Danforth.

Treading down the corridor, you finally come upon the apartment where your friend is staying; he is a guest of some mysterious, wealthy tenant, temporarily residing in a spare bedroom until his return to Charleston, South Carolina. Hesitating at the apartment, you discern strange music filtering to you from somewhere within the old building, possibly on the same floor, possibly from one of the others. It is like no other sound you have ever heard and fills you with profound dread and anxiety.

At last, you knock on the door and wait . . .

revelations—

A scream. Your own.

You awaken in a dark room, shaking. *Fever.* Your body is weak, your mouth dry. Sweat soaks the bed linens . . . you recall that you are in the hospital.

Haunted. You are a living spectre, haunting yourself, your experience. Not truly a soul inhabiting the physical realm so much as a nebulous consciousness marooned at arbitrary points in time . . . as though randomly appointed by fate to forcibly participate in various situations—that is your impression of this thing you have at times called "a life." Yet you are, from your deathbed perspective, dissociated from its causes and outcomes . . . nothing you do or have done seems to have mattered or been impactful. Your family is in ruins; your wife is gone; your life is near its end . . .

And what has it all meant? What has it amounted to? A collection of mistakes and a sheaf of anguishes . . . to what end?

Your answer: *A few childish scribblings, nothing more. Just the empty motions of a pointless existence . . . the random thrashings of a col-*

lection of cells and chemical reactions, shambling through a meandering, poorly scripted dramaturgy.

At some point you sleep again.

And the dreams come . . .

a flicker—

He stands in the doorway, smiling.

"*Welcome!*" he says and motions you in. The foyer is expansive. You feel self-conscious, shabbily dressed. You nod thanks and cross the threshold. As the door closes, the eerie music from the hallway is silenced. Your friend offers to show you around, explaining that the owner is away on unexpected business in Europe: something about trading in exotic artifacts from the Middle and Far East.

The rest of the unit is equally grand. The ceilings are high, trimmed in ornate molding, the hardwood floors as shiny, warm, and deep as a tiger's eye ring. After the tour, he offers tea and you settle in to discuss writing and the state of the world.

Everything seems almost normal for once . . .

another flash—

The landscape is at once familiar and foreign. The ground is a bitter moonscape, devoid of life. Nothing grows here; skeletons of trees loom on the fringes of the field. The wind is soft, arid. On the horizon there is a faint, otherworldly glow; the air seems at once clear and touched by some peculiar electricity. Unseen, something generates low and strange thrumming noises, more sensations than sounds. Darkness overtakes the sky.

In the distance, running toward you, a man; he is pursued by others. As he becomes more distinct, details emerge: his clothes, a sort of uniform, are ragged, his face mottled and bloody. His eyes are overly large, wild; his mouth is gaping, and his breath trails him in the cold darkness—

From the mob, queer screeching noises. Not a language you are familiar with. You are frozen in shock. They are brandishing weapons: axes, guns, bludgeons. They are also clad in tatters and appear bloodied. Far off, booming sounds—growing closer . . . *Explosions.*

The man sees you. He screams something—then his head peels apart and a piercing shriek splits the night. He seems to slough off his flesh and clothing, reaching toward you—

additional flares—

The train.

Rocking gently as is rolls through a barren stretch of terrain, you are able to relax your mind. The cares of the day fall aside . . . considerations of politics, the natural world, the sciences you so admire all drift away, absorbed into the hypnotic clacking wash of metal wheels on track.

Travel suits you. In your half-conscious state, you recall images from previous excursions: majestic old architecture, vistas of the restless sea, peaceful rustic landscapes, thunderstorms flashing on the horizon . . . even the slowly morphing faces of pen pals and friends you have met only a few times, or only seen in grainy, blurred photographs—

The train's horn sounds, snapping you back to the moment. The angle of the sun informs you that it will soon be time for dinner.

Tempus fugit.

a blast—

"Great God!"

The creature's gigantic dark wings unfurl slowly, blotting out the full moon.

Taking to the sky, it circles back on its pursuers as you watch in horror. The group fires weapons at it, but the beast—fearsome and implacable—shrugs these efforts off. It lands again on the devastated plain, just ahead of the men, using its monstrous clawed hands to grab them and bring them to its enormous, fanged mouth, swallowing the broken bodies whole—

You turn to run but are stopped by your friend—

"Are you quite all right? You look as though you've seen a ghost!" he says.

For a moment you are confused; sweat crawls down your forehead. You retrieve a handkerchief and dab at your face. You flash a nervous grin. *"I'm fine. My apologies. I must be coming down with something. My stomach has been troubling me for a time. I didn't sleep well last night, I'm afraid."*

He nods. *"No need to apologize."* He looks out the huge living-room window. His eyes are distant, dark. *"It's getting late. It was a pleasure to meet in the flesh. Perhaps you should rest, and we may reconvene at another time?"*

Surprised, you simply nod and stand to leave. *"It—it was a treat. I do hope we can continue later,"* you reply.

He walks you to the front and bids you goodbye. As he closes the heavy door you turn toward the elevator—but something macabre and decidedly misshapen seems to change his features, if only for an instant. Your skin feels clammy as you linger before the apartment, and you once more hear strange musical sonorities distantly fill in the quiet hallway.

The elevator clacks to your floor, and the weird operator opens the entrance. His face is cragged, his eyes black pits under his hat. You notice his gnarled, veiny hands are hooked on the manual controller, yellowy nails thick and dirty in the electric light of the lift.

"Going . . . *down*," he intones, his guttural voice raspy and dry.

and the light fades again . . .

None of it matters. Everything I know or have known will be forgotten. We always assume that things will remain the same, unchanging . . . and at the same time we understand the fleeting nature of time and existence . . .

Swimming in your fever dream, you begin to appreciate why you have struggled . . . why you have bothered . . . why you are being taken:

Because, equally, it all matters. I am destined to become the stuff of others' memories—even as mine are scattered through the ages. It is the fate of everyone, be they Pharaohs or paupers. We live on as reflections . . . as ripples in the aether. As remembrances. Our true value is realized in our afterlife, not our daily travails.

This curious persistence of memory is matched only by the odd dichotomy that one must have lived in order to achieve it. You were unknown . . . and now you are immortal. Physically dead, you live on as reverie, memory, projection.

You are Providence.

Dreams Are Forever

Scott Wiley

For Lily

The biting wind that swept through Providence each December brushed across her fur and the stars sparkled, in no rhythm at all, while the moon illuminated the large headstones of Little Neck cemetery—those past denizens of the city whose words and deeds had been lost to time. When the trees rattled their skeletal branches, long icicles responded with the tinkling sounds of winter like delicate copper wind-chimes. The small cat knew she was alone here.

Everywhere was dusted with a fine white powder, marking her dainty steps among the graves as she made herself comfortable under an evergreen shrub. She settled there, near the base of an angel with open palms and melancholic eyes that looked sideways upon her starving frame. On the pedestal of the statue read the words, "By His Mercy." Even if she could read, she wouldn't know what to make of it.

Alone in the cemetery, Filthy—which was not what she called herself, but the name she was so often called by others—nonetheless kept her one good eye half-open, ready to defend her territory for the night. She wouldn't be disturbed, though; the winter chill had driven most other animals to warmer sanctuaries.

Filthy had no concept of mortality as humans know it; her life was not framed in days or months or years, but in daily hunts and the cycle of birth. How many of her kittens still inhabited the streets of Providence, she'd never know, but her time here had been measured by their births and departures, and now it was growing long.

Her good eye felt heavier; she needed rest, and memories flowed fast like currents in an underground sea until she felt herself being swept away by them. Carried away to another time and place, a warm and sunny summer day when she had been much younger . . .

"Ugh, filthy rat!" yelled the butcher's wife. "Get out of here, shoo!" She swatted her broom at the black cat snaring a padded paw through the window at a pile of tripe. The woman overshot her swing and lost her balance, tripping on the stone floor and cursing the cat as she fell. Filthy took full advantage of the brief window of opportunity and snared a bit of tripe with her claw, maneuvering it masterfully through the window and into her mouth before tearing away down the alley and onto the cobblestone streets. Darting between the feet of a carriage horse, she crossed Market Square and headed toward a shady and quiet alley on Westminster where she knew she could enjoy her victory feast in peace.

After her meal, Filthy gave herself a thorough and satisfied cleaning. Fastidious to a degree that belied her name, she always kept her coat glossy and free of debris. Sated, she intended to stay in the shade of the alley until sunset; the upturned freight boxes were full of packing hay and offered an array of beds to choose from. She selected one and began to make herself comfortable, kneading down the hay with both paws. She wouldn't get a chance to sleep, though, as the peace was disturbed by two men dragging a third into the alley. They were beating him—to death, Filthy knew. She crouched low and unseen, listened as his shallow breathing slowed and stopped, then stared with dilated eyes as a white mist spilled from his mouth into a familiar and horrifying vision of a man. The man's killers were unaware of the shade finding form above him as they emptied his pockets and stripped him of his boots, but the ghost followed them as they left with their goods, its arm outstretched as it called for mercy, for help, for clarity. Its confused and plaintive cries went unheard by the thieves, but the sounds of the recently deceased would haunt Filthy for weeks after. Her fur bristling with unease, she crept down from her crate and sped stealthily toward the opposite exit, following the route through town to Roger Williams Park.

Although the park was thronged with people seeking a breeze in the humid afternoon, she knew most had come to see the geese and escape the worst of the heat and so would pay no attention to her. All the mothers and sisters and nannies, their hands full of boisterous children, had congregated near the water, so Filthy stayed up in the treeline as she sought a shady bough to sleep on. There was one tree, leafy and well-situated, but she was surprised to discover she wouldn't be alone in it; next to the tree, set apart from the other park visitors, sat a severe woman of middle age fussing over a sickly-looking boy of about eight. They had a picnic basket of provisions and a cold bottle of milk, along with a small stack of books laid carefully on their blanket. He was reading intently while his mother repeatedly offered him the snacks she'd brought. Eventually satisfied and having suitably positioned their parasol, she lay back on the blanket and closed her eyes, opening them again almost immediately.

"Howard, keep those books clean now. Your grandfather expects them back in the same condition you borrowed them." She chided the boy without unkindness, but with an oppressively anxious kind of love.

"Yes, Mother, I will. Grandfather told me they were special." The thin boy paused, then continued hopefully. "Mother, this story is about—"

She cut him off with a sigh. "Oh, Howard, you are too much like your father, always busying yourself with that nonsense."

He didn't need to be told again. He fell silent in shame and confusion, wondering whom he would ever be able to share his stories with, if not her.

But his mother continued, irritable now. "Dear, it is so hot today, I don't know how much longer until I faint in this heat. And you, you're so pale, we really must go home soon."

"Oh, please, Mother." He was desperate. "I never leave the house and it is so beautiful today! I'll read quietly, pl-please may we stay?"

With a more patient and indulgent sigh than the last, she leaned back again, closing her eyes and patting the spot beside her. "I'm going to sleep for a while. You may read, but only if you lean here next to me so I'll know if you've wandered off. Understand?"

The small boy respectfully agreed and scooted back, leaning against her shoulder as she drifted off to sleep. Her breathing slowed and the occasional snore escaped, so Howard knew she wouldn't wake. Still, he remained dutifully pressed up beside her, entranced by his book. The boy reminded Filthy of a runt: not only small in stature, but inherently weak in nature; yet there was a gentleness about him that she trusted. Still, their presence beside the tree meant there was no opportunity for her to climb it, and she debated her next move. She could return to the market, she decided, and wait for the afternoon garbage that piled up behind the kitchens to scavenge for her dinner. She was preparing her retreat with one last survey of the park when her eyes connected with the boy's.

He was gazing on her with delighted glee and admiration. Quietly, with slow and deliberate movements, the boy poured some milk into a shallow dish and set it on the grass a few feet away from him. His mother continued to sleep soundly. Filthy watched the boy. He went back to reading, settling against his mother and pretending to ignore the saucer he'd so carefully laid in the grass.

Contrary to her typical instincts, Filthy approached the tree. She was curious and could sense no danger, but even so she approached slowly and kept her large eyes locked on him. The boy smiled and called out to her, "Come here, little kitty. I poured some milk for you. Cats like milk, I think, or at least everyone says they do." Filthy sat down where she was and watched him.

His voice trembled, but he wasn't afraid of her, nor of waking his mother. He was, Filthy could tell, yearning for approval—in this case from a little street cat.

"Mother says animals are dirty and make us sick," he continued, "but I have read many books on animals, kitty, and I don't believe that at all." Howard glanced up at his mother, but she continued sleeping, and he went on. "Animals are special. They haven't forgotten their past. And animals can see special things, I think, sometimes scary things." He leaned toward Filthy with a hushed whisper. "My father saw things too. I would hear him. Sometimes he would scream about them. He would yell at the wall, and he would cry . . . He died. I think he died because of the things he saw. He was too scared of them." The boy looked down for a moment, then said, "Mother says it was lust that did it to him. I don't know what lust means, do you?" He smiled. "You can't answer because you're a cat."

Filthy couldn't understand the substance of his monologue, but she was reassured that he was no threat and dipped her paw into the milk, promptly sitting down to indicate her lack of interest in the chilled liquid. Howard laughed at the sight and, gaining in confidence while Filthy stayed close by, reached into their picnic basket and brought out some slices of thick, buttered bread, a bunch of sardines, and some cold melon. He tore off small pieces of each and set them on the grass in front of him. "What about this, kitty?"

She came closer and craned her neck to smell the fish. The boy reached to stroke her and Filthy backed away, but only slightly. She walked behind the boy and his mother, then came around to the picnic basket and rubbed her cheeks against it, marking it with her scent. The boy picked up a sardine and tossed it closer to her.

Filthy, entranced by the smell, crept up to the piece, sniffed it, and then ate it. It was fresh and delicious. Howard tossed another piece to her, and there was no deliberation this time—Filthy devoured the fish in one gulp.

The boy dangled another sardine out front of him. "Kitty, come here, I have some more for you."

Filthy walked up to the boy slowly and sniffed the treat, but did not take it. The boy held it still and reached out with his other hand to stroke her. This time, Filthy allowed the contact; she could feel his small fingers play upon the thick fur of her back. It felt comforting, a type of touch she hadn't felt since she was a kitten.

Feeling receptive, she moved in closer and stood on her hind legs, bracing her paws against his chest to stand up and reach for the fish. Howard giggled as her hair tickled his nose and dropped the fish for her. Filthy swallowed it whole, then sniffed his fingers, licking off the last of the sardine juice before crawling onto the boy's lap. He could feel her warm weight against him as the cat began to press her paws gently into his legs, circled a few times, and curled up on his lap.

Boy and cat were together on the hot New England day as birds sang, children played, and a burgeoning breeze rustled the leaves above them. Howard stroked the cat and hummed a lullaby to her. When he was scared, he would hum it to himself to quiet his fears. This time, though, Howard felt no fear; in fact, he had never felt so peaceful. As he stroked the cat and listened to the summer chorus, Filthy added her contented purr to the summer refrain, utterly relaxing in his lap.

"Mother does not care for the books I read," he continued, and Filthy would have been pleased to know that he found talking to her as soothing as she found listening to him speak. "She thinks they're a waste of time, but I don't know how you can waste time when you love something so much." He tapped the book by his side. "This book is about ancient Egypt. You don't know about Egypt, do you, kitty? It's all gone now, but I've seen pictures of the Pyramids—and of the Sphinx, which is a really big cat! Well, it's a cat everywhere except the head, but I think the head must have belonged to a Pharaoh.

"Cats were very important in Egypt, kitty, lots of their gods and statues look like cats. Black cats just like you." Saying this, Howard touched a tender fingertip to her wet nose. Filthy opened her eyes and looked up at him, letting them close again as she began to doze. Howard stroked her in a gentle rhythm until she was sleeping, then began to speak very softly so as not to wake either cat or mother.

"I dream of these places, kitty. When I dream it's as if I live there, as if I've always lived there. Sometimes the places are so nice, I dream of adventures in the jungle looking for lost cities of gold, or sometimes I dream of my father. Those dreams are not as nice, kitty. I see him in a room and he's alone. There's nothing in the room, not even a bed, but the walls are all soft like pillows. But he's screaming all the time and his words don't make sense. I don't like those dreams much, but what scares me the most are the monsters. They follow me. Every time I dream, they're there. I wake up and sometimes they're there standing over me. Watching me. I don't like thinking about it too much."

Howard tensed as he said this, pressing his hand into her fur. "It's daytime, so they're not here, kitty. We're safe, just you and me." He exhaled purposefully. "Let me tell you a story, kitty." And he picked up the book by his side, holding it to his chest as he closed his eyes. "Long ago in Egypt, before there was anything, before the Pyramids or the Sphinx, there were only the gods."

The small boy spoke words she couldn't understand, yet Filthy found herself slipping from the waking world, consumed with a rainbow of colors and shapes. Slowly, as the cadence of his voice continued, those muddled colors and shapes began to tear themselves apart, revealing distinct forms gathered inside a long hall . . .

It was a great hall of gold and white, with bright, warm light spilling in from an unidentified source. There was no ceiling but instead a canopy of new, dancing stars where a roof should have been. The shimmering walls on either side of the hall rose until they faded into black, merging with the cosmic ceiling above. The floor was a gleaming white alabaster that reflected and doubled the light inside the hall, while the light itself sang a song of creation. As these details came into focus, what were originally shapeless shadows also became more defined, indicating a mass of beings all facing the elevated platform and golden throne at one end of the hall. Seated on the throne was a stately figure dressed in white linen, the smooth golden mask of an eagle, and a hovering golden crown.

At the opposite end, filtering into the hall one by one, were a pair of beings also dressed in white linen robes. They too wore masks, but each was different. The first to enter wore the mask of a jackal, and in this hall of immense light he left a palpable, chilly darkness in his wake. He approached the throne platform and stood before it respectfully erect, his arms crossed. Another masked being entered, this time with the mask of a crocodile, and his mouth dribbled from it water that vanished before it hit the ground. He too approached the platform, and the jackal nodded to him, "Brother Sobek, welcome." His voice was cold and distant, and Sobek merely nodded his acknowledgment, while the being on the throne said nothing.

Sobek addressed him, growling, "So, Father Ra, you have summoned me and I am here. What is it you wish?"

Ra declined to shift his gaze, responding calmly, "All will be revealed when the others arrive."

Sobek began to grow flustered. "Am I Set? Do I bring chaos? I demand to know why I am here, I have the Nile to protect, I—"

He was silenced by a rush of sound, like sand being swept across the desert, as Apophis appeared on the threshold. He wore the mask of the snake and announced himself to all in the hall as he swept toward the throne. "Yesss, it isss I, brothersss, Father." Stroking his chin, he continued sarcastically, addressing the jackal, "Ahh, Anubisss. Ra hasss sssummoned you ssso it mussst be sssomething ssseriousss."

At this Ra stood, pointing at Apophis and speaking with calm authority. "I will tolerate Sobek's outbursts, Apophis; he protects my Nile. But you are only here to bear witness, for you are too close to Set and his chaos. Be silent unless you are addressed, understood?"

Apophis bowed, his eyes indignant. "Yesss, my lord."

In a burst of moonlight, the last to arrive to the hall was Bastet. In her arms she cradled a small, black, furry animal whose face resembled her own mask: large eyes with black diamond pupils, small nose, a short snout, and long, pointed ears.

"Ah, Bastet." Ra was happy to see her. "You are here with your creation, I see! So this is what took you so long; my patience has been waning." He finished with a chuckle and a wink before gliding down the steps to her, eager to see the furry creature she held.

"I hope I have not tried your patience too much, Father, and that you will be pleased with what I have brought to add to your new world," Bastet replied deferentially.

"My dearest daughter, I would have waited a millennium to see what you have created."

At this Apophis frowned and Ra turned on him fiercely. "Do you have something you would like to add?"

"No, Father." Apophis held his tongue.

Ra continued with Bastet, "I think I would like to hold this little creature." She passed it to him and he held it out, admiring its shape. "My daughter, I see the likeness!" Ra turned his head to one son and added, "It's much nicer looking than yours, eh, Sobek?"

Sobek growled but kept his anger in check. "My servants protect your Nile, Father," Sobek replied solemnly. "I did not design them to be pleasing to the eye."

"Ha!" Ra laughed, which only happened when Bastet was present; she seemed to put him in a lighter mood. "That is true, Sobek, that is true. So tell me, sweet daughter," he said, handing the animal back to her, "how will this little creature serve me and my world?"

Bastet smiled proudly and explained, "Father, my creation has claws to scratch and protect, eyes to watch over all, and a heart as light as a feather. It will be loving and it will be loyal to you and your creations from now until the gods are gone forever."

With her last declaration the room fell hushed.

Ra clapped his hands. "Well then, I approve! What about the voice of the creature? Does it sing?"

Ecstatically Bastet exclaimed, "Yes, Father! Let me show you." She dangled her fingers in front of the creature's face and swept her hand lightly. "Sing for Father, my precious thing."

With the greatest of efforts, the little creature made the slightest sound, a gentle little squeak.

"Beautiful, my daughter. This creature will sing my praises for all time. I am so proud of you," Ra beamed.

Bastet had begun to stroke the animal's black fur when it sang, and now it was purring audibly.

"What is this sound?" Ra leaned in closer.

"It's for comforting those who need it, Father, both its young and others. Others who may be alone in your beautiful world. As you know, those who are alone often cannot revel in your creation, and my creature will help they who are lost and lonely."

Ra smiled, pleased with this. "And if it is upset, or angry, or scared? Let us hear."

Bastet curled her arms around it protectively and hesitated. "Is that necessary, Father? I cannot bear to scare this precious, tiny thing."

"I am Ra, and I must know all that exists within my domain, daughter. All its sounds, all it can do. Please do not make me ask again."

Apophis, who had been leaning against the wall, sensed an opening to speak. "Let'sss sssee a dissplay, sssissster. I insssissst!" Suddenly Apophis flew at Bastet, opening his jaw and exposing his fangs at the creature in her arms. At this, the little animal opened its jaw, exposing its own four tiny fangs, and let out an angry hiss.

Apophis laughed a hideous laugh. "Sssee Father, your Bassstet hasss ssstolen *my* voiccce! Thisss beassst hasss sssoundsss you bessstowed on *me!*"

"Apophis, be silent!" Ra bellowed. With concern he continued, "Is this true, daughter? Did you steal Apophis' voice?"

Bastet held her creature close and nodded. "Yes, Father, much to my shame. It is so small and defenseless, I needed something that would frighten any who wished to harm it. Apophis and his creations have such a fearsome voice, I believed you—"

"Dessstroy it, sssissster," Apophis cried, "thisss isss an immenssse insssult! Father, I insssissst—"

"You will insist on nothing, belly-crawler!" Ra said, silencing Apophis with a hand. "Oh, my daughter, why would you steal? No, it does not matter." He silenced Bastet the same way. "What can I do?" he asked himself. "I cannot destroy this creature, which will serve my new world so well. And Apophis, after the monstrosity you created you would wish this precious thing destroyed? No, I will not do this. But still, something must be done . . . Anubis, come!"

Anubis, the jackal, ever the loyal servant to Ra, approached, and as he did his feet left footprints of frost on the otherwise warmly glowing floor. He bowed slightly, "My lord, what is your wish?"

Ra stood quiet for a moment, then decided, "It is not my wish, but I am left no choice. Anubis, remove the veil from between the dead and the living from this creature, which is as precious to me as my own daughter and cannot be destroyed. Instead, *it will forever see the world that exists beyond this world, where the restless dead roam and wail. This shall be the punishment for theft.*"

Bastet let out a wail. "No, that is not fair, Father! My precious little thing will always be afraid, it shall never be at peace in your world! Even Anubis cannot appreciate all you've created, surviving as he must in the underworld."

Ra ignored her, gesturing to Anubis, "Proceed."

Anubis turned to Bastet and the tiny creature she clung to, which squirmed and hissed in utter despair.

Apophis laughed, eliciting silent tears from Baster who stroked her precious pet's furry black neck in a comforting gesture as Anubis' hand hovered above its head. His voice was cold and hard. "You will see beyond the veil that exists between the living and dead. Shadows will follow you, they will haunt you. You will hear all that they suffer and all that is unknown, and none shall see them except your kind. This I have done in the name of Ra."

Bastet was weeping now, pressing her wet face to her furry creation. "My sweetest little one, I can never be sorry enough. I only wished to keep you safe, and instead I have cursed you all. I will watch over you forever. Please forgive me, little one. Please forgi—"

Sudden shrieking woke Filthy with a start. "Howard! What is that disgusting thing you are holding? Dear God, get rid of it!"

"Oh, please, Mother, don't scare it, it's only sleeping."

Their exchange was lost on Filthy as she tore out of Howard's lap, leaving the commotion of the horrified mother further and further behind her. She was running through the grass, faster, up into the trees and the thicket—

Filthy awoke. It was still dark, the moon still hung in the sky, and the cold was especially strong. She lacked the strength to rise, even the strength to hold onto the world.

Before Filthy, the moonlight that illuminated the cemetery seemed to flicker, binding together piece by piece until a translucent figure, clad in white robes, appeared. Loving arms reached down, and although Filthy couldn't see who it was, her ears heard the words clearly. "My precious little one, I have found you."

Bastet scooped up the old cat and pressed their noses gently together, humming a quiet song to her darling little one.

"Come with me, my precious one, it is time leave this place of pain and sadness. The old gods left long ago, yet I remain to watch over my creation. And now I will take you in my arms to a paradise, where you can dwell with the others in my garden and comfort me as I grow older. Come now, this is no home for you, but do not fear. I have read your dreams, and in time the boy will join you, and he will love you as I always have."

A warmth such as she had never felt enveloped Filthy as the world faded away and she found herself transported to a realm of light, and joy, and peace—and an unending love.

A Meeting Beneath the Moon

Mark Howard Jones

The stars overhead defiled the darkness, drawing unsettling silver patterns against the black backdrop, and the moon was larger and paler than any waking sky had ever held.

The garden stretched a long way from the house, and the man with the pale complexion wasn't sure whether he'd ever seen the full extent of it. He anticipated that some obscure, previously unseen corner of it might one day yield a sight that would fill him with wonder or joy. Or perhaps some other, less wholesome emotion.

Once he'd been certain that the sea touched the garden at one point, far distant. But when he'd tried to find it again he'd become lost, unable to revisit the place where the tang of brine and ozone in the air made him feel as if he were setting out on a long voyage of discovery.

He turned and looked back at the impossibly tall dark house from which he'd emerged. The darkened windows of the forbidding structure seemed to hold his attention for longer than they should have done.

He tore his attention away and finished tying his sturdy gardening apron at the back. Frowning slightly, he reflected on how demanding a garden this large, and this unusual, could be.

The layout of the vast garden appeared to change regularly, yet he always retained a map of sorts in his mind, so that whatever happened he could find his way back to the house from within the heart of the leafy labyrinth. But that didn't stop it from surprising him at almost every turn.

Nearby a small tree, stirred to life by a lazy breeze, sighed a sentence of alien sibilance.

On nights like this, when the starlight was so cold, he could sense the presence of a darker dreamer, reaching towards him through the icy blackness.

At first it was tiny and far away, like the sound of a single candle guttering in the vast darkness of a cathedral. Then it drew closer and closer. Finally it was as persistent as an unwelcome visitor hammering on the door of night.

It was then that he headed for a small grove of trees not very far from the house. They had tall, slender trunks crowned with upward-facing branches, and he had no idea why he had sought them out. They each bore a symbol on their trunks.

At first, he thought they had been carved into the light-coloured bark of each tree individually. But on closer examination, the strange five-pointed symbol seemed to have occurred naturally, growing there in some inexplicable fashion as each tree developed.

Whenever he stood within or near the tiny grove, the unwelcome sensation receded until he could no longer feel it. This was a place of peace that he cherished.

The gardener looked around at the plants waiting to be tended and mused that he had planted none of them. They had all seeded themselves. He had no doubt that each of them had come here from a very far-off place, seeking a very particular nourishment.

The moon tonight was so large, so bright, that he felt that it could be reached quite easily, if you had the right sort of craft. Its brightness brought an ancient coldness with it.

He was constantly surprised that those chill fingers of night had little effect, either positive or negative, upon the plants, even though they affected him quite keenly.

Indeed, the growths seemed to thrive in any sort of weather. He attributed this to their alien origins and, in no small part, to his care, which was always diligent and appropriate regardless of their uncommon demands.

Dutifully, he lifted out the implements he would need from a small box he'd secreted under a large bush. He put on a pair of heavy fabric gloves for safety's sake.

He scooped a handful of loose pellets from a small bag marked Starfeast Fertiliser Company and spread it liberally around the thick base of the nearest plant. The fat leaves spilled over the path, making it difficult to pass by without touching them.

Nearby, odd triangular insects, trailing frail tendrils behind them, flitted from flower to flower, gathering nocturnal nectar. A group of them, seemingly mesmerised, hanging in mid-air before the large purple bell of a gargantuan flower. They waited patiently as a long tongue emerged slowly to devour them one by one.

He stood and gazed at them, wanting to turn away but being held there perhaps by the same fascination that enraptured them. He found the idea of their hanging in mid-air, waiting for death, quite repugnant.

Then he paused. Was the human condition really any better?

Like all men, he knew he must someday exchange the coolness of the night for the eternal cold of the grave. Until then, he mused, I shall make the very best of this remarkable place.

He reached up to pull a flower closer, intending to inhale its unfamiliar perfume, but quickly let it go when an angry clicking began. A multi-legged creature crawled from within the bell of the flower, dropped to the floor, and scuttled away.

When he finally inhaled the flower's scent, it was disappointingly insipid.

Continuing along the path, he came across a gaping pit barring his way. The deep hole was just long enough and wide enough for a man to lie down in the pool of darkness at its bottom. A snug fit, he thought, but not tonight.

The garden had provided him with several graves in recent days. But he still had things to do. If the place really was able to anticipate his thoughts, he found this particular intervention a great impertinence.

The enormous bell of a highly scented flower nodded at him, as if in silent agreement. He scooped some food around its base as a slight reward.

He stooped now and then as he made progress to those plants that looked most in need of nourishment. Soon he found that he was some distance from the house and the air had taken on a distinct chill.

The wall was high and sturdy in that part of the garden, yet still the ice had encroached. In the snow at the vanguard of the chill whiteness, he'd noticed several giant plants, barely buried beneath the thin layer of frost. Atop their enormous bodies were large star-shaped flowers.

One day, he knew, he would have to find out exactly what sort of thing grew there. But he had more pressing matters this night.

Bending to feed a large, proud flower with an eye-like centre, he was sure he felt the ground tremble slightly beneath his feet.

He imagined the earth from the garden running through a hole in its hidden centre, like sand in an hourglass. Perhaps the garden was as temporary as everything else and, once he was no longer able to tend it in his unique way, it would fall into desolation and decay.

There was already a definite stink of rot in the air. Yet all the plants here appeared healthy. Healthier than in the average garden. Although "average" was a word that was definitely out of place here.

Following the overgrown path around a red flower-laden bush, he was somewhat startled to see a figure standing with its back to him. Hearing his approach, the man turned around.

He wore slightly old-fashioned clothes but had a kindly expression and a head crowned with silver hair that hung below his ears.

The gardener felt that he should be wary of any stranger in this place, and yet there was something curiously familiar about this person.

Although they had never met before, an odd expression of recognition appeared on the faces of both men. Stepping forward to welcome his visitor, the gardener extended his hand. "It's Arthur, isn't it?"

The older man returned the handshake with some vigour. "Yes,

yes. Hello!" he replied, as if greeting an old friend. "It's very good to see you. I was just admiring your splendid garden. It is *your* garden, I take it?"

The gardener paused for a moment as if unsure. "Yes. It must be. I am the one who always tends to it."

Arthur nodded. "Always? There is no one to help you?"

"No. I feel a compulsion to come here each night. The plants need tending. Some require a very particular sort of care."

Again a nod. "Do you never feel a little trapped by that regimen?"

The moon high above dimmed its light, making the darkness deeper and thicker. Does it somehow disapprove of our conversation? wondered Arthur.

Despite the blackness of the night, the two men could see each other clearly in the curious luminescence given off by the larger plants. It is as if they are drinking in the moonlight and then releasing it once they are sated, thought Arthur.

The gardener stood, shaking his head with a half-awake expression on his face. "No. Not trapped exactly."

From the high black house somewhere behind them came a sound like an enormous object crashing against its walls, shaking it tremendously as if something were being born. Or were dying.

Arthur and the pale man stood looking in its direction. Their expressions were a mixture of awe and fear. They waited several more moments, but the sound did not repeat itself.

"Is that a regular occurrence?" asked Arthur, once he'd found his voice.

His friend merely shook his head slowly and returned his attention to the plant at his feet.

Arthur wandered off a little way to examine more of the bizarre flora.

One plant that drew his attention seemed to be made up entirely of stalks. He nearly walked straight past but then noticed an unusual pink flower almost hidden in the centre.

Stepping closer, he saw that the flower looked uncannily like a woman's face. It looked peaceful, as if it had recently fallen asleep.

From the mouth extended a tongue-like stamen. On its surface was yet another face—this one looking as though it lay in a troubled sleep—and, if he peered even closer . . .

Arthur pulled himself upright with a jolt. He would not look at the thing.

Composing himself, he ambled over to where his companion was tending a low liquorice-scented bush with fleshy leaves.

"Yes, you have quite a remarkable collection of plants here. Did you choose them all yourself?" Given what he'd already seen, Arthur hoped the answer would be in the negative. He was more than a little relieved when his companion shook his head.

"No. Most, if not all of them, have seeded themselves. But I welcome their appearance, I must say. I believe that each of these extraordinary growths may have been drawn here by a less than arbitrary occurrence."

Arthur blew into a pipe he'd produced from his pocket, making a loud snorting noise. He considered whether to light it or not.

"A gift from the gods, you might say." He waved the pipe around, pointing at individual plants in turn to illustrate his point. Observing the look of consternation on his friend's face, Arthur stopped fumbling for his tobacco and slipped the pipe quietly back into his pocket.

"I admit that tending this garden does help me to formulate my ideas. Whether I can carry them beyond this place is another matter."

The leaves of one plant hung down like the spread pages of an oversized, inverted book. The gardener paid particular attention to this one, Arthur noticed, feeding it generously, fussing over it and picking off dead leaves.

Arthur suddenly felt compelled to look over his shoulder. A strange, tree-like shrub behind him now seemed particularly fascinating. A few steps and he was standing right in front of it. It gave off a musky scent.

On the enormous bole of the plant were a series of raised mounds with a notch running down their centre. From each ran a thin trickle of clear liquid.

To Arthur they appeared like a superfluity of vulvas. Or weeping eyes, ready to open and stare at him.

A slight sense of unease crept over him as he speculated as to what could be born from such a fecundated growth. Or what the thing would see were it to look at him—a friend, or food?

Suddenly he became aware of the gardener at his elbow. "Please come away, Arthur. I have reason to believe that this particular plant has an actively hostile nature."

Arthur looked around, unsurprised. "Really?" He was glad of an excuse to step away from the plant.

The bag of food was now empty, so the gardener folded it and put it in the pocket of his apron before brushing off his hands.

"Let me show you where this place lies." He indicated a narrow path that led off to one side, away from the main promenade through the garden. Arthur followed as the tall man led the way through a gap between the plants.

Luxuriant growths shot up on either side, and the light became dimmer as they squeezed between the narrow green walls. Leaves caressed them, and once a twig tugged at the silver hair that hung down past the older man's ears. He was beginning to feel a mild claustrophobia when the path suddenly opened out and he found himself on a stone platform.

The two men stood on a small outcrop that seemed to stand proud from the garden itself, where green walls curved back in either direction. They were within an oddly decorated stone and wood gazebo. The stone looked so ancient that Arthur feared to touch it, lest it crumble beneath his fingers. He stuffed his hands into his pockets to deter any temptation to do so.

He looked out from his vantage point, astonished at the fact that there was nothing to see. There was no landscape stretching away from the garden and its heavily overgrown walls. The strange stars seemed to fade out just as they met a horizon that was not there.

Arthur looked at his friend, who simply said "The void."

Daring to lean forward slightly to peer over the low wall, Arthur gazed down into the blackness, hoping to catch a glimpse of something. "An abyss above us and an abyss below," he muttered.

But surely there was something, he thought. Was that the sound of waves? Were they in fact on an island of some sort, lost in the wastes of some vast aetheric ocean? He turned his head to one side, listening intently to the sound, which seemed to come from miles and miles away.

Arthur turned to his friend and opened his mouth to speak. He didn't know whether it was possible to be interrupted before you'd even said anything, but that's how it felt to Arthur. "Voices," said his companion.

"But—?" began Arthur, then stopped and leaned over to listen even more intently to the sound coming from far below. "I—it . . . it . . ." he began. There were words within the faraway, echoing chaos of sound.

"I thought at first that I was hearing the sound of waves," said his friend. "I'd imagined once before that the sea lapped against the garden, but I was mistaken. It is not the sea, just an ocean of voices."

Arthur's face twisted into an expression lost somewhere in the wasteland between hope and fear. The strange, whispering siren sounds refused to let him stop listening. He wondered if this was a place of inspiration or merely desperation.

As if in answer, his friend spoke once more. "It is a place where all the voices are dead. They simply repeat empty things. Sometimes they grow louder, but they are still divorced from life. Or from what we know of our life, at least."

The pale man now stood beside Arthur. He closed his eyes and listened. Unsure of the sturdiness of the ancient stonework, Arthur stood back from the edge. He was afraid it would not support the weight of two people, and he was certainly the heavier man.

He watched his friend intently, expecting some further revelation from him about the curious nature of the phenomena. Instead, his friend's face took on an aspect of grief, as if he recognised the tones of a familiar voice in the distant tumult. It seemed to grow more profound with each passing second.

"Come, let us go back," said Arthur hastily. "I have seen—and heard—enough." He laid his hand on the pale man's arm as if to guide him away, afraid that he might succumb to some wayward instinct within him.

Back where they had begun, the two men sat on a large, decorated rock for a moment.

The gardener looked down at a plant whose dried leaves were drooping so much that they nearly touched the ground.

"Some of the more fragile plants need watering. It hasn't rained here for some time." He held a leaf gently between his fingers, but even this was too much for the plant, which crumbled at his touch.

"I will fetch the watering can from the house later. There is a well in the garden, but it has become unaccountably poisoned. Anything watered from it undergoes an unwarranted and quite bizarre transformation."

Arthur couldn't help but wonder what exactly that must look like in this hothouse of wonders and horrors.

Once they were on their feet again, the tall man led the way.

To one side of the path was an object on four sturdy iron legs. It stood on its own paved section and was about two feet long.

As the men passed by, a sound came from inside the box-like object. "What is that?" asked Arthur.

The other man shook his head. "I have no idea."

They stepped closer to examine it and saw that it was made of glass, almost completely covered with a green film. Taking his handkerchief out, Arthur tried to clean off the mouldy layer. As he did so, there was movement inside.

"There's something alive in there," noted the gardener, as he leant closer to look inside. The reverse of the glass was similarly grubby, obscuring everything but the impression of movement within. A faint blue glow penetrated the murk. A low grumble or growl accompanied it.

He and Arthur looked at each other with mild concern. "Might it be dangerous?" asked Arthur. The other man acknowledged his lack of knowledge with a slow shake of his head.

A small brass plaque was attached to the front of the odd display case, but it was impossible to read it in the gloom. Arthur struck a match so his companion could examine the sign. "We are no wiser, I'm afraid. The writing has been worn away," he said, indicating the pitted and weathered surface. The only decipherable letter was a capital 'S' at the top right-hand corner.

A dozen pinpricks of blue light appeared through the twilight inside the box, then disappeared in the blink of an eye. It was difficult to work out if they were looking at a single creature or a whole colony. Whatever it was, the commotion from inside was growing the longer the two stood looking at it.

"I don't think we'd better open it," whispered Arthur, suddenly surprised at himself for lowering his voice.

The other man checked around the back of the box. There was a curiously fashioned brass clasp at the rear, but it seemed not to have been designed to be opened—at least, not by human fingers. "I agree. There's no way to open it without breaking it, in any case."

As they walked away, the noise and movement inside the glass case grew even more frantic. They talked of other things, deliberately ignoring it until it was out of earshot. Both men secretly congratulated themselves for escaping something that would have been exceptionally unpleasant, if not deadly.

The two relaxed sufficiently to carry on their conversation as if the sinister glass case had been merely something from another dream entirely.

Arthur was regaling his companion with the finer details of an extraordinary novel that he had read recently and was not paying full attention to where his feet were going. ". . . and on the very last page, at that."

He was so absorbed in his tale that he nearly pitched forward into a deep pit that had opened up in the ground ahead of them. Only a restraining hand saved him.

"Good Lord," he muttered, recognising a grave when he saw one. There was a headstone already in place at the far end of the mortuary trench.

As the men watched, letters began to form as tiny chips of stone fell from the upright stone slab.

"Come on. We won't want to see this . . ." The gardener began to part the foliage nearest to him, finding a way around the obstruction. His companion followed, placing his feet carefully so as not to be snagged by protruding branches. *If we keep going we must come across the path again,* he reasoned, as the undergrowth crowded about them. They trod slowly and carefully in the gloom.

Neither man had anything to cut through the foliage, and the going soon became difficult. After a few minutes of struggle they came to what looked like part of an old cast-iron fence. At first glance it looked as if it had been allowed to rust, but on closer examination they saw it was entirely organic. It had grown straight out of the soil at their feet, barring the way.

"Where are we?" asked Arthur.

"I don't know," said the younger man. "I've never been here before."

On the other side of the obstruction could be seen a clearing where three or four enormous stone blocks stood. Three had become obscured almost completely by vegetation, but the fourth, which stood slightly apart, was free of any growth. It looked, in fact, as if had been freshly deposited there.

Finding their way along the obstructing plant, the men discovered that it decreased in height, then trailed off along the ground before finally disappearing into it. Having cleared the obstruction, they decided to examine the huge stone blocks. These were obviously ruins that required exploration.

As they neared the closest block they could see that, unlike its companions, its surface was smooth and clean. The dark grey block was nearly ten feet in height and looked as if it had been part of something much larger. On one side of it, picked out in the moonlight, were several large glyphs, both whole and partial. Some of the shapes were carved right up to the edge of the stone and looked incomplete, as if they were meant to join with a companion carving on another block.

As they took their next step, the indecipherable letters appeared to invert themselves for a second before returning to their former position.

"Extraordinary! Did you see that?" When no answer came, the younger man turned to his companion. He saw that the older man was standing with his head in his hands. "Arthur? Are you not well?"

The older man staggered forward a few steps before being steadied by his companion. "My head . . . it's so—"

Within a second or two, the gardener began to feel an odd pressure building behind his eyes. It was as though a huge yet silent tocsin were being rung inside his head. The pressure came and went in waves, reverberating against the inside of his skull.

The two men stumbled into each other, almost ending up on the ground. Grabbing at their clothing to support one another, they retraced their steps as quickly as they could. At a certain distance away, the throbbing waves began to ease. It was clearly a warning to stay away from the ruins.

Disoriented, Arthur staggered off to one side, bumping into the trunk of a large plant before tumbling sideways.

He suddenly found himself in a tiny space surrounded by the enormous fibrous trunks of several plants clustered together. What little space lay between the trunks was filled by the thick stalks of yet another plant.

Confused, Arthur looked around. How on earth had he got here? There was no entrance to the cramped space. He pressed against the trunks and the stalks, but neither gave way even an inch. He could only imagine that the plants had suddenly and impossibly sprung up around him.

He then noticed that each of the thick trunks had set into it a narrow, hollow space suggestive of a coffin. They were just large enough for a man to fit inside.

Standing was difficult. He had hardly any space to put his feet and, struggling for balance, he toppled backwards into one of the tight spaces.

Arthur lay still for a second or two, tilted backwards at a slight angle. He got his breath back and tried to stand. His arms were pinned at his side and he was wedged in place.

Managing to free one hand, he placed it on the side of the plant and exerted all his strength. He moved an inch or two before becoming stuck fast once again.

He felt a slight shiver run through the plant as thick, sticky liquid began to trickle down the sides of the hollow he was lying in. The smell was quite unpleasant.

Realising that the plant knew it had fresh prey to digest, Arthur was on the point of panicking when he saw a hand appear between the thick stalks directly in front of him. "Take my hand," a voice commanded.

Angling himself as best he could, he heaved his one arm free and grasped the outstretched hand with gratitude. With a tremendous effort he pulled himself up and through the plants blocking his way.

Out in the open once more, Arthur did his best to clean the viscous substance from his clothes with some large leaves from a nearby bush. "Are you all right?" asked his saviour.

"Yes. I think so. Thanks to you," he answered, before glancing back in the direction of the gigantic stones.

His companion followed his gaze. "That's one mystery that can remain a mystery for today, at least. Though I'm reluctant to give up on it altogether. After all, it may reveal that the entire garden is planted over ancient ruins."

Arthur glanced warily over his shoulder as they picked their way around the site. "Menhir of some fashion, perhaps . . ."

Within a few minutes the pair found their way back to the path. Picking tiny hair-like seeds from his clothing, the gardener indicated which direction they should take.

As they continued, the soft luminosity around them faded. The eldritch growths, fallen from the stars or risen from the seas, were suddenly aglow with a deep orange light. The effect on the two men's faces was alarming. In the infernal illumination, Arthur fumbled for his matches again. As he struck one, he noticed there were only a few left.

The halo of light returned their faces more or less to normal.

"That's never happened before." The two men looked about them warily, fearing that the odd livid light might foreshadow something more sinister. After a few minutes the light began to change once more, the previous white glow returning as the redness faded into the night around them.

Then, above them, the stars blinked out slowly, as if being obscured by gigantic petals as they closed over the garden. Soon only the doleful, ashen eye of the moon remained, gazing down at them from directly overhead.

Suddenly the taller man gasped and doubled over. He seemed helpless for a few seconds; then, panting hard, he regained control of himself.

Arthur rushed forward to help him. "Are you all right? Can I help?"

"No. No. I'll be all right, thank you. I have some pain from time to time." He stared into the distance, seemingly at nothing at all.

"How long have you been suffering from these pains?"

His shoulders moved in what might have been a small shrug or a reaction to a final small spasm of pain. "Several weeks now, if my memory is correct."

"Do you think it may have something to do with some noxious emanations put forth by these remarkable plants?" asked Arthur.

The thin man looked at his silver-haired companion. "Well . . . some kind of radiation, you mean? I hadn't considered that."

Arthur nodded, though he wasn't sure that was exactly what he'd meant.

"Have you sought your doctor's advice? After all, it might not merely be a passing problem but a more serious malady. It is not good to ignore these things."

The tall man had an uncomfortable expression on his face. "I distrust the medical community. They pretend to more knowledge than they actually possess, it seems to me."

He took in the view of the vegetal and floral kaleidoscope surrounding him. His next remarks indicated to Arthur that he had indeed considered his own mortality.

"Whatever might happen, if I have taken some of these dreams and made them real—at least for myself—then I think it may have been a price worth paying."

"They are more than dreams, I think," muttered Arthur. "I am sure they are . . ."

The gardener nodded. "Perhaps. Or perhaps I am merely storing them up against a time when there will be no more dreams."

Again an enormous crashing sound emanated from the dark house that towered over the far end of the garden.

"Your guests seem to be growing ever more restless," commented Arthur.

"I don't have any guests. At least, none that I know of."

Arthur seemed embarrassed at his friend's response. He stepped back and sat on a convenient bench, making some general remark about tiredness in order to cover his obvious error.

His companion ignored the remark. "I am tired now. If you don't mind, I believe I will go inside. Thank you for your visit, Arthur. It was so good to see you."

When no reply came, he turned to look. There was no sign of the other man. In his place on the bench was a jumble of sticks and roots, twisted together to approximate the shape of a seated man. Several lightly browned leaves, curled and misshapen, made up the face, with two dark berries beginning to wither below a brow of smooth bark. Some downy white seed heads had settled atop the plants.

After contemplating the sight for a few moments, the solitary man turned and walked away. Heavy night-borne aromas filled the air as he rounded the bend in the path, passing beneath an enormous drooping overgrowth of *Orchidaceae stellam natae,* to face whatever waited for him in the dark house.

In the near-darkness, the house opened up like an enormous flower to welcome him in.

The Return of the Night-Gaunts

Darrell Schweitzer

They bore him up, soaring, into the darkness, far beyond the lights of the city, over black mountains with pinnacles as sharp as teeth, their touch chilling, their claws hard as iron, and yet he was not afraid. The whimsical thought came to him that he was like Scrooge carried off by the spirits in Mr. Dickens's famous, if mawkish, tale. But no, it wasn't like that. Insofar as he had any volition left, he shook off that ridiculous thought and merely observed, objectively and passively, what was below him.

The Cold Waste.

He was not afraid, because he knew his companions. He knew what they were. They were familiar. They had come to him again, as he had always known they would.

He felt only a quiet sense of awe.

"Funny how early interests crop up again toward the end of one's life."

If all this had started a few months before, on what might have been the last perfect evening he would ever know, he had certainly not realized it at the time. The weather was uncommonly warm for late October, so he was not yet imprisoned within his meager dwelling. He could still go out, and did, and in the course of his wanderings discovered, much to his delight, a woodland not more than three miles from his home that he had never explored before. The city was his native place. Its streets and towers were as familiar to him, as much a part of him, as his own body; but here was a remaining pocket of the unknown, affording him one last glimpse of adventurous expectancy as he gazed through the trees at the remote urban skyline, its domes and pinnacles aglow in the fading sunset, floating in the air, like something out of a dream.

He stood there, deeply moved, as the Hunter's Moon rose, two days short of full, and if something passed across that moon briefly, it must have been a bird or a bat or a wisp of cloud, and he did not notice.

He recalled the ecstasy he had felt as a child when, in his pagan phase, in woods similar to these, he genuinely believed he had glimpsed the god Pan with his retinue of nymphs cavorting between the tree trunks. As a grown man given to reason he was of course beyond such things. He regretted that. The best he could do was try to cling to the memory of the sensation, to hold on to it as long as he could.

If, from overhead, there came a sound like a tent flap blowing in the wind, it must have been, indeed, something blowing in the wind, a mere distraction.

Only in full darkness, after the night had begun to get uncomfortably chilly, did he make his way home, into the city, and on to the ancient hill.

He let himself in quietly. His aunt had gone to bed. He was quite used to preparing late meals for himself—something out of a can, cold, a couple slices of bread, and coffee with plenty of sugar.

When he settled down to work that night, mostly catching up on letter-writing, he found it hard to concentrate. It was like dreaming while awake; he had the momentary impression that he had become weightless, like a thing of smoke, and had fallen *through* his window into the clutches of those dark things that waited for him outside, that bore him up and away.

He closed his eyes and rubbed his eyelids and shook his head to get back into focus. Out his window at the city lights twinkled. He laughed softly at the irony, that less than a year ago he'd written a tale for a friend about a much younger writer who'd sat in paralyzed horror at this very desk, gazing out over the darkened cityscape he saw now, while a hideous thing from a distant, haunted steeple merged its mind with his own as it came racing to devour him.

He held his pen above the page. Such impressions were not coherent enough, not entertaining enough, to be worth relating to his correspondents.

A gentleman, of course, knew better than to be tedious. One only shared what would be of interest to the other.

He was forty-six, but he felt like a tired old man. It wasn't a pose. No amusing self-caricature as "Grandpa." He merely felt as if all the energy had gone out of him, and such brief, imaginative flashes as he still had were like the twinges an amputee allegedly feels from a missing limb.

The cold set in. He was imprisoned now, inside his rooms. Weariness or discouragement precluded any new tales, no matter how much hordes of mostly young, naïve, and endlessly energetic fans demanded them of him. They did not understand. Perhaps one day they would, it being the fate of all random biochemical, molecular phenomena such as himself and they to pass from non-being into being and back into non-being again, gaining at best an ironic glimpse of their precarious position in an uncaring and meaningless cosmos.

Yet one must live as if it were not so. There were a few bright moments. He sent two unpublished tales to the editor who had rejected so many others, merely as a formality so that no possible source of badly needed income might be said to have been neglected, and both were purchased. That brought in enough money to keep the grim carnival going on a bit longer.

That year they had a Christmas tree. It wasn't that he had ever believed in Christ, or in Santa Claus for that matter, but the tradition soothed him, and he and his aunt amused themselves decorating it until their tiny quarters glowed with resplendent light. He hadn't been able to go to New York as he so often did to be with friends—poverty, his heath, and the cold all precluded it—so he spent the holiday with his lone aunt, surrounded by such remnants he had been able to retain from better days, the familiar furniture, pictures, and books. For the moment, again, he was content, or at least without suffering.

When he opened a package from one of his young correspondents and dust and soil trickled out onto the floor, and then the shattered remains of a human skull was revealed, his aunt exclaimed, "Disgusting!"

But he said, "No, it is an entirely appropriate gift from a young ghoul to a venerable elder of the clan."

Later, he carried the dead thing into his study and set it down on his desk, idly fitting some of the pieces together, thinking that another of his young friends, who was so clever, could probably repair it, coat it with lacquer, and mount it on a stand as a suitable *memento mori* of the sort that sorcerers always seemed to keep on their shelves amid crumbling tomes and dusty vessels.

Only after he had been sitting there for some time did he glance up and see the shape at the window.

It held his rapt attention. He knew exactly what it was, black-horned, slender, with membranous wings that flapped slowly as it floated in the air. Its bifurcated tail twitched from side to side. *It had no face,* as he had known it would not.

And yet, for the first time ever, it spoke to him, not with sound, but with a kind of merging of the mind, like what had happened to the young writer in that story of his when confronted by the horror from the steeple. He was it and it was he. He rose from his desk and went around to the window. He placed his hand on the glass and *it did the same,* the taloned claw much larger than his own hand, the nails clicking against the pane. The glass was intensely cold, and then it shattered, crumbling into powder, and he felt only numbness in his arm all the way up to the shoulder, and an undeniable dread as the thing was in the room with him now, crouching low, its folded wings scraping against the ceiling.

He stepped back, around the side of his desk, and the creature followed him. It *touched* him, its claw passing into him as if it or else his own body were made of smoke. It reached *inside* him, then withdrew, holding up its index finger—for it had, indeed, five fingers, and its claw, despite the huge talons, was surprisingly humanoid—to where its mouth should have been, as if it were *tasting* something.

You will be with us soon, it seemed to say, inside his mind. But he rejected that. He tried to rub his eyes and shake his head and force himself awake, even if this at no point had seemed like a dream.

Later, after an indeterminate interval, perhaps after a genuine lapse of memory, he was at his desk again, shivering from cold, and he realized that one of the panes in his window was gone and snow was blowing into the room. It was late. There was no sense in awakening and alarming his aunt over this, so he made do as best he could, tearing a side panel off a cardboard box and affixing this over the gap with adhesive tape. They would have to get a repairman in to replace the pane. He couldn't account for how it had become broken. There were shards underfoot. He swept them up with a broom and dustpan. He could only explain it—to anyone else—as the wind. Merely the wind.

He sat down again at his desk, gazing gloomily at his ever-increasing pile of unanswered correspondence. There was a blank sheet of paper on the desk, and his pen lay there, its cap off, ready for him to write. But, again, he could hardly find the energy. Back in his prime, such a vision as he had just experienced might have proved the basis for a story. He had once attempted an entire short novel filled with dream-quests, and winged apparitions, and strange vistas beyond our world. That failure resided in a file drawer now, even as a corpse in a morgue resides in a drawer.

Or he might at least have given a vivid account in a letter, for the appreciation of those few sensitive souls intrigued by such things.

Now, nothing. He wrote of other things. He argued politics and economics with his friends. But he did not soar.

His health grew steadily worse. Some days he could only lie about wrapped in blankets, writing or reading for a few minutes at a time.

His "grippe," which had bothered him before, now returned with real pain. It was hard to eat or sleep.

If he could not sleep, he would have no more fantastic dreams. No more visitations in the night.

They paid for the broken window pane out of the sadly depleted exchequer.

The philosopher, he told himself, must accept what comes, and merely observe in a detached way the follies and sufferings of mankind. If one could derive some momentary pleasure from an aesthetic association, immersed in one's culture-stream, that was all well and good, but even that only had meaning in the moment it was experienced.

Sometimes his feet swelled up and he could not even wear normal shoes, but had to make do with an old pair with the sides cut out, like sandals.

Then, for a while, he felt a bit better, and some of his energy returned. Miraculously, the winter had proven, overall, a mild one, so that walks in the town proved occasionally possible even as late as January. For brief moments it seemed as if somehow his life could go on as before, but each time the weakness and pain would catch up with him again. He thought of a story he'd read once, called "The Torture of Hope."

He revisited old, familiar places, the Athenaeum where Poe used to meet Sarah Helen Whitman, the house in Benefit Street that had been the subject of one of his own, failed, and never quite published stories. The graveyard below Benefit Street, which held so many associations.

To his friends he put up a brave front. He complained of piled-up work, correspondence, a massive revision job on a textbook.

But no new tales. No new visions.

Often, when he could sleep, or at least drowse, he heard wings flapping outside his windows.

He began typing his letters when his hand grew too unsteady to hold a pen reliably.

When he finally saw a doctor, the man's manner was grave.

He reported to correspondents that he was taking three "nostrums."

But they did little good.

When his condition had proven undeniable, the doctor told him and his aunt the truth. He had already known it. *As before August 20, 1890*. He looked forward only to oblivion, thinking of the old Stoic epitaph, *I was not. I was. I am not. I don't care.*

Indeed, after he had been taken to the hospital in an ambulance, and had received a few visitors, one of them said to him, "Remember the ancient philosophers." He smiled at that.

But otherwise there was only pain. He had tried to keep a diary of his symptoms, to focus his own mind, and with a vague idea that the doctors might find it useful, but some days he could write little more than the word "pain."

The rational man, the philosopher, the would-be artist understood that fancy, fantastic visions, and otherworldly things are created artificially for the amusement of one's friends. They are appealing precisely because one *cannot* believe in them, any more than we believe in Christ or Santa Claus or other such emanations of the human mind. Mere electro-chemical sparks in the darkening universe.

Therefore, what happened next must have been a dream.

The creatures were in the room with him again, several of them, their faceless faces hovering over the bed, their great wings hunched beneath the ceiling. They reached with their talons into his body and drew them out again, placing their fingers to where their mouths would be, if they had mouths, as if they were feeding around a trough. But he wasn't afraid of them. They were not hostile. They were merely impossible, things from his dreams, the subjects of one of his sonnets, and now here they were, speaking to him again, without words, as his consciousness merged with theirs, and he saw himself lying in the bed, from their perspective, a mere fragile shell, and he seemed to share some of their memories of black planets rolling in the void, and the swirling whirlpool of stars before the ultimate throne of chaos.

He was not afraid, because he did not believe. The philosopher understood that it was not a matter of belief. The philosopher accepts merely what *is*.

This wasn't a Faustian bargain when they offered to take him away with them, into their dark and strange and wonderful worlds. He wasn't at long last compromising his rationality and caving into superstition. If, in his dying mind, he had merely created one last pleasing illusion to ease his passing, let it be so. It did not matter. There was no right and wrong of it. No true and false, not anymore.

The philosopher merely observes, dispassionately.

"Yes, I will go with you," he said aloud. "I shall look forward to the journey with adventurous expectancy."

He raised both his arms and held out his hands.

Howard died this morning. Nothing to do.

Perhaps it was a little bit like *A Christmas Carol*, Scrooge carried off by the spirits, but without the moralistic ending.

They were soaring. They bore him up, a great flock of winged shapes. They carried him over the impossibly tall, dark mountains. He saw black worlds rolling in the void. He saw, too, lands he knew only in fancy, Ulthar beyond the River Skai, the Dreamlands, and Kadath in the Cold Waste.

They raced toward that distant tower with the single light in the window, where One sat waiting.

He felt that perfect balance of dread and dark wonder that he had never quite managed to capture in any of his stories.

Soon he would know the secret of the silken mask.

The Gilman Woman

Stephen Woodworth

> If ever there was a true woman it was Mollie Mathewson, yet she was wishing heart and soul she was a man.
>
> And all of a sudden she was!
>
> —CHARLOTTE PERKINS GILMAN, "If I Were a Man"

> By gazing peculiarly at a fellow-student she would often give the latter a distinct feeling of exchanged personality—as if the subject were placed momentarily in the magician's body and able to stare half across the room at her real body, whose eyes blazed and protruded with an alien expression. Asenath often made wild claims about the nature of consciousness and about its independence of the physical frame—or at least from the life-processes of the physical frame. Her crowning rage, however, was that she was not a man . . .
>
> —H. P. LOVECRAFT, "The Thing on the Doorstep"

PROVIDENCE 1887

"Come now, Lotty. Come away from that window." Walter put his hand on her shoulder. "It's time for your rest."

Charlotte did not even look up at him. "Rest? From what? I do nothing."

She continued to stare through the paned glass at the vacant lane of Humboldt Street below. Although it was nearly the end of March, the day had broken bleak and gray, and a sludge of melting snow remained in the gutters. But surely someone would walk by soon enough. Some man . . .

Walter Stetson knelt between the chair and the window, forcing her to look directly into his sweet, concerned face. "Please, Lotty. For me and Kathy, you must get better."

A gifted painter, he reminded her of Lord Byron, with a sharp cleft chin, high, cerebral forehead, and a manly mane of dark hair. Yet in her current state of enervation, the sight of his handsomeness merely exhausted her, just as the thought of tending to their daughter Katharine sank her into abject melancholy. So it had been ever since she'd given birth to the child two years earlier.

"If you would just let me *work*," Charlotte pleaded. "What harm would it do me to scribble with pencil and paper?"

Walter frowned. "You know how it tires you, my dear. Remember what Dr. Mitchell said. Do I need to summon him again?"

Charlotte turned her face away, shutting her eyes to keep from weeping again. She recalled all too well what the physician had said, and had no desire to suffer his presence again. Hailed as the finest nerve specialist in the country, Dr. S. W. Mitchell of Philadelphia seemed to believe that any mental exertion inappropriate to her sex was unhealthful for a woman, so he had prescribed the pernicious "rest cure" for Charlotte's melancholia that was now driving her mad.

"Live as domestic a life as possible," he dictated. "Have your child with you all the time. Lie down an hour after each meal. Have but two hours' intellectual life a day. And never touch pen, brush, or pencil as long as you live."

That last injunction struck her as a death sentence. Charlotte was determined to outlast this lethal "cure," even if she had to resort to subterfuge to do so.

"I suppose you're right." She rose from the chair and meekly allowed Walter to lead her to the chamber's bed.

As soon as she reclined, fully dressed, on the mattress, her husband took the rag baby that hung from the room's inside doorknob and nestled it by her cheek to comfort her. She'd fashioned the doll herself from strips of worn-out clothing—one of the few creative activities they'd permitted her during her convalescence.

"There you go, my dear," Walter cooed. "Enjoy a nice little nap, and we'll have supper when you wake."

Charlotte shut her eyes and waited until she heard his footsteps recede from the room and the door latch behind him.

Even then, she lay with her eyes shut, feigning sleep but keenly alert. When she felt sure that no one would disturb her, Charlotte crept from the bed back to the chair at the window, treading lightly on the wooden floorboards so they would not creak and attract her husband's attention downstairs. She seated herself and scanned the street below, waiting.

Before long, a solitary pedestrian came into view, but Charlotte noted with disappointment that it was a middle-aged matron, hoisting her skirts to keep from dragging them on the wet pavement. She let the woman go. What point would there be trading one imprisonment for another?

Charlotte fidgeted in an agony of impatience, darting glances at the bedroom door, wary of the slightest groan of the wooden house around her. Surely someone else would pass by before Walter came for her . . .

There! A mustachioed fellow in coveralls and galoshes sauntered past, arms swinging, mouth puckered as he whistled. He wore a flat cap and carried some kind of tool chest. A carpenter? Plumber?

It hardly mattered. Charlotte fixed her stare on him, willing all her being toward him, so much so that it seemed that the entire contents of her mind were erupting out through her eyes.

She had attempted this feat on a few prior occasions. As before, she experienced a swirling sensation of vertigo as her vision blurred, opposing perspectives overlapping as if she were peering through a stereograph at two different photographs. Previously, the impression had been fleeting, so that Charlotte wondered if her diseased fancy had fabricated the incidents.

On this occasion, however, her view through the lattice of the paned window faded, replaced by an unobstructed panorama of the surrounding neighborhood from the street level below. Charlotte felt the smooth solidity of a wooden toolbox handle in her grip, breathed cold outside air in her nostrils, smelled wet paving stones, heard the clop and rattle of a distant horse-cart.

The man in the street stopped, his swinging arms now limp at his sides. Then he turned—or, rather, *Charlotte* turned—toward the house at 21 Humboldt Street and looked up at the second-floor dormer window on the left. There she saw her own face gaping down at her, ashen and aghast. The woman in the window silently screamed, hands clawing at her face and hair.

With her free hand—sinewy and hirsute—Charlotte touched her upper lip and stroked the well-groomed whiskers of the full mustache she found there . . .

Then a hand slapped her hard across the cheek, and when she pressed her palm against the stinging skin she felt only the soft hairlessness of her own face. She opened her eyes to find Walter clutching her arms.

"*No!*" Charlotte wriggled in his grasp. "Why did you wake me?"

"*Wake* you?" Walter regarded her with a combination of ferocity and fear. "My dear, you've been raving and trying to claw my eyes out! You shouted something about 'What am I doing here? Who is this woman? What are you doing to me?'"

"I did?" Charlotte hoped he couldn't hear the eager longing in her voice. "I'm sorry . . . I lost myself for a moment."

Feigning contrition and dismay, she let Walter guide her back to bed. But secretly she exulted: it hadn't merely been her imagination. She'd succeeded in escaping the bondage of femininity, however briefly.

Charlotte decided then that she would continue to hone her ability to infiltrate and master others' bodies. And, when the time and subject were right, she would become the man of her choosing.

PROVIDENCE 1927

Howard loitered on the corner of Humboldt and Taber, peering at the house across the street. He shrugged his overcoat more tightly around himself to ward off the frigid air of early November. Already, the plunging temperature made it difficult for him to breathe, and he dreaded the imminent onset of winter. But it was not the cold alone that made him shiver.

The house at 21 Humboldt Avenue was one of those Victorian hodgepodges that had supplanted the grand old Georgian homes that Howard cherished—a gray-and-white façade cluttered with gabled dormer windows and a pillared veranda. Ordinarily, Howard would have found its excess of angles and ornamentation merely irritating, but this particular house inspired a deeper revulsion in him than its mere appearance would suggest. Perhaps it was solely the home's association with the appointment he awaited, but as his gaze wandered to the upper left dormer window, he fancied he could see a woman's face peering through the paned glass like an inmate in an asylum . . .

"Do you know the place?" a lilting voice asked.

Its feminine pitch startled Howard, and when he turned toward the speaker his skin crawled, for it was as if the woman in the window had stepped out of his phantasy to stand beside him. Her longish face bore the puffiness and etched lines of late middle age, and her dark hair was veined with silver. Her figure was still slender, however, and she wore a boater hat and a funereal black dress with a white lace collar and a cameo brooch, a rather old-fashioned outfit in this era of the flapper. She regarded Lovecraft with keen expectation—almost, one would say, an expression of suppressed amusement.

Howard glanced at 21 Humboldt Avenue again. "I've never really noticed it before," he said. "And you?"

"Oh, I'm quite familiar with it. I nearly went mad there."

Her implication dawned on Howard. He pointed to the house. "You mean . . . ?"

"Yes. The wall paper wasn't yellow, but the rest of the experience was very much as I described."

Howard tipped his fedora to her. Now he understood why she'd asked him to meet her here. "Mrs. Gilman, I presume."

"Mr. Lovecraft. A pleasure. I do apologize for keeping you waiting. You look about frozen. May I offer you a cup of coffee to warm up? And then we may discuss my business proposal." She lifted what appeared to be an artist's portfolio that she carried.

Howard sheepishly accepted her generosity. He'd been skipping meals to buy stamps for his correspondence again, and so was grateful when she added a slice of pie to the offer.

Once they were seated with their refreshments at a table in a nearby drugstore soda fountain, Mrs. Gilman opened the portfolio and took out the recent debut issue of *The Recluse*, in which Lovecraft's essay "Supernatural Horror in Literature" had appeared.

"I wanted to thank you and your publisher for sending this to me." She tapped the cover of the magazine. "And for your kind words about my work."

"I'm never kind—merely honest. 'The Yellow Wall Paper' is the finest depiction of creeping insanity since Poe."

Mrs. Gilman smiled. "Again you flatter me. But I wished to let you know I enjoyed your entire essay, not merely the praise directed to me." She again gave Howard that look of secret mischief. "I noted your mention of a tale by Barry Pain. By any chance, have you read his novel *An Exchange of Souls*?"

"Why, yes. A memorably disturbing treatment of a particularly repulsive idea." The narrative concerned a scientist who, to confirm that the human soul exists independently of the body, transfers his consciousness into the person of his female lover and assistant. The girl does not survive her displacement into the scientist's body, leaving him trapped in her corporeal form. He subsequently degenerates into a horrid sort of hermaphrodite, a creature so repellant to Nature as to be an atrocity.

Mrs. Gilman giggled at Howard's grimace of disgust. "Indeed! How much more monstrous than turning into a vampire or werewolf would it be to become . . . a *woman*."

Her schoolgirl teasing nettled him. "Does this have some bearing on the business you wanted to discuss?"

"Actually, it does. I was curious what insights you might have into the feminine mind."

"I would hardly claim to fathom that insoluble mystery." Howard had never felt any particular kinship with females, even Sonia Greene, the one to whom he'd briefly been married.

"But you do occasionally edit other writers, do you not?"

"Occasionally. With proper compensation."

"Would you have any objection to collaborating with a woman?"

"No," he said without enthusiasm, "but I insist on being given a free hand to amend the work as I see fit."

"Of course." With another of her maddening, impish smiles, Mrs. Gilman withdrew a thick manuscript from the portfolio. "I have here a work-in-progress that I am unable to bring to a satisfactory conclusion. I would like you to complete it for me."

She placed the sheaf of typewritten pages on the table between them, but when Howard leaned forward to look at the top page, Mrs. Gilman folded her hands over the title, hiding it from view.

"I would be happy to take a look at it . . . for my usual fee," he said. "But I doubt you require my assistance. You seem quite a capable writer and successful in your own right."

"On the contrary, Mr. Lovecraft—you are essential to achieve the aim I have in mind." Her mirth vanished, effaced by an expression of such piercing intensity that Howard wondered if she might be having some kind of seizure.

Then a shimmering starburst blotted his own vision, akin to the afterimage of a photographer's flash bulb. His consciousness lapsed for what seemed only an instant, as though he had nodded off during the conversation, but he gradually became aware that a radical alteration in his visual perspective had occurred, suggesting that he had been moved without his knowledge. A moment before, he had been facing the entrance of the drugstore and could look past Mrs. Gilman to see patrons entering and leaving; now he faced the soda fountain's far end, and Mrs. Gilman was nowhere in view. His body seemed strangely light yet inert, and he felt like a patient roused from general anesthesia with no knowledge of how much time had passed or what operation had been performed.

"Mrs. Gilman?" a male voice said. "Are you all right?"

Howard glanced around, eager to see where she was and how she would answer. Instead, he found a man standing over him. The stranger struck Howard as familiar—the fedora and dark wool suit, the elongated countenance and round spectacles—but the unexpected context prevented him from acknowledging the obvious. If the image had been reversed and imprisoned behind the silvered glass of a mirror, he would instantly have recognized the visage as his own.

"Mrs. Gilman?" the *doppelgänger* repeated in a nasally tone that Howard thought a poor imitation of his speech. "Can you hear me?"

The impostor aimed the question directly at Howard, who squinted in disbelief. "Who do you think—?"

Howard wasn't sure whether he should ask "you are" or "I am," but it didn't matter because he never completed the question. The wrong voice came out of his throat, as if thrown there via ventriloquism—high-pitched, gravelly with age, yet unmistakably female.

Trembling, Howard lifted his left hand. Fine-boned, hairless, and smooth-skinned, it did not seem a part of him, and raising it was akin to an act of levitation. The hand jutted from a black sleeve with a frilly cuff, and the ring finger bore both a wedding band and a diamond solitaire.

Lovecraft's entire universe inverted.

"Mrs. Gilman?" the impostor reiterated, as if to impress the name upon Howard through hypnotic conditioning.

Howard would have screamed, but he feared the sound of his own voice. He'd also become acutely aware that several of the other customers and even the soda jerk behind the counter had begun to stare at him.

Howard peered up at the face that used to be his. Its expression was one of superficial concern, but he could discern a trace of Charlotte Gilman's guile there. It reminded Howard of the novel he'd recently completed but had yet to show anyone, in which the ancient wizard Joseph Curwen pretends to be his look-alike descendent, Charles Dexter Ward.

"Mr. . . . Lovecraft," he ventured in that alien voice that now belonged to him.

The charlatan smiled, confirming Howard's most awful suspicions. "I feared you might have suffered a recurrence of your nervous prostration. Shall I get you a doctor?"

The offer of medical attention had the insinuation of a threat. It brought to mind the madwoman confined to her ghastly yellow room, condemned by her physician to "rest" in a miasma of jaundiced delusion.

Howard's gaze again darted to the surrounding people, who peered at him with growing alarm. If he protested about his transposed identity, whom would they likely believe? The gentleman who claimed and to all appearances seemed to be Howard Phillips Lovecraft? Or the hysterical woman who had once been a lunatic and might well be so again?

"No . . . thank you." Howard spoke in a hoarse whisper to mute its soprano register. "I'm fine now."

"Ah! I'm glad to hear it. Would you like me to escort you back to the Biltmore?"

The charlatan was evidently attempting to cue Howard on where to go next, since returning in his present guise to the house at 10 Barnes Street where he lived with his Aunt Lillian was impossible.

Howard glared at the thief wearing his flesh. "I think I can find my way."

"Excellent. Well, I must get home before dinner." The impostor doffed his hat. "By the way . . . I believe if you review your manuscript there, you'll hit upon a suitable ending. I wish you the best of luck with it."

The stranger in his body gave a slight bow and strode out of the drugstore.

For several minutes Howard sat in paralysis, staring straight ahead. He didn't dare to look downward, didn't even want to move because he would feel the unnatural contours of this form into which he'd been condemned. Perhaps, if he sat very still and concentrated, he could stop his heart and need never accept the reality of—

"Get you anything else, ma'am?" The soda jerk had come from behind the counter to Howard's table.

Howard shook his head. *Ma'am.*

The soda jerk scribbled a total on Howard's check and left it on the table.

To delay the inevitable shock of seeing his altered anatomy, Howard focused instead on the title of the manuscript in front of him—the unfinished work he was chosen to complete:

THE LIVING OF CHARLOTTE PERKINS GILMAN.

Charlotte returned to the lodging house on Barnes Street, the "home" she had never entered before. Although she had no difficulty in manipulating the body of Howard Lovecraft, its unaccustomed heaviness weighted her like a suit of armor, and the stride of its long legs felt as if she were walking on stilts. Yet she reveled in the freedom from the encumbrance of skirts and the confinement of corsets, the latter of which she'd continued to wear out of habit even though they were falling out of fashion. Lovecraft's loose-fitting wool suit hung lightly on her, and with each step she took in the comfortable, flat-footed shoes she became more intoxicated with the sensation of power and independence of being this young giant.

The Barnes Street boarding house was another Victorian, with an odd assemblage of angles and appendages that made it resemble a Cubist hybrid of several different structures. Larger than the one Charlotte had inhabited on Humboldt Street, it nevertheless unsettled her with its similarity to the residence where she'd spent the darkest days of her life. She much preferred the California ranch-style house in Pasadena where she'd written "The Yellow Wall Paper" after her divorce from Walter Stetson or the stolid family manse in Connecticut where she'd lived with her second husband, Houghton Gilman. No doubt she would get used to her new abode in time, however. After all, her situation was entirely different now.

Now she was a man.

Charlotte hesitated outside the boarding house's side entrance, her breath steaming in the cold. She'd surreptitiously observed Lovecraft's comings and goings over the past several days as part of her woefully incomplete research into his character and history. But the prospect of actually having to masquerade as Howard Lovecraft with his family and intimate acquaintances intimidated her.

Who else would they think you are? she chided herself. *No one would believe the truth.*

Reassured, she entered through the side door, Lovecraft's eyeglasses fogging at the sudden change in temperature. She wiped them on her shirt as she made her way down a brief passage to the ground-floor rooms Lovecraft shared with his maiden aunt, whom Charlotte found toiling in the apartment's kitchenette.

The elderly woman stirred stew in a saucepan on the stove. "Ah, Howard! I was beginning to worry you wouldn't make it home in time for dinner."

Charlotte removed her hat. "Hope I didn't keep you waiting, Aunt Lillian. It smells wonderful."

"So? Did you meet that Gilman woman you talked about?"

"I did indeed."

"Well? Is she going to give you some work?"

Charlotte smiled. "I believe I shall profit from our acquaintance."

Movement outside the window caught her attention: a figure in a black dress had stopped on the street to peer into the house. For a moment the reflection of her new face on the inside of the glass superimposed itself over her previous visage, creating an androgyne of her past and present selves. Charlotte feared that Lovecraft might try to come inside and create an unpleasant scene, forcing her to call in the authorities.

But the figure merely stood there, a forlorn specter in the deepening dusk.

Good man, she thought. He understood his position.

Aunt Lillian crept forward to squint out the window. "What is it? Is someone out there?"

Charlotte took her hand and pulled her away. "No. It's no one."

After dinner, she retreated to Lovecraft's bedroom and its walls of bookshelves. The sight of Lovecraft in her cast-off skin preyed on her, for it was a nasty trick to commandeer a man's life and leave him with the dregs of her own. But at the age of sixty-seven, if she hadn't acted now, she might never have had the opportunity to learn what life would be like as the unfettered male sex.

Despite her copious publications, Charlotte felt her work had never received the attention it would have if it had been written by a man. When she'd received her copy of *The Recluse* and read the "Supernatural Horror in Literature" essay, she decided that Howard Lovecraft would be the ideal subject to test her hypothesis: an up-and-coming young male writer, of similar interests to her own and with a devoted readership, who happened to live in the city she already knew so well. Although it was bittersweet to leave behind her husband Houghton and her grown daughter Katherine, Charlotte consoled herself with the thought that they would have lost her to death within a few years anyway, and she looked forward with enthusiasm to her new life as a man.

To that end, she moved to examine the sheaves of manuscripts and correspondence collected on the shelves around her. She needed to learn as much as possible about Howard Lovecraft in order to be him.

As for Lovecraft himself—well, he was a bright fellow. Charlotte was sure he'd get by somehow.

When Howard peered through the window of 10 Barnes Street and saw himself fraternizing with his Aunt Lillian, he knew there was no way he could return home—at least, not yet. If the impostor could fool his nearest kin, how could he hope that anyone would believe that a madwoman had usurped his life, particularly when he now looked like that madwoman?

Somehow, Howard needed to figure out how the Gilman woman had transposed their identities in hopes of reversing the travesty. Until then, he would have to join her in the masquerade.

With no place else to start, he made his way to the Biltmore Hotel, the nineteen-story modern monstrosity that dominated Dorrance Street downtown. His shrunken stature made him feel like an outsider in the city of his birth, the familiar landscape of the streets looming Cyclopean on either side of him, the strange garments and even stranger flesh he wore alienating him even from himself.

When Howard finally made it to the hotel, a uniformed doorman grinned and opened the Biltmore's entrance for him. "Ma'am!"

Lovecraft glared at him. Howard had already come to hate the word "ma'am," and gestures that he had once believed chivalrous he now perceived as insufferably patronizing, a constant reminder of his presumed weakness and inferiority. As though he were not perfectly capable of opening the door for himself!

Once inside the lobby, Howard reached into the portfolio Mrs. Gilman had left him and fished out the hotel key he'd found there. The number on the fob said "329," so he took the elevator to the third floor to find the room she had once occupied.

The room's bed had already been turned down for the night, and a worn leather portmanteau lay on a rack to one side. Lovecraft shut and locked the door, dropped the portfolio, and sank onto the bed. He wanted to bury his face in his hands and weep for all he had lost, but the instant his fingers contacted the unnaturally soft skin he jerked his hands away, holding them out from his body, afraid to touch any part of himself, as if he had been drenched in some nauseous ichor.

At that moment, Howard would either have sprawled on the bed and cried himself to sleep or flung himself out the third-story window, seeking whatever oblivion would end this abomination. His perverse new anatomy foiled him, however, for Mrs. Gilman had drunk so much coffee that afternoon that Howard was forced to hobble to the en suite lavatory to empty his bladder.

He cringed at the high-pitched squeal of frustration that escaped his mouth as he fumbled both to hitch up his skirts and to pull down his drawers before awkwardly plopping on the toilet. The urine sprayed like that of the female cats he'd seen, spattering the insides of his thighs. Whimpering with repugnance, he tore some sanitary paper off the nearby roll and frantically dabbed himself dry. The act forced him to fold back the skirts and confront the naked actuality of his emasculation, the downy thatch and leering lips of his crotch.

An odor assaulted him, one he had not endured since separating from his wife—a fetor akin to rotting fish. Small wonder he loathed seafood! He sniffed his hand, and his gorge rose when he smelled the stink on his fingers.

Howard yanked up the underwear, let the skirts swish back into place, and rushed to wash his hands in the adjacent basin, scrubbing them as maniacally as Lady Macbeth. But it was useless—this reek was now a part of him. He exuded it, just as Sonia had. He took cold comfort in the fact that Mrs. Gilman was most likely past the age of menstruation, so he would not have to suffer that particular horror, although Sonia had treated the monthly exsanguination as nothing more than a mild nuisance.

As Howard toweled his hands dry, he froze at the sight of his face in the gilt-framed mirror over the sink. Circumstance had kept him from confronting his reflection until then, and the image teased him with features similar to his own: the oval visage, the prominent, patrician nose, the elongated jaw. The skin was surprisingly smooth and unlined for its age—far *too* smooth, with pores too fine to see and not a hint of stubble on the chin. The long, loose tresses of hair, gray at the temples, had been parted in the middle and pulled back into a haphazard bun.

Howard stretched out his fingers and touched the cold and unyielding surface of polished glass. He could no longer hope to deny what he had become.

With grim urgency, he rushed to snatch up the portfolio he'd dropped by the bed and took out the manuscript inside.

THE LIVING OF CHARLOTTE PERKINS GILMAN. It appeared to be the author's memoir. Perhaps she had written it for his benefit, so he would not be completely ignorant of the life she was forcing upon him. At least it would provide a sort of script for the part he would have to play. He would go to the woman's home and find out as much as he could about her, and perhaps he would unearth what sort of witchcraft she'd used upon him.

As he sat on the bed and turned the pages, Howard did not allow himself to think about the wedding band he now wore on his left ring finger.

Norwich 1928

"Charlotte?" Houghton Gilman lowered his evening paper. "Charlotte!"

It took a moment for Howard to respond. Even after three months in his new identity, he still had difficulty recognizing the name when it was applied to him.

At last he glanced up from the open book on his lap. "I'm sorry . . . dear. What did you say?"

It made Lovecraft profoundly uncomfortable to play wife to this stranger, yet he had to maintain appearances lest the man think him mad.

Houghton eyed him quizzically. "I merely asked what you were reading."

"Oh!" Howard laughed and brandished the volume so Gilman could read the cover. "*Herland*, again."

Houghton harrumphed. "I had no idea you were such an avid reader of your own work."

Howard essayed one of Mrs. Gilman's puckish smiles, which he'd become quite adept at imitating. "Trying to learn from my past mistakes."

In truth, since "returning" to this Connecticut home where he'd never been before, Lovecraft had been devouring as much of Mrs. Gilman's writing as he could lay hands on. Her memoir had provided him with at least a rudimentary knowledge of her life that he could use to perpetuate the charade of being her, but he wanted to learn as much as possible about her so his apparent lapses in memory would not be too blatant.

Not that Houghton would suspect the truth. How could he? Even Howard could not believe the daily nightmare in which he lived.

Fortunately, Houghton Gilman was an easygoing chap. Nearly seven years younger than his wife, Charlotte Perkins's first cousin and second husband had dark hair parted in the middle, jutting ears, and a thick handlebar mustache that gave him a severe appearance until he grinned. A shrewd attorney, he was well-read and a good conversationalist, albeit a bit pedestrian and unimaginative for Lovecraft's taste. Ironically, Howard sometimes found it easier to converse with his new spouse than with Sonia, his previous one. Lovecraft had always been more at ease in the company of men than that of women, whose moods and mentality he found capricious and inscrutable.

"Seems to me you'd be better off writing something new," Gilman said as he shook out his newspaper and folded it. "Didn't that Lovecraft fellow help you with your latest book?"

"In a manner of speaking."

"Well, I think it was a mistake for you to go back to that place. You've been so distant since you came home. The memories have clearly upset you."

"Yes." Howard's face fell as he wondered if he would ever see his beloved Providence again. If only he could find some clue as to how that cursed Gilman woman had worked her blasphemous magic, perhaps he could undo it . . .

Lovecraft rose from his wingback chair, careful to lift the hem of his infernal dress so as not to step on it, and crossed the library to the bookcase laden with Charlotte Gilman's voluminous published works. A perpetually slow and hesitant writer, Howard envied her prodigious literary output. He'd been impressed with much of her fiction, particularly *Herland*, which told of a trio of male explorers who happen upon a Utopian civilization inhabited only by women. Because the women have the capacity to reproduce asexually—a notion that appealed to Howard, particularly in his present state—they can flourish without the violent, base, and corrupting influence of men.

He equally admired her copious nonfiction. In works such as *Women and Economics* and *The Man-Made World; or, Our Androcentric Culture*, she argued persuasively that women possessed skills and intelligence equivalent to those of men that were suppressed or ignored by a society that favored female domesticity and male dominance. Lovecraft himself had once believed the female mind to be too flighty and emotional to equal male rationality and achievement, and yet here he was, possessed of a female anatomy but with his intellect and personality intact. As Charlotte Gilman herself had put it, "There is no female mind. The brain is not an organ of sex. Might as well speak of a female liver."

Howard also approved of Mrs. Gilman's sensible attitude toward race and the detrimental influx of foreigners to the nation, as expressed in cogent essays such as "A Suggestion on the Negro Problem" and "Is America Too Hospitable?" "I am an Anglo-Saxon before everything," she declared, and Lovecraft could not help but nod in agreement.

Yet nothing he'd read told him how she'd stolen his life.

Howard set *Herland* on a shelf and scanned the adjacent titles, none of which hinted at transmigration of the soul. An overwhelming sense of futility exhausted him, and he turned away from the bookcase without selecting another volume. "I think I'll get ready for bed."

Houghton still perused his paper. "Very well, darling. I'll be up shortly."

"No hurry." Lovecraft hastened from the library and up the stairs, eager to be alone when changing for bed so Houghton would not see him undress. So far, he had managed to forestall any physical intimacy between the two of them, pleading fatigue and melancholy from the recent sojourn in Providence.

The sight of the broad bed in the upstairs chamber filled him with the dread that some sort of connubial contact might be inevitable. Howard had naively hoped that, given Mrs. Gilman's advanced age of sixty-seven, her marriage might have settled into a staid, celibate friendship. But Houghton Gilman was nearly six years her junior, and the flame of his libido had not yet burnt to ashes. Howard didn't know how he could continue to deny the man his conjugal rights as a husband forever.

The thought repulsed him, and he struggled out of his dress, shoes, and drawers as quickly as possible. With a groan of relief, he next unhooked the front of his corset. Despite his discomfort, he appreciated the undergarment during the day, for it minimized the viscosity of his breasts, an intolerable sensation akin to having two enormous, pus-filled boils on his chest. At night, however, he welcomed the opportunity to breathe without constriction.

Naked, he took a floor-length cotton nightgown from the wardrobe and put it on. His nearly hairless skin prickled at the touch of the fabric, as though layers had been scraped from its epidermis, and the enlarged teats of his breasts puckered slightly in response. As a man, Howard had had almost no sensitivity in his chest, and this combination of voluptuousness and vulnerability unsettled him.

Standing in front of the mirror on the inside of the wardrobe door, he pulled the hairpins from the tight bun on the back of his head and brushed out his long tresses with his fingers. Given his choice, he would have taken a scissors to the hair, for it pulled at his scalp when tied up and fell in his eyes when let loose. He dared not change it, though, lest Houghton think he'd lost his mind.

Though threaded with gray, the loose tangles of hair softened the evidence of age in his face and mitigated the schoolmarmish quality of the visage. Lovecraft touched the cheek and thought, not for the first time, that Mrs. Gilman must have been quite the beauty in her youth. Even now, with breasts drooping, her body remained slender and smooth-skinned, its porcelain whiteness largely unwrinkled and unravaged by time.

By necessity, Howard had overcome his aversion to touching this flesh in order to dress and wash himself, yet his mind still felt removed from it, as though it were a marionette he manipulated from a distance. Tonight, however, an insidious curiosity crept over him. He was about to button the front of the nightgown when, instead, he slid his hand beneath the open neckline to cup the underside of the left breast.

Howard had never understood the impulse to fondle women's mammae, an act from which he'd derived no particular pleasure even when copulating with his wife, nor could he fathom why women would wish to be pawed in that way. As he lightly grazed the underside of the breast with his fingertips, though, the softness of the skin gave him a tactile comfort akin to that he savored while stroking a cat. At the same time, the sensitivity of the female flesh made him feel as though he were the cat being stroked, a purring thrill that raised the fine hairs along his ivory white arms. He shut his eyes, the better to appreciate the experimental caresses.

"You should let me do that, my dear."

Howard gasped and jerked away as Houghton Gilman tried to grasp him around the waist. He hastened to button up the nightgown. "It wasn't anything. I have an itch . . ."

Houghton grinned. "So do I."

The man pulled Howard close, would have kissed him full on the lips if Lovecraft hadn't swiveled his head. He pushed Houghton away. "Please! I can't."

Houghton growled in frustration. "What *is* it? Are you getting ill again? Do I need to call the nerve specialist?"

The threat of a doctor made Howard think of asylums, barred windows, and yellow-papered walls.

He folded his arms over his torso. "I just need some time."

"But you were fine before you went to Providence!" Houghton drew a deep breath and his expression softened. "What happened there is past—a whole other life. *I'm* your husband now." He gently took hold of Howard's upper arms. "Let me be a husband to you."

Petrified, Howard couldn't think of a way to refuse without sounding like an utter lunatic. He quaked as Houghton peeled back the nightgown and kissed Howard's bare shoulder, a shudder both of horror and . . . stimulation? Houghton's voluminous mustache tickled slightly, not unlike the light, pleasant brush of a cat's tail when it caught Lovecraft by surprise.

Howard shivered, but relaxed his arms. In his limited experience with Sonia, lovemaking had been a marital chore to be performed, which he had done in dutiful if perfunctory fashion. From his perspective, the entire act seemed entirely for the benefit of the female, its success hinging on her satisfaction, and he had never been comfortable with the masculine role of aggressor in passion.

Houghton Gilman had no such inhibition. He brushed the sides of the nightgown off Howard's shoulders with such deft subtlety that Lovecraft did not realize he was naked until the gown was in a heap at his feet. Howard felt no obligation to do anything other than receive the tender caresses that Houghton lavished upon him.

But it was *wrong*. Sodomy was aberrant to society, abhorrent to Nature. Although Lovecraft did not subscribe to any morality dictated by an imagined divinity, copulation between men ran counter to the inviolable dictates of biology.

Yet this was not fornication between males. As far as Houghton Gilman was aware, he was making love to his lawfully wedded wife. And, anatomically at least, Howard was that wife. Society and Nature would not only encourage the union; they would virtually mandate it. Even the God in whom Lovecraft did not believe would have given His Almighty blessing.

Reason abandoned Howard. Houghton was suckling at his right breast, the wet tongue undulating over the stiffening nipple like some mollusk that had attached itself to him. The unprecedented sensation dizzied Howard with its strangeness. Then Houghton glided his hand down the soft convexity of Howard's belly to the cleft below, where his finger located the tiny button of nerves that even Howard had not yet dared to touch, and all conscious thought in Lovecraft's mind dissolved into a discharge of blissful static oblivion.

Houghton pushed him back toward the bed . . . or did he simply carry Howard there? All Lovecraft knew was that one moment he was standing and the next he had reclined on the mattress. He looked up to see Gilman shedding the last of his own clothes before climbing into bed on top of him.

Howard had always valued intimate male friendships above every other human acquaintance—had celebrated them repeatedly in such stories as "Pickman's Model," "Hypnos," and "The Hound"—but he had never been physically attracted to another man simply because it did not occur to him that such a desire was possible. Now, however, as Houghton reared up over him—muscles tensed, nostrils flared, arms and chest virile with hair—the man seemed a priapic satyr of ancient Greece, fearsome, feral, and beguiling all at once. His tumid phallus jutted toward Howard.

Raised largely by women, Lovecraft had never seen the sex organs of a living man other than his own, and had certainly never witnessed an erection that was not his. The sight of it flooded Howard with fear of its unknown potency and promise, and he finally understood the awful fascination of the blood-red tentacles that had haunted his dreams since youth.

Then Houghton crouched on top of him with a grunt. A fat tendril of engorged meat invaded the cavity between Lovecraft's legs and, with each thrust, sent gelatinous pulsations throughout his viscera.

Iä! Iä! Cthulhu fhtagn!

Shutting his eyes, Howard moaned in surrender, allowing the tentacles to take him at last.

DELAND 1934

Cthulhu's octopoid appendages twined over the surface of the bas-relief, the texture of the hardened clay so sinuous that it felt almost viscid beneath Charlotte's fingertips. The sculptor had lavished the same loving detail on the god's scales, wings, and claws.

"Do you like it?" The boy seated beside her on the bed—for what else could she call him but a boy?—smiled with pride, but the eyes behind the thick round lenses of his glasses betrayed anxiety as well as eagerness. "I tried to make it just like you described it in the story."

He didn't know that Charlotte had nothing to do with the creation of "The Call of Cthulhu." From what she'd read in Lovecraft's tale, however, the bas-relief might have been "The Horror in Clay" made real.

She smiled. "It's a perfect likeness."

The boy beamed, and the expression of delight made him look even younger than he did with his usual studious and melancholy demeanor. He gazed at her with a puppy-dog yearning that made her feel as though she were a young girl again—made her feel as though he could *see* the young girl she was inside.

"I can't tell you how happy I am you could come stay with us, Mr. Lovecraft," he said.

Charlotte grimaced. The boy had taken to calling her *Mr. Lovecraft* ever since she'd arrived, perpetually reminding her not only of the difference in their ages but also of her current male sex. "Please, call me . . . Howard."

The boy swallowed and smiled sheepishly. "Yes, sir. I mean, Howard."

The boy's name was Robert Hayward Barlow, and he had corresponded with Charlotte—or, rather, with "Mr. Lovecraft"—incessantly for nearly three years before he invited her to vacation at his family's dark log house down in Florida. The diction and erudition of the letters made Charlotte assume their author must be in his twenties, so she was taken aback when a slight, baby-faced lad of sixteen with peach-fuzz on his cheeks and slicked-back black hair arrived in a pickup truck to meet her at the bus station in DeLand.

Charlotte had accepted his invitation in large part because she'd wearied of life as Lovecraft, with its constant and often fruitless struggle to earn a living from her literary work. The frustration had become so acute that she'd suffered a wistful homesickness for her original identity. To recapture her true self, she'd befriended and mentored other female writers such as Zealia Bishop and Hazel Heald, and while she emulated Lovecraft's previous themes and styles, she endeavored to put her own stamp on the work, as if to shout to the world, "It's me, Charlotte, behind this mask!"

To begin with, she actually incorporated women in the stories. To read Lovecraft's early work, one would have thought the world completely devoid of the female sex—what Charlotte derisively thought of as "Himland." So she populated her stories with women she could admire: Keziah Mason, an unrepentant "witch" who is actually a genius of arcane mathematics and physics and a traveler through unknown dimensions of space and time; Pth'thya-l'yi, immortal matriarch of the Olmstead family, and Mother Hydra, goddess of the Deep Ones; and, of course, Asenath Waite, a formidable sorcerer who, like Charlotte herself, yearned to shed the strictures of femininity in order to unleash her true power.

Indeed, "The Thing on the Doorstep" was virtually Charlotte's confession. Her fictional account of Asenath's theft of Edward Derby's body and identity so closely mirrored the truth that she assumed it would be obvious to one and all that she had done the same to Lovecraft. As if that weren't hint enough, Charlotte had even placed her actual name in the stories, like a signature hidden in the swirls of a painting. She'd christened "Walter Gilman," the protagonist of "The Dreams in the Witch House," with the combined names of her first and second husbands, respectively. And Robert Olmstead, the narrator of "The Shadow over Innsmouth," takes up lodging at—where else?—the Gilman House.

Despite these self-indulgent ploys to alert the world to her true self, no one suspected a thing, for when she stood in front of them they saw Howard Lovecraft.

Being a man—at least a man like Lovecraft—did not confer the advantages that Charlotte imagined it would. She'd become frustrated in her efforts to make a living as Lovecraft and realized, with bitter irony, that she'd been a far more successful writer as a woman. And with each rejection she collected, she inherited more of Lovecraft's poisonous insecurity about her talent. She hadn't even bothered to submit "Innsmouth" to magazines, for the tale now seemed supremely silly to her. A fish story, indeed!

She almost wished she were herself again.

As for intimate relationships, Charlotte hadn't given them a second thought since becoming Lovecraft. After her two marriages, she'd generally assumed that part of her life was finished, and that she would devote herself wholly to her one true mate: her muse.

Then she'd met Robert.

"My folks say you can stay as long as you like," he told her. "Dad says we could even build you a cabin out back."

Again, Charlotte had the impression that he could see *her* through the façade of flesh she wore. But she knew the look of adoration he gave her was because he saw her as a surrogate father, not as a lover. As a former lieutenant colonel in the Army, Robert's own father was too much of a martinet to be a sympathetic parent to such a sensitive aesthete of a son, so Robert had gravitated toward Lovecraft as an avuncular authority figure.

Little did he know, Charlotte had more than paternal feelings toward him.

They had recently returned to the house from a long walk through the woods that surrounded the nearby lake, and Charlotte still felt drenched with perspiration from the humid Floridian air. Dressed in matching white Oxford shirts and gray trousers, she and Robert could easily have been mistaken for father and son. The boy had brought her into his bedroom to show her some of his artwork—paintings, sculptures, and even marionettes he'd made—and that was when Robert surprised her with the Cthulhu bas-relief. Now that she'd learned how young he was, the depth and range of his precocity astounded her. His talent and passion reminded her of Walter in his youth, but Robert was even more gifted, more brilliant. If she were a young girl again . . .

No. She couldn't allow herself to think like that.

"You and your family are very kind," she said, "but, much as I appreciate the warm weather, I'm afraid a born New Englander like me would wither if transplanted to your Southern soil. I have to go back." She held out the bas-relief. "Here—you'd best put this in a safe place."

Robert cupped his hands around hers, his fingers thin and delicate as a girl's compared to her thick, rough digits. "No, take it. I made it for you."

"I couldn't—"

"Please." He kept his hands closed around hers, their palms sweaty and feverish. The look of longing in his eyes intensified. "Maybe I could go with you."

She shook her head. "Your parents . . ."

"I want to be with *you*, Howard."

Charlotte now regretted encouraging him to call her by that name. She looked up and discovered that he had leaned so close to her that their faces were no more than an inch apart. Robert's lips parted, panting breath, and his pale cheeks had flushed.

Charlotte stared at him, and for an instant she forgot who she was supposed to be and who she ever was.

Then a hideous swelling stirred in her groin.

She knew perfectly well what it was and what it meant. A woman always knows when a man is aroused.

Charlotte yanked her hands from Robert's grasp. The Cthulhu bas-relief fell to the floor and shattered.

"Howard, wait!" Robert pleaded as she bolted from the room. "Mr. Lovecraft—I'm sorry!"

She ran to the makeshift guest room the family had arranged for her and shut herself inside. Charlotte had fled not only because she feared Robert might see the telltale bulge in the fly of her trousers.

She had also seen the bulge in his.

Charlotte lay on the cot in her room until dark. When Robert quietly knocked on the door and asked her to come to dinner, she told him she felt sick. The statement was not entirely untrue. He stood outside the door for some time but did not say anything, and eventually she heard his footsteps retreat.

As the room sank further into gloom, Charlotte decided she might as well get ready for bed. She stripped down to her undershirt and boxer shorts, and for the first time her borrowed body repulsed her with its overlong simian limbs and ugly, matted hair. She buried her face in her hands but immediately recoiled from the touch of stubble-covered jaw and brutish bone structure.

How could Robert ever desire such an odious creature?

She lay back on the cot and shut her eyes, straining to put the world to right in her mind. Again she pictured Robert yearning toward her, but this time their lips touched, and she was a blushing girl of fifteen, and their love was pure, innocent, and true.

Unbidden, her male appendage engorged itself. The effect seemed the opposite of her arousal as a woman, which was a drawing inward, a warmth that spread from the pubic mound to suffuse the entire body. Instead, all the energy within her flowed out and up to concentrate in the peninsula of that phallus.

With two marriages behind her, Charlotte had had extensive experience and enjoyment of the male member. She had not held an erection since she'd left Houghton, however, and did not realize how much she'd missed that contact until now.

Sliding a hand into her underwear, she gripped the organ with the gentle caress she'd used to please her lovers, imagining that it was

Robert's manhood she stroked with dainty, feminine fingers. As her excitement increased, so too did her desperation to resolve her impossible desire.

What if she traded lives again, took up residence in the body of a young girl Robert's age? No one could object to their being together then.

The moment she conceived the notion, though, she realized it was futile. Robert wanted Howard Lovecraft, not despite the fact that he was a man, but *because* he was a man. And he would not want Charlotte any other way.

She could not believe—could not accept—that her tender, thoughtful prodigy Robert could be a sodomite.

But if he were a degenerate, what did that make her? A filthy old man, a contemptible pederast.

No! I'm a woman!

The sticky male seed that oozed onto her hand said otherwise, however.

With the release of climax, she went flaccid on the cot, sobbing, aware how completely love was now lost to her.

PROVIDENCE 1935

The letter in the mailbox that August afternoon bore no return address, but Charlotte knew immediately from whom it came. The envelope was postmarked Pasadena, California, and she recognized the handwriting on it even though it appeared cramped and shrunken, having been scrawled by smaller, thinner fingers. The sight of it clawed at her insides as if it were an unpaid bill or a summons to appear in court, yet she could neither bring herself to open it nor to destroy it unread. Instead, she tucked it into the breast pocket of her linen suit coat to delay the inevitable reckoning.

Despondency welled within her, and she decided to treat herself to some coffee ice cream in the hope that it might quell her gnawing dyspepsia. Charlotte had nearly depleted the small inheritance Lovecraft had received, so she'd taken to skipping meals to save money and was now afraid her perpetually empty stomach might be developing ulcers.

Although it was nearly September, the weather was still quite warm, and the drugstore to which Charlotte strolled had filled with perspiring townsfolk and noisy children all seeking root beers and chocolate sundaes. Only after she'd seated herself on a stool at the counter and taken her first bite of ice cream did it occur to her that this was the same shop where she'd traded destinies with Lovecraft. Perhaps it was true that criminals are subconsciously compelled to return to the scene of their crime.

Charlotte spooned more ice cream into her mouth, but it suddenly seemed tasteless and unappetizing. She idly slipped the envelope from her pocket and tore it open. Best to get it over with, she thought.

"My dear *Mr. Lovecraft,*" the letter inside began, the name underscored with sarcastic emphasis. "I trust this note finds you better than myself. I have perused your recent publications whenever I have come across them and must admit a grudging admiration of your extrapolation of the themes I once addressed. Since you seem intent upon assuming my literary mantle, no matter how tattered, I bequeath it to you wholly. You may declare ownership over all the earlier works in my name. I give them gladly.

"In return, however, I lay claim to your entire, impressive *oeuvre*: 'The Yellow Wall Paper,' *Herland, Women and Economics*—all of it. I shall be proud to have history think me the mother of such a distinguished progeny. You may have thrust this identity upon me against my will, but I now make it mine by choice.

"Speaking of which, I am about to conclude your unfinished masterpiece, as you requested. Perhaps you heard that I became a widow when Houghton passed away last year. This January, my doctors diagnosed me with incurable cancer of the breast, and it is now in its final stages. I find it oddly appropriate that my inherited femininity should prove my undoing. Yet even in this I shall be the master—or would that be mistress?—of my own fate. I have sufficient chloroform here to ensure that I may welcome oblivion before the disease devours me.

"I cannot honestly say I have no regrets about our acquaintance, but rest assured that I leave this world at ease with the person I have become. I hope for your sake you may say the same.

"Respectfully yours, I *am*—

"Charlotte Perkins Gilman"

The pain in the pit of Charlotte's stomach intensified, and the ice cream melted into uneaten slush in the dish in front of her. She reread the suicide note and felt a hideous emptiness open within her, a vacuum left by an essence of herself that she'd allowed to slip away.

When she'd first assumed Lovecraft's body, Charlotte had unconsciously nurtured the notion that somehow she would retain possession of both their lives, enjoying the benefits of both identities. She now saw how foolish she'd been.

The author of that letter was Charlotte Perkins Gilman, recently deceased.

And for better or worse, he—*he* was Howard Phillips Lovecraft.

In His Own Handwriting

S. T. Joshi

1

Harry had left for the day. Given the intense, almost unbearable pain Howard was experiencing, he had scarcely been aware of Harry's presence in the room, and all he could do was give him a weak smile when Harry gently advised him to "remember the Greek philosophers." He was referring, of course to the Stoics—the originators of the stiff upper lip in the face of overwhelming pain, grief, or sorrow. Or was he thinking of the Epicureans, who with equal sense said, "Death is nothing to us"? You're either alive or you're not; and once you're dead, you just return to that native infinity of crystal oblivion from which the demon Life has called you for one brief and desolate hour.

He thought he had written something like that once, long ago, but he now couldn't remember.

He knew his time was up—had known for weeks, perhaps months. Oh, sure, he told his many and far-flung correspondents that he just had indigestion or "grippe," that he would be ill "for a long time" but would somehow recover to write more stories and lend advice to young and old; but it was a lie, and he knew it.

So his life would end before his forty-seventh birthday. Well, Poe was forty when he died, Mozart thirty-five. His own father had barely reached the age of fifty-three. The memory of him slapping his father across the knees and saying, "Papa, you look just like a young man!" suddenly popped irrelevantly into his head. His father *had* been a dashing young man—no wonder Susie had fallen under his spell. Naïve, innocent, and—as he learned later—petrified of sex and physical intimacy, she had probably welcomed Winfield's early demise, loathsome as it was. Where else did the images of putrescent horror in his own tales come from?

The door of his cheerless, sterile room opened tentatively, as if the new and unexpected guest wasn't certain he had come to the right place. But the moment Howard caught a glimpse of him, he knew this was no mistake. That balding, roly-poly man who had haunted him all his life—a man whose appearance was so grotesque that it would have evoked laughter in anyone who didn't know who he was and what he stood for—slipped into the room and stood stone-faced at the foot of the bed, plump as Capt. Norrys and hardly less ominous. *What am I afraid of? What can he do to me* now?

But he sensed, with a sinking of what remained of his spirits, that the demon had one more trick up his sleeve.

2

It wasn't difficult to keep Frank preoccupied. His young, incandescent mind fluttered about from one topic to the next like a crazed butterfly, and all Howard had to do was to give him general instructions to pick out as many Machen and Dunsany titles as he could find and let him roam in the bookstore where he wished. Howard made it clear that he was determined to spend a good many minutes in the architecture section, knowing that, for all Frank's multifarious interests, the architecture of colonial America was not one of them. When Howard later showed him Singleton's *Furniture of Our Forefathers* as one of the several books on the subject he had secured, Frank sniffed in disdain and countered with Harper Williams's *The Thing in the Woods*—the book that he claimed as his reward for helping Howard use up the pestiferous Henneberger's sixty-dollar credit at the Scribner Book Shop. In his desperate financial condition, Howard had begged the bookstore to convert the credit into cash, but it had refused.

Howard didn't know what led him to suspect that the phenomenon he both welcomed and dreaded would happen again, and happen here. Perhaps it was the telltale tingling in his fingers; perhaps it was nothing more than the fact that it hadn't happened for a good many months, and *never* in this pest zone. To his friends, his colleagues, his new wife, and especially his devoted but austerely frugal aunts, he had felt an increasing need to prove that his coming to New York was not a mistake—and yet, what did he have to show for the six or seven months he had been here? A few mediocre poems, an article or two for the amateur press, and bootless attempts to secure work through a literary agency and that criminally expensive *New York Times* advertisement.

Perhaps he should have accepted the editorship of *Weird Tales* after all, even though it would have meant his moving to the supremely uncolonial wilderness of Chicago. But he had refused, and now that ass Wright was in charge.

The architecture shelves were brimming with new titles on matters relating to the colonial era, and Howard took heart at how many people were experiencing a new or revived interest in this field. He himself had only begun his explorations of colonial oases up and down the East Coast: New England he knew well, but he was irked that he hadn't even gotten as far south as the nation's capital, although his honeymoon in Philadelphia—after they had spent the night typing the Houdini manuscript—was invigorating, even if much of it was spent on that rubberneck bus.

It was as he was reaching for a copy of Dyer's *Early American Craftsmen* that the roly-poly man materialised as if out of nowhere.

It is important to emphasise that Howard did not feel terror, fear, dread, or even apprehension. What he felt most of all was . . . *shame.*

Why can't this man leave me alone? How can I continue living a lie?

As on so many previous occasions, the man said nothing—*did* nothing, or almost nothing. Just the slightest hint of a nod, a beckon, and a swift turn on his heels as he stalked silently off to some remote corner of the bookshop.

Howard had to follow. There was really no choice in the matter.

The roly-poly man came to a door—one Howard had never noticed before, however many times he had been in this establishment—and *drifted right through it.* No, that's too preposterous: a trick of the light or some kind of auto-hypnosis. No one believes in ghosts today, do they?

The doorknob that Howard clutched spasmodically with his right hand was chilly. But that's natural, isn't it?

He opened the door. The roly-poly man was inside, unsmiling as always. He had never seen that expression change—indeed, could it even be said that the creature *had* an expression? Wasn't it possible that that face was merely a cunningly devised *mask?*

But that hardly mattered now. The room seemed to be nothing more unusual than a storeroom for excess books—perhaps books that had not yet been catalogued or priced. But the mundanity of the place was not at all reassuring. *All these episodes take place in mundane surroundings.* It was not the setting that was the source of his terror—no, his shame. It was something else entirely.

The roly-poly man, raising his arm with infinite, excruciating slowness, pointed to a high shelf. The symbolism of the gesture struck Howard with a sense of bitter irony: he couldn't possibly feel lower than he did at this moment.

It took only the most token glance to see what the man was indicating. Amidst all the books, new or old, dusty or pristine, octavo or folio, was one item that manifestly did not belong. It was the same crumbling brown scrapbook that he had seen so many times before.

Howard was tall—a head taller than his unwelcome companion—and he had no difficulty taking the object down.

What's the point of looking? I know what is in here.

He flipped through the scrapbook. Page upon thick page of spidery, almost indecipherable handwriting. Words and sentences leaped out at him, even as he struggled not to read them: "From even the greatest of horrors irony is seldom absent" . . . "To Malone the sense of latent mystery in existence was always present" . . . "Back, back—forward, *forward*—look, ye puling lack-wit!"

Howard closed the book with a slam, releasing a tiny and derisive cloud of dust. His fingers, then his whole body shook, and he had to reach out with one hand and cling to the tall bookshelf so that he wouldn't collapse in a heap (*fainting—just the way I (or someone) made Houdini faint over and over in that Pyramids story*).

When he regained some modicum of self-composure and looked around him, the roly-poly man had disappeared.

That was also par for the course. All Howard now knew was that he had more stories to type up to send to *Weird Tales.*

3

He cast his mind back to the time when he had first seen that roly-poly man.

It was a June day in 1917, and he was walking through Swan Point Cemetery with his aunt Lillian. Suddenly he saw a crumbling tombstone with a skull and crossbones dimly traced upon its slaty surface; the date, 1711, was still plainly visible. It set him thinking. Here was a link with his favourite era of periwigs—the body of a man who had worn a full-bottomed wig and had perhaps read the original sheets of *The Spectator*. Here lay a man who had lived in Joseph Addison's day, and who might easily have seen John Dryden had he been in the right part of London at the right time. Why could Howard not talk with him, and enter more intimately into the life of his chosen age?

He remembered how his boyhood friends—Harold and Chester and Ronald and Stuart—had laughed at his obsession with the eighteenth century. *Howard, here we are in a new and dynamic era! You'll never get anywhere if you moon about dwelling in the past. Get a job, get a motorcar, get a wife*—that's *the way to make something of yourself in the world.*

Perhaps it was—but perhaps he didn't *want* to make anything of himself in this fundamentally tawdry age.

He was staring off into the distance, thinking of periwigs and small-clothes and the coffee shops of London. His yearning for that era sometimes became overwhelming: *this must be what it's like to be in love*. But no mere female could ever evoke that kind of longing.

It was then that he saw the roly-poly man, leaning next to a gaudy marble mausoleum in the distance.

"What is it, Howard?" Lillian said. When he made no reply, she repeated the query a little more sharply.

"I wonder who that man is," Howard said dreamily.

"What man?"

Howard couldn't believe it. Lillian's distance vision was usually much better than his own.

"Right there!" Howard cried, gesturing stiffly.

"Howard," Lillian said with some asperity, "there's no one there. Come on—we should be getting along home. You know how your mother worries when you're out too late."

Howard looked at her uncomprehendingly. *There's something wrong here*. He was too devoted to reason to think that anything supernatural was occurring, although the tingle in his fingers was certainly anomalous. But he felt an unaccountable desire—no, *need*—to understand the nature of this situation. And that roly-poly man was at the heart of it.

"Just wait a moment—I'll be right back." And before she could protest, he stalked off on his long legs in the direction of the man, who remained motionless and expressionless, utterly unconcerned at his rapid approach.

Within seconds they stood face to face. Howard looked down at his antagonist—he instinctively thought of him as such—and took heart in the fact that the man was a full head shorter than himself. Howard was not at all used to fisticuffs, although in school he had managed to ward off that bully "Monk" McCurdy by assuming a dramatically ferocious aspect frightening to the nervous . . . the "by God, I'll kill you!" stuff.

Why Howard even thought he would have to resort to this sort of behaviour, he couldn't have begun to explain to himself. But he instinctively sensed that the man was up to no good. So he spoke sharply and aggressively.

"Who are you? What are you doing here?"

For all Howard knew, the roly-poly man had just as much right to be here as he did. Perhaps this mausoleum housed a relative—but somehow Howard knew otherwise. But perhaps his hostile tone would allow him to get to the bottom of the matter before he had to run along home to Mother.

All that the roly-poly man did was to gesture faintly, almost imperceptibly, with his head, as if urging Howard to stroll around to the front of the mausoleum.

What good would that do? he wondered. *Surely he doesn't want to take me inside. It's locked, and I can't believe this fellow has the key.*

The man himself led the way as he sensed Howard's reluctance to act on his unspoken command. As they faced the locked wrought-iron gate that led into the mausoleum, the man only had to nod for the gate to open of its own accord, with a predictable metallic creak.

Very clever bit of prestidigitation, old chap! I don't know how you did that, but you're not going to flummox me with some two-bit sleight-of-hand.

Howard nevertheless followed his guide into the place. No, it wasn't dank, the walls weren't covered with nitre, there were no stone steps leading down into the bowels of the earth. It was, in fact, a single narrow room with slabs holding half-a-dozen or more coffins—expensive and lead-lined, no doubt—with a few empty spaces for additional interments. If anything, the place was dry as dust, and a few cobwebs were festooned in dark corners.

Once again, the two men—one short and plump, the other tall and lanky—faced each other. Howard had suddenly lost any sense that a dramatic confrontation would take place; in fact, he now felt a bit foolish. This comical-looking man couldn't possibly be a threat to him: he had no visible weapon of any kind, and his pudgy face and body were the antipodal opposite of threatening. Maybe Howard should just apologize and beat a hasty retreat.

But why doesn't he ever speak?

As if he had read Howard's mind, the roly-poly man gestured with his head to one of the empty spaces in the room. Howard had, upon his initial entrance into the place, quickly canvassed it for any possible booby-traps or other signs of danger, and had seen nothing. Now, he was almost reluctant to turn his head in the direction of the man's gesture, wondering—in a sudden resurgence of a sense of threat—whether he was trying to distract his attention for nefarious purposes.

I think I've read too many dime novels.

He felt that a quick look at the empty space couldn't hurt. There had been nothing there before, he had been certain of that; and there could be nothing there now.

But there was.

It was a crumbling brown scrapbook—large in dimensions, but apparently quite thin, as if holding only a small number of pages.

There's some trick here. I must now be very careful.

Without letting his eyes leave the man's face—or, more properly, the top of the man's bald pate—Howard snaked to his right in the direction of the scrapbook. What he expected the scrapbook to be, he couldn't begin to imagine; but once again he sensed the overriding folly of this entire episode, and almost burst out laughing at the grotesquerie of it.

Only when he reached the flat marble surface on which the scrapbook rested did he turn his head to give it a hasty examination. It was harmless enough, but he still felt the need to maintain vigilance.

He picked up the scrapbook, then quickly turned back to his companion.

The roly-poly man had disappeared.

Howard was not afraid. *Another clever trick, no doubt.* Since there was no place the man could have hidden in this solidly built room, he must have slipped away when Howard's attention was focused elsewhere. *Well, good riddance to him. I might as well see what my prize in this ridiculous adventure could possibly be.*

The scrapbook, as he had predicted, had a remarkably small number of pages—perhaps only fifteen or twenty. But every page was covered from top to bottom with spidery, almost indecipherable handwriting. Only random sentences leaped out at him when he flipped through the pages: "In relating the circumstances which have led to my confinement within this refuge for the demented, I am aware that my present position will create a natural doubt of the authenticity of my narrative" . . . "I am writing this under an appreciable mental strain, since by tonight I shall be no more" . . . "Into the north window of my chamber glows the Pole Star with uncanny light" . . .

The passages sent a shiver through him. *This is exactly the kind of work I've wanted all my life to write.* With intense embarrassment he thought of the stories he had written as a child and adolescent—crude, inane, bombastic specimens that his mother had made him save. Two years earlier he had said to a friend, "I wish that I could write fiction, but it seems almost an impossibility." It still seemed impossible—and yet, this scrapbook contained tales that a Poe—or at least a competent disciple of Poe—could have written.

All of a sudden, Howard felt a hot surge of perplexity and nervous apprehension. Now he was grateful that that peculiar man, whoever he was, had so mysteriously vanished; for he did not wish to have any eyewitness to his pilfering. He was going to take this scrapbook, read it in his leisure, and then . . . maybe transcribe those stories on his 1906 Remington.

And pass them off as his own.

It was this final thought that made him flush. *I must adhere to the standards of honesty and dignity of my beloved eighteenth century.* But the thirst for literary greatness—even the most fleeting soupçon of recognition—coursed constantly through his mind. *My poetry is rubbish, my essays and editorials not much better. What else can I do but establish a foothold in the lowly realm of weird fiction?*

He made haste to emerge from the mausoleum, hoping Lillian hadn't utterly lost her patience with his tardiness. But, as he stumbled out of the place, awkwardly slipping the scrapbook underneath his shirt, he saw her standing patiently by that 1711 gravestone, even if looking a bit sharply in his direction.

They walked home in silence. Susie greeted them with a kind of alarmed effusiveness, as if irrationally worried that they would never return. She was, Howard had to confess, starting to get a bit odd. He remembered how she had spoken to him about weird and fantastic creatures that rushed out from behind buildings and from corners at dark, and how she shivered and looked about apprehensively as she told her story. Now she seemed to want to embrace Howard, but he quickly turned his body aside and clumsily embraced her in such a way that she wouldn't feel the scrapbook still stuffed under his shirt.

As he read the stories in the solitude of his room—the room he had occupied ever since the family had had to give up his lavish three-story birthplace in 1904—he did indeed sense a thrill of the supernatural. *How could anyone have captured my thoughts, feelings, moods, and images in exactly the language I wish to use but know I can't?* The tingling that had affected his fingers at the time he saw the scrapbook now seemed to cover his entire frame, and he began to tremble as if in a fit of ague. As he turned the last page—there were indeed only three stories, filling eighteen stiff cardboard pages—he closed his eyes, expelled an immense sigh, and contemplated the morality of the situation.

How can I claim these stories as my own? But if I didn't write them, who did? What violation of natural law has allowed these tales to fall into my hands?

He decided to prepare just one of the stories and send it to his new friend Paul. Paul had the greatest private collection of weird fiction he had ever seen, and he also edited a little amateur magazine where, he had clearly implied, he would be happy to see some of Howard's stories appear.

If only I had any stories to send . . .

Howard typed up the story, sent it to Paul. Paul waxed rapturous over it and published it, preceded by a ludicrous paean to his own impending greatness as a writer of weird fiction.

4

And that's how it had begun.

At key moments in his life, that roly-poly man would show up, never to be seen by anyone but himself. Every time, he would lead him to some obscure, hidden corner, point silently at that same brown scrapbook (same, but with different stories each time!), and then vanish without a trace.

There was the time when he and Clifford, his friend from North Providence, had gone to Arthur Eddy's bookstore downtown. That was when, flipping through the pages, he had come upon sentences that seemed plucked from the innermost recesses of his heart and mind: "Unhappy is he to whom the memories of childhood bring only fear and sadness" . . . "I have never seen another street as narrow and steep as the Rue d'Auseil" . . . "Fool that I was to plunge with such unsanctioned phrensy into mysteries no man was meant to penetrate" . . . "History, indeed, was all I had after everything else ended in mocking Satanism" . . .

And every time, he dutifully typed up those stories, affixing his name to them, sending them out to publishers amateur and professional as his own. The frequency of the act did not make it any easier—did not lessen the sense of guilt and shame that he was absconding with the work of some other man, brashly claiming credit that belonged to another.

Once he was wandering among the stacks of the John Carter Brown Library, looking for rare tomes on antiquarian Americana that could not be found even in the main student library at Brown. He had once hoped to matriculate to Brown, but illness and nerves had gotten the better of him, and he had to be content to be a non-university barbarian and alien. But that telltale tingling in the fingers came again, and the roly-poly man this time actually touched the scrapbook—on a high shelf he could reach only by absurdly standing on a chair (*why aren't the librarians making a fuss?*)—and giving him that balefully significant look.

"Curse you, Thornton, I'll teach you to faint at what my family do!" . . . "Carter, *it was the unnamable!*" . . . "It was the Yuletide, that men call Christmas though they know in their hearts it is older than Bethlehem and Babylon, older than Memphis and mankind" . . .

Then had come the move to New York. Sonia had been as kind and wonderful as a wife could be, but it had all been a mistake. His fleeing back to Providence like a dog with its tail between his legs had been undignified, but necessary for the very salvation of his mind and spirit. But he knew that, just as that roly-poly man had followed him to the metropolis, he would inevitably make his way back to this New England backwater—the only place he could consider home.

"The most merciful thing in the world, I think, is the inability of the human mind to correlate all its contents" . . . "But by God, Eliot, *it was a photograph from life*" . . . "In the morning mist comes up from the sea by the cliffs beyond Kingsport" . . . "West of Arkham the hills rise wild, and there are valleys with deep woods that no axe has ever cut" . . .

His illegitimate, undeserved fame—if, indeed, it could be called that—was growing. New friends, fellow writers of weird fiction—August, Donald, Two-Gun—wanted to make his acquaintance. Even book publishers expressed some faint interest. Was it because he knew those stories really weren't his that he spoke so modestly, even disparagingly, of them?

"When a traveller in north central Massachusetts takes the wrong fork at the junction of the Aylesbury pike just beyond Dean's Corners he comes upon a lonely and curious country" . . .

In later years the scrapbook—brown and crumbling as always—

at times attained immense thickness, filling dozens, perhaps hundreds of pages. He couldn't imagine how it even stayed in one piece. Some of the stories were so long it took him weeks, months to type them. He couldn't imagine the effort it must have taken to write them. Certainly that was well beyond his own capacities.

"Bear in mind closely that I did not see any actual visual horror at the end" . . .

Sometimes he would be so mortified at this literary theft that he hid the scrapbook behind bookshelves, under cabinets, once between the mattresses of his bed. As the years progressed he could only bring himself to send out a single story in a whole year. *No one can accuse me of profiting from another man's work. Can they?*

"I am forced into speech because men of science have refused to follow my advice without knowing why" . . . "and in that lair of the Deep Ones we shall dwell amidst wonder and glory for ever" . . . "What they finally found inside Edward's oddly assorted clothes was mostly liquescent horror" . . . "They were, instead, the letters of our familiar alphabet, spelling out the words of the English language in my own handwriting" . . . "I am it and it is I" . . .

And then he was stricken. He held off going to the doctor as long as possible, but finally his aunt Annie had summoned Dr. Dustin, who in turn had called in a specialist, Dr. Leet. But by then it was too late.

Howard was dying.

5

"Why have you come?"

He had no idea why he was even speaking to the roly-poly man—the man who had never spoken a word to him. That blank, deadpan face—maybe a mask—should have been terrifying, but he was now beyond the reach of fear or joy, dread or ecstasy.

There was only the intense, almost unbearable pain.

"What do you want with me?"

He could barely get the words out, but he felt the need for some kind of final confrontation with this creature—this source and focus of all his shame and mortification. Why had this man harried him all his adult life? What had he done to deserve it?

Without warning, the man's figure began to blur, change, transform; and in a matter of seconds there stood before him a tall, slim figure with the young face of an antique Pharaoh, gay with prismatic robes and crowned with a golden pshent that glowed with inherent light.

But somehow there was no terror here, only a transcendent awe and wonder. Howard took the spectacular metamorphosis in stride—but what truly stunned him was that words at long last began to pour forth from the entity's mouth.

"You have reached the end," he—or it—said. The statement was uttered with an ineffable mildness, as of the peace that surpasseth all understanding. It was only a confirmation of what Howard already knew, but the words nonetheless carried a blissful finality that comforted, soothed, reassured.

"I know," Howard managed to say in a whisper. "I just wish . . ."

"Wish what?" the figure queried.

Howard paused for many moments. For some strange reason he did not wish to annoy or alienate his companion—all he wanted was an explanation.

"Why have you . . . done what you have done?"

The figure turned his head to one side, as if in query. "What have I done?"

Howard couldn't believe he would have to explain what to him was so obvious. At the same time he sensed that even a mildly accusatory tone or implication would be problematical, even dangerous.

"You . . . you *tempted* me. You made me pass off the work of another as my own. You knew I could not resist the urge to see my name in print, plastered over tales that I could not possibly have written. Why did you do that? Why?"

The speech exhausted him, and he no longer cared what repercussions his words might have on his antagonist. He had, after all, reached the end.

But to his surprise, the figure did nothing but smile. He was, Howard sensed, enjoying a secret joke—a joke of such cosmic hilarity that the stars could not encompass it.

"I made you claim the work of another? Who? Who is this other you speak of?"

"I don't know!" Howard cried out in a final burst of strength. "The scrapbook . . . the writing . . . not mine . . ."

"Not yours? Then whose? Who else could have written those stories but you? Who else had the imagination, the learning, the grasp of the physiology of fear to set those tales down? It was you—no one but you. You 'found' that scrapbook on your own—I only led you to it, time and time again. It was in your dreams that you found that book, found that spidery, almost indecipherable writing. That writing came from your heart, your mind, your soul—no one else's. I know, for I am Nyarlathotep, the Crawling Chaos."

And with that, the figure gathered up the folds of his robe, made a curious gesture with his right hand, and vanished from the room in a blaze of light and a flurry of wind.

And, as he died, Howard Phillips Lovecraft knew at last that his life had not been lived in vain.

Avenging Angela

Jonathan Thomas

Something bounced off the back of her head and pinged against the hardwood floor. She whipped around, ready with a choice word or three for the lame-ass joker or jokers. Everyone knew she'd been jumpy, like much of the waitstaff, ever since the Club had reopened after renovations. Lights went on and off, glassware staged suicide dives off counters; Cheryl, too psychically sensitive for her own good, was especially on edge.

And now? Oh, hell no. Either the offending party had set a land-speed record exiting the gallery before she'd turned or it was no earthly joker. She slid her tray of empty wineglasses next to the gallery assistant's computer, and off the floor scooped up half of a little old-fashioned mother-of-pearl button, from a cuff or lapel maybe. It spooked her out of all proportion to its size and physical impact. Striving to keep a lid on her jangled nerves, she hollered to her coworker, tromping upstairs from the Café, "Hey, Jackie?"

Cheryl's best efforts to tamp down anxiety never fooled anyone. Jackie rushed the rest of the way up, and chalky-faced Cheryl greeted her on the landing by holding out the half-button between thumb and forefinger. "What's that?" asked Jackie.

"Someone threw this at me!" After the Art Club hosted a private party, the skeleton crew folding up furniture, washing dinnerware, dousing lights was always leery of the bogeyman, likelier a sex criminal than lurking ectoplasm in the mazy, olden, scary building. Therefore Jackie, an avowed skeptic on the ghostly front, hadn't braced herself for Cheryl's idea of an emergency, and only ticked her off by gaping at the projectile and voicing what instantly sprang to mind. "Where's the other half?"

"Why don't you ask Angela?" Cheryl shot back. And don't tell her Jackie didn't know who that was!

The tremor called time out. No boneshaker, but the glasses on the tray rattled; what reading on the Richter scale wouldn't derail trains of thought? This must have been the fourth around the East Side after the Club's relaunch, and its shockwave had come up through the girls' insteps, as if a fault-line were underfoot. They adjourned to the kitchen and joined the dishwashers at the fire-escape door overlooking the parking lot and the massive iron barrier behind it that sealed off an ancient railroad tunnel. No visible damage, but everyone kept staring into the night as if something was wrong and they were missing it.

Harry's wistful gaze wandered among the myriad details of the Cabaret. He wondered idly if, for all his celebrity, he was in a club he'd be welcome to join. Not that he played Providence enough to bother trying. This cozy sanctum to one side of the Café would have qualified as a snug in Merry Old England, and its charms were considerable: the quaint Mitteleuropa chairs and table, the Colonial hearth replete with bread oven, the silhouettes of esteemed members on the walls, the sooty mural of Mephisto under the low ceiling, leering at dusty, empty Chianti bottles dangling from the rafters.

He'd dined in the Cabaret before as honored guest of Sydney Burleigh and other Art Club bigwigs; Burleigh had requested his company for lunch today. Harry hoped his host wouldn't show till he'd had a minute to get a handle on his pal Cliff Eddy's pal Howard Lovecraft. Curious name!

Harry's wish came true. A tall, gaunt, diffident fellow, thirtyish but with a callow air, led with his sizeable chin as he scuffed in. He fit inside his charcoal suit as if it were the uniform of a Brahmin, worn though it was and far from modish. He carried himself with the certainty of moving through his rightful element, his inalienable home grounds, yet with the guardedness of an infiltrator. He bowed slightly and proffered a deferentially unassertive handshake. "Mr. Houdini? It is an honor." His voice was both boyishly high and weighted with gravitas.

What to make of this rare Yankee bird, this man of conflicting parts? "Call me Harry, will you, so long as it's all right if I call you Howard? After all, we may be working together."

Howard nodded—a bit warily, perhaps? Attempting to put him more at ease, Harry brought up their mutual acquaintances, Cliff and Muriel Eddy, who'd commended Howard's cerebral approach to the supernatural. Without warming particularly, Howard professed meeting them face-to-face only recently, after corresponding a while. Harry curbed his surprise that apparently like-minded folk who lived scant miles apart would send letters instead of arranging a rendezvous or at least phoning.

After several rudderless seconds of silence, Harry rose to the challenge of a tough nut to crack and pressed on, "Your worthy debut in the newest *Weird Tales* aside, your feud with some astrologer in a local paper convinced me you were the man for a peculiar job. I take it you haven't softened your position on astrology."

"Astrology?" Howard huffed. "It's the bunk!" Ah, the tight-wound Yankee was loosening up at last. Just give him something to denounce!

"Yes, Howard, precisely. And as you may know, I've applied myself lately to debunking spiritualism, a much more villainous racket. It's in that capacity I've been retained at the Art Club."

Howard perked up, almost to the point of flippancy. "Someone's saying the old place is haunted?"

"In a word, yes. Are you familiar with this 'old place'?"

Howard gave the Cabaret a once-over redolent of a townie's familiarity. "My Aunt Lillian exhibited some watercolors in the gallery not long ago."

"So creativity runs in your family!" When this bid at personability also sank without a ripple, Harry punted, "I'm here at the invitation of Sydney Burleigh. Quite the accomplished artist in these parts. Maybe you've crossed paths?"

"I know who he is," Howard stated noncommittally.

"A man of wide-ranging repute, wouldn't you agree?" Howard's nod was pure politeness, with nary a trace of conviction. Harry soldiered on. "Besides his success as a painter, he's been a very generous patron of the arts, and he even designed that distinctive Fleur-de-Lys house two doors down." Uh-oh, was the green-eyed monster fussing at Howard's cuffs, glinting behind his wire-rims? Or was something else eating him?

"Oh, that?" Howard intoned at length. "A distinctive eyesore, if you'll pardon my opinion, the silliest, most misguided excuse for revivalism. That Tudor half-timbered freak does not belong in our beautiful Colonial environs, and adding insult to aesthetic injury, it flouts itself directly across the street from the finest Georgian steeple in America! He just should have fixed up whatever used to occupy that address."

"I stand corrected, but please soft-pedal your disapproval when Mr. Burleigh arrives. He's due anytime now."

"Of course." Howard, the old-line gentleman, smiled complaisantly. Harry entertained the possibility he might be a pedant. Conversely, might Howard, on architectural grounds, have branded Harry a philistine?

The seats beneath them and everything on the table trembled; the shrieking whistle, the stupendous chugging and clatter of a train might have erupted from the adjacent room. "Good God, Howard, it sounds as if we're on top of a railroad track!"

"Basically, we are," Howard affirmed. "Several trains per day go by behind the Club, to and from Bristol. There's a tunnel into the hillside out back that runs all the way through the East Side. The dishes in here have been rattling since 1908, if I'm not mistaken."

Harry didn't suppose he would be. And then as foretold, Burleigh entered, filling the doorway with expansive presence rather than bodily stature. Everyone was cordial as Harry made the introductions. Burleigh's baggy white casual attire and trim, birdlike frame imperfectly offset a patrician bearing; likewise, the sprightliness he projected imperfectly offset his bushy gray Van Dyke and the inroads of frailty. Howard, Harry observed, unfavorably eyed the floppy beret Burleigh wore indoors, even after sitting down, but thankfully let this lapse of decorum pass.

Fixing his glance on Howard and Harry in turn, Burleigh fairly whispered, "Gentlemen, I've been the target of a cruel imposition, of a sort that put me in mind of Mr. Houdini's skill in exposing occult hoaxes. I'll be profoundly in your debt for whatever light you can throw on my situation. And, of course, for bringing any culprits to justice." That last clause sounded strangely like an afterthought. Was Burleigh absolutely positive a hoax was involved?

"I shouldn't assume you know this, but going on two years ago a dear, longtime friend of mine cut her own life tragically short, in the studio directly above mine." Both Harry and Howard nodded because they knew exactly whom he meant.

"Well, for about a month I've entered my studio several evenings to discover a divan turned toward the door with a mannequin lounging upon it. It was wearing the same Arabian Nights ensemble my absent friend, Angela O'Leary, had worn on that divan for a series of charcoal sketches I'd dashed off in the month before her death. I found the mannequin in a different pose each time, mimicking a different sketch, but with the costume in a state of vulgar dishabille. The uncanny part is, I destroyed those studies after she died; the associations they conjured were too painful. Nobody alive has seen them."

Was Burleigh out to recruit debunkers or convert them to goose-pimpled believers? "Furthermore, my studio door and the casement windows in the wall opposite were always locked, and though I lack Mr. Houdini's expertise in these matters, none of the hasps or latches appear to have been forced." Harry nodded thoughtfully, whereas keen interest was writ plain on Howard's features. Perhaps the prospect of a real-life "locked room mystery" excited him.

"Any other spirit activity, so to speak?" Harry asked.

"Yes, one other thing: twice now an easel with a blank canvas has been positioned as if for the mannequin's inspection. On the canvases were messages in greasepaint, of a sickly green I've never worked with, and without a wet brush anywhere around."

"And the messages?" Howard chimed in.

Burleigh was unfolding a notepad sheet from his shirt pocket. "I've transcribed them. Gibberish, as best I can make out."

Harry accepted the paper, arched his eyebrows in capitulation, and passed the paper to Howard, who gave it a more searching appraisal. "It's Gaelic. I don't understand it, but perhaps your friend Miss O'Leary, or relatives at her funeral, could have?"

"So can either of you produce a scholar of obscure languages? Or an Irish cop maybe?" Harry and Howard feigned mild amusement at Burleigh's attempted humor.

At the doorway someone cleared his throat as if waiting to be noticed. "Ah! Young John, come to receive our orders!" Harry and Howard traded discreet looks of bemusement. "Young John" was squarely mired in middle age, hairline in retreat, wan indoor complexion, garb like a banker's on seaside holiday, except for the white apron over his incipient paunch. He was, be it said, around a decade younger than Burleigh. The two of them briefly conferred sotto voce with their backs to their guests.

"Gentlemen, we're in luck!" Burleigh announced as John stood by with arms folded. "John's brought some excellent swordfish, caught off Little Compton yesterday."

"Sounds wonderful!" beamed Harry, only to bite his tongue on glimpsing Howard's queasy expression and sudden pallor, worse than John's. "But I'm afraid Mr. Lovecraft is allergic to seafood. I don't suppose you can rustle up anything else?"

"Um, there are some leftover beans and franks," Burleigh ventured.

"Yes, that would be most appreciated, thank you!" Color returned to Howard's cheeks.

Burleigh ill concealed his amazement at a fellow Rhode Islander spurning such a feast, till the thought of his own more important problem retook center stage. "I don't mind telling you this is preying on my nerves. Why am I being victimized?" Hah! If Burleigh didn't know that in his heart of hearts, Harry reflected, who did he expect to clue him in? "Is there anything you can do?"

"I'll want to confer with my colleague before going out on any limbs, and naturally we'll need to examine your studio. But let me declare categorically, you are the target of an imposition, as you say, and not of the supernatural. If I may ask, has anyone approached you offering to solve your problem?"

"No, no," Burleigh shook his head, overtly unsure of Harry's drift. "I've broached this business with nobody beyond you two and Young John."

"But as the proverb goes, it is no secret if three people know of it," Howard pointed out. "Especially in Providence."

Before the insinuation that "Young John" was a blabbermouth could sink in, Harry proposed, "And maybe someone's waiting for word of your 'haunting' to get out, and when it's common knowledge, he or she won't sound as suspicious contacting you."

"You're implying someone is staging these incidents to trade on my bereavement?" Burleigh stammered.

"What a callous fraud!" Howard exclaimed. "Yet people stoop so low as to trade, as Mr. Burleigh puts it, on bereavement?"

Harry was thrilled Howard hadn't blurted "guilt" as opposed to "bereavement." "It's their bread and butter," Harry shrugged.

Burleigh, as if flustered at his failure to get Harry's drift sooner, sustained a slight quaver as he said, "Pardon me, I just want to see what's delaying Young John at the stove."

Once Burleigh was out of earshot, Harry speculated, "On the other hand, it may not be extortion. Considering the circumstances of Miss O'Leary's death, friends or relatives mightn't be above some macabre retribution. You're probably aware of rumors she and Burleigh were romantically involved?"

"Burleigh's bohemian tendencies are known to me. Perhaps other jilted paramours are playing tricks on him. Or a cuckolded husband. Or Burleigh's wife?"

"Other paramours, pray tell! And I suppose the suicide spawned no less gossip than the affair?"

Howard drew a voluminous breath. "Since you ask, Burleigh had broken off their affair a few days earlier, which she deemed unacceptable. That Friday the Art Club threw a Halloween gala, just as it will two days from now. While the party was in full swing, Miss O'Leary locked herself in her studio and 'took the pipe,' as they say. She inhaled enough gas to lose consciousness, but not enough to kill her outright because of a kink in the tube. Perhaps she twisted the tube herself in the expectation she'd be found in time. Sadly, she was not.

"In fact, not until the next morning did someone show up, a friend named Aldrich, and he went away on receiving no answer to his knocks. He thought nothing of it, but grew worried on trying twice more to no effect. He forced his way in, and she was lying on the floor, unresponsive, the tube in her mouth. She lingered a while in hospital, but was too far gone and passed away a day later. I imagine Aldrich might have harbored some guilt for acting no sooner, and some resentment that Burleigh hadn't checked on her when she sat out Friday's party. This Aldrich who discovered her, by the way, is the same Young John grilling your swordfish. And his profile in silhouette is on the wall right above my head."

"My God, Howard, this is a small town, isn't it? Still, how are you so well versed? Many of those details weren't in the obituary."

Howard's shrug was as world-weary in its way as Harry's had been. "As I said, this is Providence. And how are you so well informed of our small-town doings?"

"A clipping service, Howard. An investment I've never regretted. You might want to hire one as a research tool in your writing."

"If only!" Howard lamented. "The sole way I could afford that would be as a plotting device in a story."

They dummied up as their extempore waiters trouped in, Burleigh with his own swordfish, John with Harry's plus Howard's beans and franks. John, with nary a peep, turned on his heel and departed. No sooner was Burleigh seated than a succulent pungency overspread the chamber and Howard blanched, clamping a desperate hand over nose and mouth. Harry was about to quiz Burleigh further about Miss O'Leary, but paused while Howard grabbed his plate and utensils, wheezing, "I'm sorry, the air has become too close in here. I'll be at a table in the next room." He was out before anyone could utter a syllable.

By the time Harry and Burleigh had adjourned from the Cabaret, Howard had cleaned his plate like a trencherman and was admiring Latin graffiti on the plaster above the walnut paneling. He and Burleigh nodded at each other as Burleigh, ashen and shaky, plodded out; Harry sat opposite Howard and apologized, "I had no idea seafood made you so nauseous."

Howard smiled benignly. "I had a thoroughly delightful repast, thank you, and respite enough to contemplate the dimensions of Miss O'Leary's tragedy. By all reports, she was intelligent, beautiful, vivacious, cultured, well traveled, abundantly talented, and poised to achieve fame on a national scale. Can you imagine someone of such sophistication and promise acting so rashly under the influence of an emotion, especially one as transient as romantic love?"

"Of course I can, Howard! But the truth may be somewhat less straightforward. Burleigh may have been more of a last straw. She'd become much more 'begrudging' of him, as he put it, after her mother died a few months earlier. An older brother, a doctor, died several years previously, having contracted TB from a patient at the sanatorium where he practiced, and her oldest brother died in 1911 soon after turning forty-four. That was Miss O'Leary's age as of her birthday, which fell on the same Friday as the Art Club party."

"She committed suicide on her birthday, then," Howard clarified, "during a soirée she may have viewed as antipodal to a birthday party."

"Could be, but anyhow, she may have seen forty-four as a tipping point: middle age breathing down her neck, her best years squandered on a married man decades her senior, and she very much alone in the world. Losing Burleigh may have brought on her ultimate despair, as he confessed just now through gushing tears, though he may be taking too much credit for that. The wondrous male ego! It actually craves the guilt, to prove it's tough as nails and can stand it. But I digress. If you have time, would you mind inspecting Burleigh's studio with me?"

The studio, on the Fleur-de-Lys' ground floor, comprised two bright, high-ceilinged rooms, a palatial space where nobody lived and one ego chased glory, Harry noted ruefully, recalling the cramped tinderboxes where his family of nine had sweltered and frozen during his boyhood. In the front room was a balcony of zigzag wooden slats, perfect for staging *Romeo and Juliet*. It overlooked Burleigh's atelier, the walls chockablock with framed landscapes and portraits and people in landscapes. Beyond a partition wall punctuated by horseshoe arches was a classroom with easels, cabinets of art supplies, trunks of costumes and props. In one corner leaned a jumble of naked, jointed, sexless plaster mannequins. Too bad Burleigh hadn't preserved the dummy more recently *en déshabillé* for examination.

"Already," Harry proclaimed with a cavalier wave, "I can puncture the argument for a supernatural agency, or even a 'locked room mystery.' With students and associates coming and going, a nimble intruder could easily secrete himself on the balcony or in a hamper while Mr. Burleigh was distracted. Once the intruder was alone, he'd be free to work his mischief. He could let himself out or, if he were locked in, sneak out whenever Mr. Burleigh reëntered and his back was turned. A good hoaxer is supremely gifted at covering his tracks. Nothing more cryptic here than the same principle of misdirection behind most magic and escapes!"

Burleigh heaved a dolorous sigh. "I'm afraid I've withheld something that may forestall dismissing the supernatural." His tone had a hapless ring. "During her final poses for me, Miss O'Leary recounted nightmares she ascribed to her Celtic second sight. They presaged doom and a rift between us, as symbolized by her futile search for me in a deserted, squalid city of colossal masonry, which she accessed via the train tunnel out back. She'd entertained no self-destructive urges prior to these dreams, which perhaps merely signaled the onset of nervous collapse. But I've been having these same dreams, as if her troubled spirit has invaded mine."

"Mr. Burleigh," Howard essayed, "while I am no alienist, I'd conjecture Freud might be able to explain why both you and Miss O'Leary had those dreams, without invoking the spirit world. Perhaps it would be of consolation, reducing them to mundane subconscious origins."

"I'm no Freud either," Harry leapt in, "but I concur: don't go looking for the occult where it's not thrust upon you." Besides, he was raring to jettison the intangibles of dreams and psychology and get back onto the solid ground of fakery, where he had a firm grip on the reins. "And if ever the occult were to be thrust upon you, let's consider Friday. Your masquerade will occur too near the anniversary of Miss O'Leary's death for your harassers to resist. After taunting you all month, chances are they're plotting some bolder, nastier stunt during the party. Mr. Lovecraft and I, with your permission, will be in attendance. I presume you can lend us disguises."

Harry and Burleigh arranged to reconvene in the studio Friday after nightfall, but before ill-prepared partygoers typically came begging Burleigh for last-minute costumes. Burleigh tendered his two pillars of composure profuse thanks and damp handshakes. Filing out the door, Harry espied Howard critically eyeing Burleigh's beret on a coatrack. The preening old duffer hadn't seen fit to doff the headgear till he was in his own bailiwick. Yes, Burleigh did hone affectations to promote his Boho image, forsaking polite custom in the process.

Out on the herringbone brick sidewalk, Howard beckoned Harry to step uphill and into an alley between the Fleur-de-Lys and a spruce Colonial mansion.

"Howard, I gather our client doesn't strike you as 100% sympathetic?" They both squinted sidelong on passing by the casement windows, and relaxed on determining Burleigh's attention was elsewhere.

"Is he not a bit of a fop?" Howard countered. "Even for a traditionalist like myself, he represents a stodgy, passé vision of art. And you may have noticed, he never directly addressed me. Hardly the ploy to win my sympathies!" They were schlepping across a swath of saplings, weeds, and litter beyond the alley.

"No, I'll grant that, but people under pressure are seldom at their best, and he'd be lost without us."

Howard grunted noncommittally and extended his arm to block Harry from tumbling down a little graveled slope and onto the tracks. To the right was the ominously gaping mouth of the tunnel. "Unless I'm also prey to overactive imagination, this railroad portal may have a role in our business. Burleigh's tormentors used some outwardly preternatural knowledge of Miss O'Leary's poses in positioning the mannequin, and as we just learned, it's no feat to peek into Burleigh's windows unbeknownst to him. Furthermore, might there be something to Miss O'Leary's apprehensions, at least in her dreams, about the tunnel, based on a glimpse she may have unconsciously absorbed of skulkers within? As a hidey-hole it appears foolhardy, but a mindful scoundrel with a timetable would be relatively safe."

Harry stared into the dark as if seeking a rejoinder. "Even if we establish a clear sightline between the tunnel entrance and Burleigh's windows, aren't you putting the cart in front of the horse? Why would Peeping Toms have spied on Burleigh before they had the motivation of Miss O'Leary's suicide to avenge?"

"True, true," Howard admitted, "but as the adage goes, 'When you have eliminated the impossible, whatever remains, however improbable, must be the truth.' And haven't we eliminated occult influence as impossible?"

"Ah, the wisdom of Conan Doyle," acknowledged Harry, "before the crooked mediums got to him."

"Exactly," Howard nodded genially, one autodidact high-signing another. "Yet the point remains: Burleigh has evidently been under unfriendly surveillance for two or more years, and he never the wiser. We've come this far. Might as well poke our heads in."

Harry shrugged, and Howard gingerly planted his right foot upon the slope. The vaguest trembling, the faintest of rumbles prompted Harry to grab Howard's sleeve. "Hold on! Must be a train approaching."

Howard nodded, and five minutes later they realized they were straining their ears at nothing, that no train was about to materialize. "What was that? Do you get tremors around here?" Bewilderment was something Harry instilled in others; he seldom had to weather it himself.

"Rarely." Howard scooted back from the brink. "But whatever it was, if anything, it coincided with an attack of dizziness and a feverish spell. Those franks may have lain on the stove too long. I had better hurry home." They beat a retreat through the weeds, trod the alley undetected again.

Howard's stance betrayed a remnant wobble as they paused on the steep incline of Thomas Street. "They must have a phone at the Club. Please, let me call a cab for you. I feel responsible."

Howard waved off Harry's solicitude. "I'm just up the street. Don't worry, I'll be home by shank's mare in twenty minutes. If it's all the same to you, though, could I borrow that sample of Gaelic? Easy as pie to scare up an Irish cop, or a well-versed equivalent, in my neighborhood." When Howard loped away, it was at the intrepid pace of a career pedestrian. Harry had preferred not to fuel Howard's potentially volatile imagination by mentioning how Howard's symptoms had coincided with weak knees of his own and a headache fleeting but like an icepick.

In addition, he hadn't entirely blinked away a mirage like a double-exposure superimposed on the tunnel entrance, of a vast cavern's cylindrical interior, with a ledge that corkscrewed up the wall, and a floor rife with gushing plumes of steam or smoke. What's more, the cavern was apparently submarine, but in what kind of water did stone blocks, slabs, and pillars drift like twigs? This must have been a hodgepodge of images sunburnt onto his retina, transiently visible against the portal's utter blackness. Or had Howard shared Harry's vision and said nothing lest Harry question his levelheadedness?

Come Thursday afternoon, Harry pressed the doorbell on Howard's side of the prim Angell Street duplex at the corner of Butler. Again, what a luxury of elbow room by New York standards, however deprecatory Howard had been of the place. Harry admired the red and yellow foliage of curbside oaks and maples, positively Arcadian compared with Manhattan, till Howard popped out the door like a cuckoo-clock automaton. He sported the charcoal suit once more, a wardrobe choice Harry couldn't envy, heated as he was in shirtsleeves and chinos. "It's such a nice day, Howard. Care to join me on my rounds before we collate notes?" Howard seemed well pleased to pound the pavement.

They headed west down Angell and north up Wayland. "I find walking invaluable in getting the brain to fire on all cylinders, don't you?" Before Harry could frame an answer, Howard resumed, "But if you're gathering information on the QT, aren't you afraid you'll be recognized?"

Harry wedged his clipboard under one arm, putting on a pair of spectacles from his shirt pocket and a tam-o'-shanter from a trouser pocket. "Less is better. Nobody tries seeing through so thin a disguise, whereas beards and the like look more like concealment and command more probing attention. And who would expect the famous Houdini to turn up as a surveyor for the Providence House Directory?"

On Wayland Avenue, Harry counted several Victorian hulks. Mostly, variants on bungalows and Dutch colonials catered to the new century's middle-class tastes. "Be on the lookout for Doane Avenue. Angela's niece and nephew, with their spouses, are renting in adjacent houses there, so to that degree they're a close-knit family. They'll be the last of her relations to canvass around here. Do you know many people in this neck of the woods?"

Howard gravely shook his head and dourly imparted, "When I was a boy, this whole section was woods, and I loved playing in them. A more halcyon era!"

Harry let the topic lapse. Yep, he reckoned, whenever anything used to be how Howard liked it, change was a heaping portion of bitter fruit.

Halfway along Doane, the entirety of which ran one short block, Harry stayed their course between two blandly utilitarian new houses divided into two flats each. "Howard, would you please have a seat on those porch steps across the street? Yep, that house with the scary vine up one wall. Since we are in your part of town, best to keep your plausibly familiar face at a distance. If anyone asks, I'll say you're my field assistant and wave. You just wave back. At one address they did act a mite suspicious, because these door-to-door guys usually travel in pairs."

In a few minutes, reattaching a pencil to his clipboard, Harry strolled over to Howard. "Their response was in line with everybody else's. You and I were speculating that an aggrieved relative of Angela's might have it in for Burleigh. I lucked out. Both her niece and nephew were home, but when I inquired if any household members or close kin had died in the past year or two, they each drew a blank and had to be finessed into remembering their dear departed aunt. Maybe the shame and scandal of a suicide in the family encouraged willful amnesia. But in a nutshell, I'd say clan O'Leary is in the clear."

"And I have some results as well," Howard reported as they turned left onto Elmgrove.

"Great! First, though, I have to confess all this sleuthing has put me in need of refreshment. A good soda fountain between here and downtown would do nicely. My treat." Howard led them back to Angell, where he fixed longing, morose eyes upon the faded glory of a Victorian mansion at the corner.

As they proceeded, Howard tore his gaze away and explained, "That house is my birthplace. I spent a wonderful childhood there. A *much* more halcyon era!"

"But home is wherever you have family, isn't it? Do you still live with the folks?"

"My mother passed away a few months before Angela O'Leary, but you don't catch me blubbering in public like Sydney Burleigh!"

They ambled down Angell in silence a while. To go nonverbal too long felt, reasonably or not, like defeatism, and at length Harry had to venture, "My word, Howard, I do hope you aren't alone in the world."

"In point of fact," Howard brightened, "I am affianced to a smart, attractive correspondent and authoress, more cosmopolitan and pragmatic than myself. I'll have to pull up stakes for some far-flung clime, though, upon our nuptials. She is a businesswoman of the Hebrew persuasion, and my aunts may never approve of her."

Was Howard even aware Harry was of the same "persuasion"? What to do except forge on, in for a penny, in for a pound? "A nice Jewish girl, eh? Good for you, Howard. May she make you very happy, wherever you settle down. Anti-Semitism is such a blot on humanity. I'm delighted it's not a prejudice you condone!"

Howard nodded circumspectly and said no more, though Harry was suddenly obliged to step up his pace to match Howard's. In a trice they were surrounded by a shopping district, and with a flourish Howard indicated a black door opening onto one corner of a busy intersection. "Here we are. E. P. Anthony's. It's been around almost as long as I have."

Which, Harry deduced, qualified as a virtue in itself. He couldn't help noting the door belonged to yet another pseudo-Tudor building, but Howard was quite unperturbed by this one, perhaps because Burleigh had nothing to do with it, perhaps because Howard couldn't indulge a sweet tooth every day. The midafternoon lull afforded them an unrestricted choice of stools at the counter. Howard, Harry readily allowed, hadn't steered him wrong: black marble and ornate brass made for classier decor than, say, Woolworth's. A slow-moving fogy with pince-nez and double-chins got around to them. "Sirs?"

Howard recommended the Rhode Island delicacy of a "coffee cabinet," whatever that was, and for himself, blueberry pie à la mode, "with vanilla of course! And coffee, four sugars, please." The soda clerk laboriously rolled up his white sleeves and shuffled off. Howard already had a cancelled, letter-size envelope out of his vest pocket, and was unfolding it to expose his smudgy scribble across its backside. "My mother and I, when she was feeling flush, used to hire an Irish kid down the street for odd jobs. I stopped by his house, and begorrah but didn't his grandpa from the Old Sod retain the Erse enough for our purposes."

He also extracted Burleigh's transcription from his jacket, where it had subbed as a pocket square. "For your files, along with my translations. I can tell you, both phrases raised every eyebrow in the parlor, and it was an uphill battle to trivialize them as obscure literary quotes, which indeed they may be." Howard's coffee slid into sight, and he took an eager slurp. "The top line," he expounded, with a finger on *Seo an doras isteach purgadóra,* "means 'Here is the door into purgatory.'" His finger hopped to *Anois a thosaíonn do leorgníomh.* "Even less auspicious is the second: 'Now your atonement begins.' Shuddersome, yes, had only Burleigh been able to understand them."

"Do you understand them? Or rather, what they're getting at?" Howard, Harry decided, wasn't striving for pedantry. It just bodied forth from him as automatically as showmanship from Harry.

"The reference to purgatory does fit a genuine Irish locale that Angela or her avenger could have visited or read about. An islet in a lough of County Donegal was reputed to have a cave or pit frequented by medieval pilgrims from across Europe. The cave owed its popularity to a legend about Jesus showing it to St. Patrick, vouchsafing that anyone who abided within for three days would witness visions of purgatory. These harrowing visions were equated with time spent in actual purgatory, so that the longer one withstood them, the sooner one would attain heaven post mortem." With extraordinary stealth, meanwhile, the decrepit soda clerk delivered their orders, as Howard lectured on, none the wiser.

"The etiology of these visions was never established, be it noxious gases leaking from the earth's bowels, or the toll of too much hunger, thirst, or darkness, or simple power of suggestion, mass hysteria if you will. And the cave was extolled by myriad authors, Marie de France in the twelfth century, William Staunton in the fifteenth, Thomas Carve's *Lyra Hibernica* in 1666, Edward Ledwich's *Antiquities of Ireland* in 1790, to cite a few. The cave either collapsed in 1632 or was plugged up by the Church following a scandal over admission fees. A monastery still dominates the island; monks nowadays charge pilgrims for a gander at the plugged-up opening."

"Howard, your pie's getting cold and your ice cream's melting." Furthermore, the "coffee cabinet" came in a sundae glass but had a deceptively bitter quality because the ice cream in it and the milk were alike coffee-flavored, and were those coffee grounds in the foam? Not that the name hadn't been a tipoff! An acquired taste, and one for another day, if ever.

"Oh!" Howard gave a start as if the pie had magically substantialized. "Thank you, Harry. But as I was saying, whatever the source of the Gaelic, it would have been entirely appropriate above the cave entrance, though no text I've consulted alludes to any epigraph." Howard picked up his fork and zealously tucked in.

"Be that as it may," Harry contended, "harassing Burleigh in terms he didn't even perceive as language could only seem like a savvy move to an outright lunatic, well-educated or not." He could choke down no more spoonfuls of "coffee cabinet" and shoved his sundae glass a scritching inch away. The tiny noise alerted Howard as if he had the ears of a bat; his plate was well-nigh clean. He eyed Harry's leftovers, and with a discreet gesture Harry consigned them to him. Technically, Howard was guilty of scavenging, yet nothing in his deportment ever qualified as graceless.

"Madman or no," Howard conjectured, dragging the cabinet closer, "the culprit is employing phrases that can apply equally to the train tunnel, is he not? I might propose he regards it and St. Patrick's

Purgatory as interchangeable, to some purpose nefarious as it is opaque. Poor Burleigh!"

Harry nodded pensively. He was most struck by the correspondence between the Irish cave's nightmare visions and his mirage in the tunnel mouth. Had St. Patrick's Purgatory occurred to Howard in the first place because he'd also experienced that illusion? And if it had beset them both, was it simply illusion? Whoa there! That line of thought led to some murky harum-scarum waters. Still, he couldn't just brush off the possibility Howard had beheld the ghastly marine cavern and dared not speak of it, dwelling instead on some remote counterpart. Talk about Freudian sublimation!

The clink of spoon upon the bottom of the sundae glass distracted Harry from his woolgathering. Howard paused in polishing off Harry's confection. "I wish my commonplace book were handy. Naturally my first concern is Burleigh's welfare, but my imagination keeps spinning aspects of his case into a wilder, more fantastic yarn, wherein I'd assign Miss O'Leary a minor role at best. The drilling, blasting, and quarrying that went into the tunnel's construction, and the ongoing din and disturbance of trains hurtling through it, would make for a much grander threshold onto the weird."

Howard gulped coffee with the gusto of a bon vivant, an enthusiast in his element again, as when he'd knocked the Fleur-de-Lys. "The railway has plumbed subterranean depths that languished in hermetic darkness for aeons. These depths, moreover, lay under a hill, the storied abode of non-human races and primeval creatures. Which of them would the noise jar awake after dormant ages, ravenous and incensed: a manitou of the Algonquins, the last survivor of Paleozoic titans, a spectral guardian of a Stygian city under abyssal floodwaters? You must agree there's more promise along these lines than in the bedevilment of an old aesthete by a ghost impersonator."

Harry suppressed a double-take. Did allusion to "a Stygian city" imply that Howard too had visualized masonry aswirl in a submerged cavern? If not, though, what would Harry gain by volunteering he'd encountered barmy hallucinations? Meanwhile, were

Howard's "giants in the earth" really more promising story material than the hopeless struggle of human beings—Burleigh in this instance—against their sphinxlike, albeit self-inflicted, fates? Tactfully he bunted, "I leave the literary judgments to you."

"And haven't I been digressing shamelessly!" As if underscoring a job well done, Howard plunked his spoon into thoroughly grubbed-out sundae glass. "But to treat of Miss O'Leary's recurring nightmares, I find it apposite that she resided in her studio, and *ipso facto* slept and dreamed there. As such, it's plausible that her dreams, and her state of mind overall, had their genesis in a gas leak from her fixtures or a discharge of noxious exhaust that accumulated in the tunnel. Toxic fumes may at least have reinforced her suicidal impulses."

Harry harrumphed soberly. These were natural, measurable causes that hadn't crossed his mind.

"Putting aside Freudian complexes for the nonce," Howard added, "the same alleged dreams on Burleigh's part may indicate a buildup of poison gas in his studio as well. Certainly to warn him of this possibility would be prudent." He filled his lungs, as Harry beckoned over the sluggish clerk, to elaborate, "Were Miss O'Leary and Burleigh to serve me as characters, though, I would posit that their nightmares were psychic emanations from the subterrene malignity, to whose influence artistic temperaments would be especially susceptible."

Harry had divided his attention between Howard's ramblings and paying the tab. "Keep the change," he said as he swung off the stool. Howard followed suit after a dubious blink at Harry for shoving off while Howard was still declaiming. Out on the corner they reconfirmed the specifics of Friday's rendezvous and shook hands, at which point a soundless tremor shivered through Harry's soles and up his legs. Howard's eyebrows conveyed he'd felt it too. "Could that have been a train?" Harry grimaced, "Or a quake?"

Howard spread indecisive hands. "The tunnel is pretty much underfoot. But I've never ascertained whether railway vibrations could travel through two-hundred-odd feet of rock and earth. Perhaps it's our manitou!" Harry wished Howard had grinned more broadly at that ostensible jest.

For better or worse, Harry had scant time for any jests to get under his skin. After twenty-four hours of catering to Burleigh, he had correspondence to dash off, contracts to pore over, tour dates to iron out. He did, when concentration flagged, lapse into gazing vacantly upon Thomas Street from his suite in the Biltmore; that was the closest he came to mulling Burleigh's predicament. Hence, seasonably mild and fine as Friday evening was, he felt too ill-prepared to enjoy it. Out in front of the Fleur-de-Lys, he surveyed its glut of whimsical bas-reliefs, and perhaps his blue mood made them seem annoyingly fey.

Howard and his charcoal suit were, needless to say, punctual. "Why the long face, Harry?"

"Sorry it shows, Howard." Harry tried waving away his blues as if they were mosquitoes, smiled morosely. "I just wish we'd had time for proper legwork. We should have reconnoitered local mediums sizing Burleigh up as fat pickings, or vindictive pals of Angela, or 'Young John' while we're at it, or the tenant currently upstairs in Angela's former studio, though Burleigh insists he's renting to someone unacquainted with her."

"I wouldn't feel bad," Howard opined. "You came here on extremely short notice, despite your hectic schedule. Whatever Burleigh is paying you, I cannot doubt he's getting his money's worth from the 'Great Houdini.'"

Harry had to curb a wince. "Thank you, Howard, but on principle any debunking I perform is pro bono, even for landed gentry like Burleigh." The issue of sordid lucre hadn't previously come up; Howard nodded understandingly, but too hard-set a pokerface telegraphed his disappointment. Good heavens, had he expected remuneration, he should have brought that up at the outset.

The Fleur-de-Lys' ponderous, faux-medieval door burst open and Burleigh barreled out, jittery, hands aflutter as if baffled over what to do with them. He lurched to an abrupt, swaying halt and spouted from the rustic portico, "Why are you standing around? It's happened again! Come in, come in!" Harry and Howard traded a put-upon glance. Burleigh had cause to be high-strung, but the bossy, petulant act wasn't helpful, especially outside if he meant to keep his troubles private. Just as well he wasn't wise to Howard's translation of the baleful Gaelic.

"Look!" exclaimed Burleigh, preceding them into his studio, flailing one arm toward something nobody could see from the doorway. "The street door and my door and the windows were locked all day, even when I was here. This happened when I went over to the Art Club for ten minutes an hour ago."

In the middle of the atelier, a mannequin in black Cleopatra wig and diaphanous harem garb sprawled upon a divan. Who could tell if those duds were dishabille or not? Its hands melodramatically shielded its featureless face from the implicitly overwhelming canvas on the easel confronting it. Harry and Howard stepped around tremulous Burleigh to read the superficially banal "Teach Domh." The scribble had apparently been squeezed from a tube of slimy green pigment, more conducive to a shiver than the rest of the tableau. Burleigh betrayed no reaction to its rancid, fishy reek; age must have blunted his sense of smell.

"My nerves are going to snap!" Burleigh quavered. "Whoever or whatever is persecuting me, their timing could not be more excruciating. I cannot attend this masquerade without fearing for my life. An enemy could approach unbeknownst, and then it will be too late. No, I shan't go. I can hardly stir from this spot."

"Or is that how your enemy is hoping you'll behave?" Harry argued. "Remember, Miss O'Leary came to grief alone in her studio. If you stay here or go home by yourself, you may be setting yourself up for a lunatic's fulfillment of poetic justice. Mr. Lovecraft and I will not be with you. We're going to the party, as agreed earlier, to nab your tormentor whenever, and however, he shows his hand." Burleigh sucked on his luxuriant mustache as if about to protest or bark counterorders, but refrained, perhaps recalling Harry and Howard weren't servants.

"I understand your trepidation," Harry continued, "but you'll be less vulnerable in a crowd, and we won't let you out of our sight. If you want to be rid of these 'impositions' once and for all, tonight's our best opportunity, and you'll have to trust us."

Eyes downcast, Burleigh affected a martyrly submission to the vagaries of fate. Four measured knocks on the studio door tabled further discussion. "Hello? It's locked!" Oak panels muffled the patrician accents of a caller patently unused to obstructed entry.

"Young John," mouthed Burleigh, "borrowing a costume." His guests nodded and stole off to the classroom and makeshift concealment between an armoire and a window seat. Snatches of back-and-forth over the merits of various steamer trunks' contents wafted to them.

"Young John," whispered Harry. "Speak of the devil." They listened a minute for any nuggets of self-incrimination, till Howard pursed despairing lips and breathed, "Has it dawned on you, given Burleigh's precautions and the narrow time frame available to today's malefactor, that Burleigh himself may have posed the mannequins and inscribed the poison-pen canvases—perhaps in a fugue state or while sleepwalking or immersed in recurrent nightmares—in any case, guilt-ridden over Miss O'Leary's suicide? Far-fetched, yes, but preferable to crediting an occult agency, wouldn't you say?"

"As you and Conan Doyle recommend," Harry restated, "we have to do every improbability justice. That leaves the riddle, though, of where Burleigh got his Gaelic."

The studio door thumped shut and its key clattered in the lock. Good! Harry preferred nobody from the Art Club barge in before he and Howard were incognito. Burleigh bustled back, temporarily chipper while he reprised his traditional role of costumier. He grabbed Howard's wrist and beckoned him along. "Mr. Lovecraft, let's get you gussied up!"

For a lark, Harry eavesdropped till the two hidebound Yankees wrangling over sartorial minutiae reminded him of squabbling yentas. How they'd splutter were he to pronounce them two peas in a provincial pod! He drifted to the classroom's diamond-paned windows, then after the fact decided to check for Peeping Toms, gauge the quality of sightline between tunnel and studio. From this angle, only a thin crescent of the portal showed, but were his nerves more tightly wound than he'd perceived? Though he couldn't peer into the aperture at all, his retinas were treating him to the same head-on mirage as yesterday.

Except today, it was definitely worse. More vents in the submarine floor were gushing more convulsively; fragmentary cornices, columns, lintels spun frantically as in a gigantic eggbeater's mixing bowl. Yet unnaturally, no lesser debris or silt clouded the water. The parallel, diagonal striations of the corkscrew ledge stood out starkly on the wall, and from his brow the question sprang unbidden: of what behemoth pattern was the thing that burrowed so prodigiously into the world? And did the mounting agitation of the whirlpool and the gushers mean that thing was flexing fitfully to burst through constrictive sediments? As for the lay of the seabed, he wouldn't swear on a Bible it had been as convex.

The longer he stared, the more real the vision felt till he was confident Howard would see it too, were he not busy humoring Burleigh. Would Howard also intuit their vision was of no literal space, was rather a breach into a nonphysical realm that would nonetheless impinge catastrophically on mortal existence? Yet none but "creative" types like Howard or Burleigh or, yes, Harry himself would harbor any perception of this impingement via nightmares or their mind's eyes.

Burleigh swept back in, presumably with Howard in reluctant tow, based on balky demeanor. He was also self-consciously jangling and clanking. Harry mightn't have laughed as heartily had he not needed a laugh in the worst way. "Mr. Houdini," Burleigh sighed archly, "your assistant did not warmly embrace the theme of tonight's gala, which is 'Wonders in the Deep.'" Howard framed no rebuttal. "I did finally coax Mr. Lovecraft into donning a souvenir of my travels, by touting its relationship to mythology and classical culture. It came from the Aegean island of Skyros, where it enlivened the pre-Lenten carnival, really a festival of Dionysus under a flimsy veil of Christianity."

Burleigh's motions toward Howard were like an anatomy instructor's. "The hooded smock of black goat hair and the belt of bells hearken to herdsmen and fauns. Mr. Lovecraft should be thankful this exemplar is tailored for the tourist trade, or else the bells would weigh upward of fifty pounds. The white trousers are traditionally Greek. The black mask is the cured skin of a stillborn kid. Those who dance and caper in these ensembles are dubbed Ancient Ones."

Harry fervently hoped Howard had stripped down to BVDs before submitting to such stifling, bulky garb. He further had to credit Howard, doubtless doing a slow burn behind the mask, for mute stoicism in the line of duty. And if Howard had taken umbrage at the evening's unpalatable theme, with its promise of odious seafood hors d'oeuvres, his choice of costume didn't altogether detach him from it: the mask with two round eyeholes was tasseled with the flayings of embryonic goat limbs and the tatters of long wear, which had come to resemble a fringe of tentacles.

Harry couldn't resist teasing, "Good God, Howard, it looks as if someone dumped a plate of *pasta salsa nera* over your head. That's 'spaghetti in squid ink' down in Little Italy."

"What a hideous waste of spaghetti!" Howard huffed through his quivering mask.

"The hell of it is," Burleigh interposed, "I distinctly remember packing two outfits from Skyros in the trunk, and I'd have lent Mr. Lovecraft the nicer one, with a white mask, but I must have mislaid it sometime. Another mystery for another day, I guess. Mr. Houdini, come, let's get you dressed."

Burleigh did not make bold to grab Harry's wrist, instead bustling ahead into the atelier. Harry, sauntering past Howard, became the second person that evening to mouth "Young John." It must have crossed Howard's mind too that Angela's inhibited pal might have filched apparel while Burleigh was rummaging through chests, or weeks beforehand. Howard nodded delphically. If Young John were impersonating an Ancient One, his reasons would emerge soon enough. Howard wasn't, at any rate, pacing around while ruminating, or Harry would have heard him clanging.

Howard's tongue finally loosened at the spectacle of Harry strutting in with pearl-tipped golden crown, luxuriant wig and beard, matching yellow sarong, and garlands of dried kelp and scallop shells. His sandals were studded with little crabs and starfish. "As I live and breathe, King Neptune!" Howard hailed him. "Avast!"

Harry goggled and bashed the butt-end of his trident against the floor in mock indignation at Howard's flippancy. Burleigh bounced over and chimed in, "Apropos for Mr. Houdini, is it not, an artiste who has bested the aqueous element everywhere, from inside milk cans to the East River?"

"Just watch how you slam that pitchfork around, Your Majesty," Howard joshed. "Neptune was god of earthquakes too, remember."

"Gentlemen, if you'll relax in here for the nonce," Burleigh requested, "it's incumbent on me to throw something on, and dole out disguises to any ill-prepared revelers who come knocking." Hah! Burleigh was a fine one advising others to relax.

He hustled off, as Harry called after him, "Mr. Burleigh, please don't let anyone in till you find out who it is!"

Burleigh signed okey-dokey without breaking his stride, and his de facto shamuses retreated to the windowseat. Howard sat with an emphatic dissonance.

"You'll have to lose the bells," Harry insisted in hushed tones. "I've no idea what Burleigh was thinking, but you won't be any good as an eavesdropper or a bushwhacker."

Howard leaned forward for Harry to undo the noisy belt at the back. Harry remarked while he tinkered, "Burleigh's acting relatively composed. We can count our blessings he never pestered us for translations of the Gaelic. He'd be a neurasthenic wreck. But to slake my own curiosity, I do wish we had an Irishman to explain that 'Teach Donn,' not that I see much jeopardy in two words that might be some sort of classroom reminder note."

Harry got the sense Howard was frowning gravely behind the kidskin. "I needed no Officer Clancy this time. If I recall my Padraic Colum correctly, that new message is as inauspicious as the rest, if not more so. It derives from Irish myth, and its two innocuous-seeming syllables can be rendered as 'House of the Dead' or 'House of Death,' or more literally, 'House of the God of Death.' It's certainly no improvement over 'gateway to purgatory' in terms of the train tunnel, or if you'd rather keep the railroad out of it, the Fleur-de-Lys or the Art Club."

Harry let the jingling belt clink upon the floor. He subjected Howard's eyeholes to unspoken chagrin at this extra turn of the screw he could have done without. Burleigh, at this juncture, may have been the happiest among them, bumping, clattering, pacing amid his props and garments, oblivious to the palaver about him. On striding back in, he sported seven-league boots, tricorn hat over a bandana, a papier-mâché parrot on his shoulder, and the rest of a pirate's standard accoutrements: frankly, an uninspired letdown. On the bright side, he hadn't decried, or else noticed, Howard's forsaken belt.

"Gentlemen, in the interests of expediting our plans, I resorted to the convenient fallback of Long John Silver. Should we adjourn to the Club before any tardy guests come demanding I dress them? Into the breach, eh?" His bravado was as admirable as it was ersatz.

Harry and Howard rose briskly from the windowseat. "By all means," agreed Harry, unsure if he was calling Burleigh's bluff or stoking moral support. "If we're not violating a rule of the game, though, how did you outfit Young John, and, as you say, expeditiously at that?"

They trooped through the atelier, where the exotic mannequin had landed askew in a corner. The cryptic canvas was facedown on butcher paper. Suddenly sheepish, Burleigh muttered, "I did him up as a pirate too. Nothing easier when you're in a hurry."

Harry and Howard nodded without comment. Burleigh locked the studio, and the front door, and on the stoop, Harry enjoined, "Mr. Burleigh, why don't you go a few steps ahead so people don't necessarily get the impression we're with you, leastwise as bodyguards?" Burleigh grunted amenably and set off, joining the uphill trickle of partiers in undersea guises.

Bringing up the rear, Harry said sidelong to Howard, "So it's Young John and Long John, is it?"

"Just so's we can tell them apart. And wonder of wonders, Long John Silver's amputated leg grew back for the occasion."

"Why, that's right! He did use to have a pegleg. But speaking of wonders, I'm not sold on pirates as 'Wonders in the Deep.'"

"Not that any of this is consonant with our biblical theme."

Nearing the Art Club's green door, they dawdled as a knot of chatty attendees maladroitly tried unraveling into single file to go in. "Biblical?" Harry asked.

"Yes, absolutely, it's a quote from Psalm 107."

"Howard, I'm amazed a skeptic of your caliber would have the Scriptures at his fingertips."

Howard shrugged a tad coyly. "Why not? I know 'em as well as I do anyone else's primitive mythology."

They briefly lost sight of Burleigh in the untidy knot of merrymakers squeezing indoors, but squandered no energy rushing after him. The preceding month's "impositions" had been signposts toward a more dramatic, elaborate outrage than a sneaking assault in the foyer before the party was in full swing. Instead of traipsing into the Café and Cabaret again, Harry and Howard loitered to one side as Burleigh hobnobbed at the foot of commodious oaken stairs with a gaggle of mermaid, fish, and crustacean mimics.

For Harry, a blond wig and beard proved as effective as a tam and cheaters at saving him from being buttonholed as the "Great Houdini." If anything, as part of no clique, theirs was the status of wallflowers—all the better, really, for sleuthing without let or hindrance. Howard's getup probably deserved major credit for deterring small talk: in an atmosphere of whimsy and effervescence, it was uniquely repulsive. The silly jangle of his belt might have offset the freakishness, made him a little more approachable.

Oops, Burleigh and associates were lollygagging up the steps like water up an Archimedes' screw. Once they'd ascended from view, Harry and Howard moseyed along in their wake; an impartial onlooker, Harry reflected, would tag the two of them, if anybody, for skulking suspiciously. Atop the stairs they rubbernecked in dismay. Drat, they'd lost him again! The gallery-cum-ballroom would have flummoxed them a minute in any event, its capacious dimensions packed with boisterous gabbing and laughter, with shiny scales, lacquered fish heads, rayon tentacles, leatherette chitin, in a kaleidoscopic ferment of angles and curves. And ratcheting up the bedlam, a jazz orchestra commenced blaring from a stage at one end.

Halfway across the sea of chaos, a black tricorn bobbed in and out of visibility. Harry glimpsed it first and clutched Howard's shaggy forearm, pointed his trident thataway, and plowed forward like an ice-cutter, clacking his glorified fork just hard enough to split the sea without offending it. Before Harry was within range to poke his objective with the tines, though, he imagined Howard's heart sinking like his, for no parrot bedecked this pirate's shoulder.

Howard hung back as Harry tapped Young John on the pudgy bicep and shook hands as if that had been his aim all along. "Wanted to thank you again for that delectable swordfish!" he ad-libbed at a roar to beat the thunderous band.

Young John went blank a disoriented second, then smiled—for a buccaneer—blandly. "Ah, Mr. Houdini! You're very welcome! Have you seen Sydney?" Harry flinched, furtively checked around, relaxed; nope, it'd take a megaphone for his name to carry in this ruckus.

"When I do, I'll pass along you have a weather eye out for him!" He had a hunch it didn't matter what he said; as the band inched closer to a crazed fortissimo, John would have beamed and nodded at anything. Harry bowed curtly and rejoined Howard.

"At least you've reduced the likelihood Young John nicked the other Greek disguise," Howard shouted over the tumult. Newfangled hot rhythms had inflamed a few couples to dance, fishtails and claws swinging recklessly.

"Could be, but I won't lie to you," Harry volleyed back, "the mystery of Burleigh's whereabouts is making me nervous. Let's find him."

"These raucous so-called musicians aren't doing us any favors!" Howard complained. "Footpads could get away with murder and we'd be the last to know!"

Harry told Howard to stay put and clacked an Olympian path toward the stage. By his return, strident jazz no longer enriched the general pandemonium. "I slipped the maestro a C-note to take ten," Harry explained. "That should give us a chance to locate Burleigh before it's too loud again to think."

As they gazed hither and yon, Howard asked with overtones of awe, "Did you say you shelled out a hundred bucks? I bet the Club didn't pay 'em that much."

"Seems like a princely sum, but the bandleader has to divvy it up with a lot of guys, and as you said, this may be a matter of life and death. Considering the stakes, I shelled out gladly and of my own free will, though it annihilated the stash in my sarong." Now that the initial shellshock of the bacchanal had waned, they were casing the maroon, windowless room more stringently.

"Harry, I'm not criticizing you, but I hate to see that excuse for musicianship receive so much encouragement."

Harry half listened to Howard while studying the decor of curtains and partitions of undulating seagrass and kelp suspended from tracking lights and crown molding, adorned with crabs, seahorses, oysters, starfish, lobsters. "Not a jazz baby, I take it?"

Howard was likewise absorbed in a slow 360° scan of the environs. "Don't get me wrong, I was a drummer in my tender youth, but we played the time-tested chestnuts, 'Bedelia,' 'Sweet Adeline,' and the ilk. I simply cannot condone— Harry, turn around! Not ten feet from us, in that corner with the screen of seaweed across it, are those the toes of seven-league boots peeking out from under?"

They hastened over and each batted away half of the dried seagrass strands, which crackled like glass beads, and there trembled Burleigh like a caged bird in a lion's den. He shuddered more acutely at their encroachment, but otherwise maintained his hundred-yard stare, according them no eye contact, no show of recognition. "Mr. Burleigh!" Harry entreated. "Are you all right?"

Obviously he wasn't, but from Burleigh's mouth to Harry's ear, what kind of shape did he think he was in? "She's here!" Burleigh gasped, with more of an Ancient Mariner's compulsion to vent than a willingness to converse with his mystified allies or anyone else. "I've seen her!"

Howard blurted "What?" the same instant as Harry's "Where?"

"Pacing back and forth across the room, back and forth in front of me the way she might have done that night, desperate for me to come and be with her. Then she stopped, maybe at the time she gave in to despair. She was looking straight through everyone between her and me. She saw none of them, they didn't see her. She took a step toward me, I couldn't stand it, I broke and ran for cover."

"Where is she now?" Harry demanded.

"On Skyros I told her I loved her," Burleigh related to nobody in particular. "In Ireland I told her that didn't mean I could afford to abandon my wife."

Harry's hapless frown mirrored Howard's. Burleigh was contributing zip toward getting past square one in flushing out the ghostly hoaxer. But then his eyes bulged and he hoisted a shaky arm and feebly wagged his hand from side to side, as if warding off a fiend who, going by the rictus on Burleigh's face, wasn't going to desist so coöperatively.

Harry and Howard turned precipitately, and Harry assumed Howard had also descried nothing macabre. As one, they implored, "Mr. Burleigh? Mr. Burleigh? Sydney!" Was their borderline paralytic in the grip of trance or trauma? Under the circumstances, the difference amounted to semantics. And was Burleigh unhinged enough to hallucinate, or were they up against an adversary who could hotfoot it like a flea?

In nothing like an answer to their pleas, and in a lilt diametrically unlike himself, Burleigh chanted, "Anois a thosaíonn do leorgníomh."

"What?" Once before had been plenty, but again this Burleigh business was coercing Harry to admit bewilderment.

"'Now your atonement begins.' It's one of those Gaelic phrases. And that's how it's supposed to sound. When did he learn the correct pronunciation of a language he condemned as gibberish?"

In the face of this imponderable, both men obeyed an impulse to survey the ballroom and ascertain whether Burleigh was drawing problematic attention. Some scattered cliques were ogling them, but with curiosity or concern or reproach Harry couldn't tell because of the sea-monster heads, carnival masks, pancake makeup. One further figure, alone in the crowd, was gazing at them. "Harry!" he heard as through a wall of batting. "The purloined costume! Our culprit's hiding in plain sight!" Yes, but where had their culprit been ten seconds ago, when his eyes had raked that same space?

Never mind. What mattered now was keeping their quarry in the crosshairs, and Howard had already elbowed a beeline halfway there. But the piratical Young John had also homed in on the statuesque miscreant, and damn him, he was hallooing, "Angela! Angela!" My God, how many gullible neurotics were on tonight's guest list?

Burleigh, meanwhile, reacted as if the repetition of her name was driving a spike into his ears. A good many more attendees were watching because he was emitting unselfconsciously shrill jabber, unless that too were Gaelic, as he shot forward among the spectators before Harry could budge. Younger, fitter Harry sped after him, but Burleigh was perversely more proficient at snaking breakneck through the crowd. Harry was no longer banging the trident's butt-end and brandishing its prongs with any polite reservation.

Howard, unfortunately, had forfeited momentum in colliding with a waiter as narrowly focused as himself. A tray of canapés that Harry took to be scallops and bacon on toast was adhering all over Howard's hairy outfit. Before the waiter could regain bodily or inner balance, Howard, who'd lost neither, snarled, "Damn you and those rotten skate wings!" As he plowed onward, sights still fixed on his impassive target, he peeled off kidskin mask and besmirched outerwear, quick to exploit the silver lining of an excuse to ditch them like an insect moult. And yes, he'd never doffed his white, starchy shirt.

Harry was far from catching Burleigh, who sprinted babbling like one possessed toward the service door behind the band, whence the waiter had emerged. Harry, in midflight, stole a look at Howard collaring the costume thief; on his vision was etched a "minute movie" to haunt him forever. Burleigh had been right: this other ensemble from Skyros had been nicer, its mask a pristine white, its tunic a checkerboard of black fur and dappled calfskin. The torso had been stuffed to promote the illusion of breasts.

The heat of the moment must have endowed Howard with an impetuosity as surprising to himself as to Harry, for he tore off the white mask by its fringe of tentacles. He then turned to virtual stone, mask in his outstretched arm, as he boggled at the nothingness beneath the mask, while the remainder of the costume collapsed in a clangor of cowbells to the floor. Harry's last fleeting glimpse in passing was of bystanders with hands on hips or arms folded irksomely. Who was this gatecrasher, pulling silly stunts while people were trying to have fun? And wherever Young John had gone, it was likeliest in deference to the better part of valor.

Harry raced down the backstairs into the Café, where clutches of maskless revelers were lounging on the Mitteleuropa furniture, circulating communal hipflasks, precious pre-Volstead fifths, trays of hors-d'oeuvres commandeered from the caterers in the kitchen. No time to process Howard's uncanny incident till Burleigh was safe! A door through the Café's west wall was clicking shut, and he could picture nobody beyond except Burleigh, since none of the sprawling carousers even rose to the challenge of acknowledging him as he scuttled past them and out.

Nor could he imagine Burleigh heading anywhere except the tunnel. Till Harry's pupils adjusted to the weakly starlit darkness,

Burleigh would blend seamlessly with the night; but hooray, his grunting incoherence made him a cinch to pinpoint. On top of which, the embankment here was steeper than behind the Fleur-de-Lys, obliging Burleigh to slow down or plunge headlong onto the tracks. Harry's night vision began to discern Burleigh's vague, lurching silhouette, along with a source of light in front of him so dim that his anatomy all but eclipsed it.

Burleigh slipped, went down on his backside, slid to the foot of the slope, shedding tricorn and parrot. His mishap afforded Harry an unobstructed view of that toward which Burleigh had been staggering, and it nearly jolted Harry off his feet too. From upslope he heard Howard exclaim, "What the hell?"

The white ensemble from Skyros was a heap on the ballroom floor, so how could someone balancing on the track's nearer steel rail have it on? And did the outfit stand out in the dark thanks to its snowy whiteness alone, or did a wan radiance generated by the wearer suffuse it? Don't stop and think! Such enigmas, however fascinating, couldn't be allowed to distract him while Burleigh posed a blatant danger to himself, over and above the danger enemies intended for him.

Howard was scuffing through the gravel right behind Harry, Burleigh was picking himself up, and the masquerader on the rail had a wavering hand uplifted, a gesture that served equally well to ward off or to beckon. To Burleigh, as a man possessed, it was all the same as he shambled on, deaf to Harry bellowing at him to wait. The second Howard skidded to his side, Harry had to dash ahead and risk a potentially deadly plummet, counting on the dubious merits of his three-pronged staff to stabilize him, for Burleigh, arms outspread, was scant paces away from embracing "Angela," who carried on ambiguously gesturing.

And as if Ossa needed Pelion's weight upon it, the din and reverberation of an oncoming train throbbed in Harry's feet, bombarded his ears, convulsed his stomach. He was still inches shy of closing the gap between his frantic reach and Burleigh as the fan of headlamp brilliance preceded the engine. Knowing he'd be blind and useless in a heartbeat when the lamp's full glare burst from the portal, he rashly hooked his trident in the junction of Burleigh's crisscrossed bandoliers and tugged with all his might. Then the headlamp bleached everything a harrowing white, mercifully blotting out the slaughter of Angela's impersonator, or whatever wore the costume, but also nixing any certainty he'd saved Burleigh.

In the thunder of the train's onrush, Harry may have made out Burleigh fussing, "Where am I? What the deuce is going on?" Or it may have been an acoustic effect of too much noise bouncing around Harry's auditory canal. The trident, he tardily realized, was out of his hands, and in the throes of tinnitus, slow-fading dazzle, and numbing stupor, he sensed Howard's mitt around his arm and pulling on it, with the reproof, "Back off, both of you, you make me anxious! The wheels will kick traprock in your faces."

Harry recovered the wherewithal to apprehend Howard had him and Burleigh in tow, and they were ascending the gravel slope. Suddenly feeling more self-conscious than ever in his wig and sarong, Harry observed, "Y'know, Sydney, you've outdone me. That was more of a miraculous escape than I ever managed."

Burleigh was still poking along unresponsive. Harry hazarded a backward squint. The only sign a train had been and gone was its squeal of brakes a quarter mile away at Union Station, and he was surprised no submarine grotto fronted the portal, after all the other eeriness. Instead, he noted a spring in his step, the dispersal of a burden that registered on his consciousness solely in its absence. Whatever had inflicted recurring mirages was quiescent again after failing to claim a victim; surely nothing primordial would strain against seafloor captivity for decades. But egad, how had such tommyrot sullied his mind? He was giddy with relief, nothing more, at overcoming danger.

Of course, the foregoing five minutes of phantasmagory weren't so easily dismissed. And on reflection, was it natural that his backward glance had shown no blood on the tracks, no shred of carnage or Bacchic disguise? Had a sham Angela been atomized—and if not, he'd careened down one slippery slope tonight, did he really have to navigate another already?

Harry was glad Howard had at some point let him toddle under his own steam, as opposed to Burleigh, whom Howard was piloting by the elbow toward the nearest door ajar, into the Café. "Howard, I'm still looking through a layer of gauze on account of that headlamp, unlike you, apparently. What are you, part cat?"

"Very flattering, but no. I shut my eyes before the engine exited the tunnel. Nothing else for me to do, was there?"

They had Burleigh's back as he doddered indoors, his conduct elderly beyond his age, no less so as he fussed, "Bring me upstairs! Bring me upstairs! This is my party and that's where I want to go! I have to see how Young John is doing!"

Howard threw up his hands in resignation. Better to humor the poor duffer; less stress all around. They had, in any event, a grossly more fraught issue to resolve. Harry cleared his throat as they piloted their hatless and disheveled Long John past the tables of roués-for-a-day with their stocking feet half-blocking the path. "I saw what happened with you in the ballroom." A logy couple of hail-fellows tossed at Burleigh fell on miles-away ears. Harry took it as a blessing he and Howard were ciphers.

Howard met Harry's dourness with his own. "And there's what happened with you outside."

"You think she was trying to warn him off or destroy him?"

"We'll never know. No use even asking." Nor was Howard dragging in the whole other issue of the lurker within the mirage, if indeed any such issue was in his purview. Another thing Harry would never know, because he wasn't about to broach it.

"Couldn't agree more, Howard, and that goes for everything else the last five minutes have wrought. We'd be damn fools to let five minutes undermine a lifetime of healthy skepticism and critical thinking, wouldn't we?"

"Couldn't agree more, Harry."

"And till we can articulate a rational explanation for what we've been through, and sooner or later we will, I propose we speak of this with nobody."

"It's a deal, Harry."

Harry and Howard were herding Burleigh up the backstairs, a step below him in case he faltered and tipped over. A dull awareness of the orchestra blatting furiously again had nagged at Harry on reëntering the Café. At the head of the stairs, the prospect of reimmersing himself in the racket and congestion so soon after cheating death set his teeth on edge. Howard's tense shoulders hinted he too was girding himself.

Flanking Burleigh, blinkering him in effect, his escorts maneuvered him past the band, off the stage to the main floor, through the gauntlet of partygoers to a wooden folding chair up against the nearest seaweed-screened wall. The clutter of white costume on the floor was gone; out of sight, out of mind, Harry decided, was the best policy. Had Burleigh had the clarity to realize he was being herded, he'd probably have taken umbrage, but the appeal of sitting down was too strong to question. And several rasping breaths later, he'd rebounded sufficiently to fret, "Where is that Young John?"

Harry, for the sake of appearing cooperative, craned his neck to and fro. Annoyingly, despite the solipsism rampant everywhere, the tableau of Howard in sweaty shirtsleeves, a scruffy King Neptune, and a bedraggled Long John was drawing an audience, its sentiments opaque behind fishy disguises. Oh, for his trident whose judicious twirling might secure a perimeter and give Burleigh air!

"You there, in the dirty shirt," motioned Burleigh toward Howard, "go fetch Young John! How hard do I have to beg?"

Exasperated Howard melted into the throng, clearly not sorry to be off and running. Harry, sighing, curbed his own exasperation, strove to be more understanding. Burleigh was old and delicate, however gamely or stubbornly he pretended otherwise, and he'd been through a brutal wringer, both bodily and psychic. Still, as he huddled ornery enough to keep his audience at bay, Harry's vision latched onto that dandified Van Dyke and he couldn't help musing, Was the tragic Angela, in the deepest recess of his heart, ever more than a mannequin to him? Or was she anyway not without reason fearing that?

Burleigh yelped and put a hand to his nose. With downcast eyes and mumbled imprecations, he fished around the baggy lap of his knee-breeches and enclosed something tiny in his fist. Whatever it was, he wasn't disposed to say, and Harry was in no mood for Twenty Questions.

By the time Howard emerged, nudging Young John before him, the interest of onlookers had strayed from Burleigh and Harry, who'd fed their appetites for drama on nothing but sullen pouting. Howard had plausibly flushed Young John from some remote fastness of the Café: he tottered along at least two sheets to the wind, his condition redounding to piratical glory no more than Burleigh's.

Yet for all Burleigh's nonstop pother about his chum, Howard was the object of his passions. "Young man," he railed, whirling back their fickle audience, "that was a mean and petty gesture on your part, the more so in light of my trials this evening!"

Howard stared dumbfounded; nor had Young John insight into recent developments, going by his slackjawed stance.

Burleigh at last held up the upsetting item between thumb and forefinger. "Don't play coy with me, Mr. Lakefront or whoever you are. You deliberately flung this in my face from across the room!" "This" was half of a mother-of-pearl cuff button.

"Why would I do that?" Howard's temper was audibly fraying. "What makes you think I threw anything?"

"Look at your cuff!" Burleigh sputtered. "It's unbuttoned. And the button is missing! Why did you do it? Why does flaming youth do anything? Envy, ignorance, hubris? To tear down to the foundations and rebuild so as to steal all the credit and condemn the true builder to oblivion?"

Harry was nearing the end of his rope himself, and thank God nobody in the gawking semicircle recognized him, not positively enough to broadcast his name anyway. Young John was no less groggy than a minute ago. Harry clapped him on the unsteady shoulder. "He's all yours, Young John!" Fed-up Harry blazed a trail into the nonplussed oglers, Howard at his heels, gratitude writ large on his features. None of the smart set could summon the chutzpah to stop them.

Atop the commodious front stairway, Howard remarked, "Harry, thank you! The reek from the hors-d'oeuvres was really getting to me."

Harry nodded, though he'd smelled nothing of a gustatory character. "I'd say we've done everything we could here." They pounded down the stairs with juggernaut willfulness.

"Our duty and then some! I hope this line of work isn't always as thankless."

"Let's say tonight was exceptional in a number of respects." They were out the green door, and Harry pointed downhill with his palm flat out. "I have a key to Burleigh's. Let's reclaim our civvies."

No further occult activity had disturbed the studio. They disrobed in front of each other; why stand on bashful ceremony after the ordeal they'd been through? While tying his brogues, Howard, with a tinge of reticence, declared, "Harry, I don't know what to say about that flying button. I'd never do anything of that boorish stripe. And why the devil would I break the button in two first? And where's the other half?"

Harry bit his upper lip philosophically. "On top of everything tonight, what's one more little enigma?"

Wisdom dictated leaving it at that while they dressed. Some seconds of awkward silence followed, and then with dispatch, as if he'd been remiss, Harry whipped out his wallet. He extracted a wad of sawbucks, skipped up to Howard, grabbed his wrist with one hand, and pressed the money into his palm with the other before Howard could react. "For your wedding!" Harry announced. "Mazel tov! Sorry it's not more, but it's all I have after bribing the orchestra."

Howard goggled as if at a heaping platter of manna. He was, if nothing else, too thunderstruck to refuse it. Good! Harry felt pretty bad that Howard had misunderstood the pro bono nature of debunking. "Thanks, Harry, thanks a million," Howard intoned as if the cash had mesmerized him, "if you're absolutely sure?"

Harry threw up his hands for Howard to stop, please.

"And frankly," Howard went on, "I've been recompensed already in a less quantifiable way. Since Wednesday—good lord, have we been at this a mere two days?—I've been jotting notes on several aspects of this case: the prophetic nightmares that trigger suicides, the ruinous undersea city Burleigh mentioned, the netherworld monstrosity that awakens once in an aeon. These are threads that should be invaluable in tying together some ideas I've had kicking around, so please accept my humble thanks for including me in this inspiring business!"

Harry nodded, choosing not to call him out on his little lapsus linguae. Burleigh had described a colossal deserted city, but never had he placed it underwater. That was a detail solely in Harry's mirage, and, as Howard had inadvertently admitted, in his mirage too. But why open that can of worms now, get into a profitless flap over figments that had come and, for the foreseeable future, gone?

Harry locked up as they departed the Fleur-de-Lys. Thank goodness Howard hadn't quizzed him about the provenance of the key. It would as easily have opened another thousand doors in Providence. Just one of his tools of the trade! He also knew better than to offer Howard the committed pedestrian a taxi home. The diehard Yankee would have branded it a profligacy for sure. Only one loose end pestered meticulous Harry.

"By the by, Howard, a mutual acquaintance told me Henneberger at *Weird Tales* wants you to ghost a story for me. When he gets in touch, maybe it's best not to let on we were ever introduced."

"Mum's the word. And would that acquaintance be Cliff Eddy? I thought so. He's off in the hinterlands of East Providence, so he won't hear anything about tonight in the normal course of things. I'll have to tell him all this brouhaha with Burleigh was a false alarm, and swear him to secrecy about the little he knows because the least whiff of gossip would cause grave embarrassment for all concerned."

"True enough, Howard. By the same logic, I won't divulge anything now about the story we're to cook up together: safest if the particulars came as news to you."

Howard nodded reflectively. They shook hands with more warmth than Harry figured was typical of Howard. Parting words were called for, but brief goodbyes were best, weren't they?

"It'll be a pleasure meeting you in the future, Mr. Lovecraft!"

"Likewise, Mr. Houdini. It'll be a pleasure working with you."

The dishwashers had drifted out to the poor man's balcony of the kitchen fire escape, taking the load off their aching feet, which they dangled in the cool, muggy autumn night. Behind them, Cheryl and the other waitresses rested their arms on the railing or leaned against the wall. The fire escape overlooked the Art Club parking lot, and to one side of that, the sealed-off train tunnel. Granted, they could have picked a wiser surveillance post for aftershocks; nothing else was proceeding along sensible lines, though, Cheryl brooded, fingering the half button of mother-of-pearl that had beaned her a minute ago.

It was common knowledge, whether people believed it or not, that the suicide flapper Angela O'Leary had been psychically active ever since months of major renovations had created disturbances in and around the premises. But really, what was the deal with flinging half a button? Poltergeist mischief or some screwy kind of warning? And where was the other half of the button?

When the aftermath of the tremor happened, it didn't shift anyone an inch. It did startle everyone something awful, though, because it was, rather than an aftershock, a furious banging on the tunnel's corrugated steel plug, like King Kong busting the gate on his dinosaur island. Or was it gas under pressure escaping from underground or chunks of ceiling bouncing around because the cement was bound to crumble someday?

No, one of the dishwashers was pointing at the gate and exclaiming something in Portuguese. The only word Cheryl got was "kazinga," suggesting to her they were good as in the toilet. Scattered cracks were showing in the steel, some yards higher than a man's reach. From hairline zigzags water was seeping, but what kind of water didn't trickle down as gravity commanded, instead fanning out all around as if welling from a fissure in the ground and not a vertical wall? It couldn't be water, could it, whatever it was?

That liquid, on top of everything else, cranked tonight's weirdness up to 11 and jogged her memory of a nightmare, no, a bunch of nightmares she'd had for weeks about wandering squalid streets in some city of giants. And with that, she realized what was pounding to get out, what would crash through very soon and very, very hangry.

By the same token she knew that screaming and running would make no difference. But for lack of other options, she grabbed Jackie by the wrist and did both, towing her full-tilt into the kitchen, ahead of panicky coworkers following her lead and stampeding right behind.

Meanwhile, at 4 A.M. on a bleak little island in Lough Derg, County Donegal, watery plumes spurted from a grassy mound surmounted by a rectangular bell tower, the alleged site of St. Patrick's Cave. The tower sank like a finger into cake as the gushers proliferated around it till the earth disintegrated, and like one massive, translucent clump of tentacles they ravenously strained sky-high. Bats were powerless to echolocate them, stuck to them on impact, and came apart like stew meat.

To Paige—I couldn't have done it without you!

Notes on Contributors

Jason V Brock is an award-winning writer, editor, filmmaker, composer, artist, scholar, and speaker. He is the author of two short story collections, *Simulacrum and Other Possible Realities* (2013) and *The Dark Sea Within* (2017), both from Hippocampus Press, and a nonfiction treatise, *Disorders of Magnitude* (Rowman & Littlefield, 2014; nonfiction finalist for the Bram Stoker and Rondo Hatton Classic Horror Awards). He has been widely published online, in comic books, magazines, and anthologies, such as *You, Human; Fungi; Weird Fiction Review* (print edition); *Fangoria;* S. T. Joshi's *Black Wings* series, and many others. Brock loves his wife, Sunni, their family of herptiles, travel, and vegan/vegetarianism.

Donald R. Burleson is a professional mathematician, retired since 2017 after fifty years of teaching mathematics at various universities, and the author of twenty-four books, most recently the essay collection *Lovecraft: An American Allegory*, the short story collection *Wait for the Thunder*, and the novella *The Roswell Genes*. His fiction has appeared in *Twilight Zone, Fantasy & Science Fiction*, and many other magazines, and in three *Black Wings* anthologies and others including *Gothic Lovecraft* and *Horror for the Holidays*. Dr. Burleson and his wife, the writer Mollie L. Burleson, live in Roswell, New Mexico.

Richard Gavin's writing explores the intersections of fear and the sacred, of nightmare and Gnosis. He has written five collections of horror fiction, including *Sylvan Dread* (Three Hands Press, 2016) and *At Fear's Altar* (Hippocampus Press, 2012), and *Grotesquerie* (Undertow, 2020). His stories have been chosen for *Best New Horror, Best Horror of the Year*, and *The Year's Best Weird Fiction*. Richard has also published numerous works of esotericism, such as *The Moribund Portal* (Three Hands Press, 2018). His meditations on the macabre have appeared in *Rue Morgue, The Teeming Brain,* and *Dead Reckonings.* He lives in Ontario, Canada.

David Hambling is a journalist and author based in Norwood, South London. His fiction, starting with a collection, *The Dulwich Horror and Others,* explores the Cthulhu Mythos in his own locale. His novels include the popular Harry Stubbs adventures, also set in the 1920s, and he has previously contributed to S. T. Joshi's *Black Wings* anthologies.

Mark Howard Jones was born in South Wales on the twenty-sixth anniversary of H. P. Lovecraft's death. He is the editor of the anthologies *Cthulhu Cymraeg: Lovecraftian Tales from Wales* (SD Publishing, 2013) and *Cthulhu Cymraeg II* (Fugitive Fiction, 2017). His Lovecraftian fiction appears in the anthologies *Black Wings III, V,* and *VI* (PS Publishing), *The Madness of Cthulhu II* (Titan Books, 2015) and *Gothic Lovecraft* (Cycatrix Press, 2016). He lives in Cardiff, the capital of Wales.

S. T. Joshi has written an exhaustive biography, *I Am Providence: The Life and Times of H. P. Lovecraft* (2010), and edited Lovecraft's complete fiction, poetry, essays, and letters. His novel *The Assaults of Chaos* (Hippocampus Press, 2013) features Lovecraft as a character. He has also written two short hard-boiled detective novels, *The Removal Company* (Borgo Press, 2009) and *Conspiracy of Silence* (Borgo Press, 2010), along with several weird and detective tales, including the novella *Something from Below* (PS Publishing, 2019). His collected fiction was gathered in the omnibus volume *The Recurring Doom: Tales of Mystery and Horror* (Sarnath Press, 2019).

Wilum Hopfrog Pugmire wrote tales of Lovecraftian horror since his days as a Mormon missionary in Northern Ireland in 1972. He published several books in the small press and had worked published in several anthologies. A German translation of his Sesqua Valley stories, *Der dunkle Fremde*, was recently released. An illustrated hardcover edition of his finest work, *An Ecstasy of Fears and Others*, was published by Centipede Press in 2019.

Mark Samuels lives in Kings Langley, England. He is the author of six short story collections; *The White Hands and Other Weird Tales* (2003), *Black Altars* (2003), *Glyphotech and Other Macabre Processes* (2008), *The Man Who Collected Machen* (2010), *Written in Darkness* (2014), and *The Prozess Manifestations* (2017), and the author of two novels: *The Face of Twilight* (2006) and *A Pilgrim Stranger* (2017). *Prophecies and Dooms* (2018) is a compilation of recondite essays on some classic authors of weird fiction under the title. Hippocampus Press released a "best of" short story collection, *The Age of Decayed Futurity*, in 2020.

Darrell Schweitzer remarks that his career seems to be growing tentacles of late. This is recently evidenced by a collection of his Lovecraftian and weird fictions, *Awaiting Strange Gods*, published by Fedogan & Bremer in August 2015. His historical Cthulhu Mythos anthology, *That Is Not Dead*, was published by PS Publishing in 2015 and was followed by *Tales from the Miskatonic Library* (co-edited with John Ashmead) and *Mountains of Madness Revealed*. His stories have appeared in numerous Lovecraft-related anthologies in the past few years. He co-edited *Weird Tales* for nineteen years and is the author of three novels, *The White Isle*, *The Shattered Goddess*, and *The Mask of the Sorcerer*, in addition to about 300 published stories.

John Shirley is the author of numerous novels, including *Demons*, *Crawlers*, *Bleak History*, *City Come A-Walkin'*, and the *A Song Called Youth* cyberpunk trilogy. His story collections include *Black Butterflies*, which won the Bram Stoker Award from the Horror Writers Association, and *Lovecraft Alive!* (Hippocampus Press, 2016). He is co-screenwriter of *The Crow* and has written teleplays—e.g., for *Deep Space Nine*—and animation scripts.

Simon Strantzas is the author of five collections of short fiction, including *Nothing Is Everything* (Undertow Publications, 2018), and is editor of the award-winning anthology *Aickman's Heirs* as well as *Year's Best Weird Fiction, Volume 3*. His fiction has appeared in numerous annual best-of anthologies, in venues such as *Nightmare, Postscripts,* and *Cemetery Dance,* and has been nominated for both the British Fantasy and Shirley Jackson Awards. He lives with his wife in Toronto, Canada.

Jonathan Thomas was born and has dwelt most of his life in Providence, Rhode Island, discounting a childhood misspent in Woonsocket and three challenging years in Manhattan. Thanks to his wife, the musician, artist, and arts administrator Angel Dean, he has gained some familiarity with the lore of the Providence Art Club, in which both Houdini and persistent hauntings figure, as elaborated in the tale in this volume. Thomas has enjoyed the great good fortune of living in the zipcode where he (inevitably) follows in HPL's footsteps more than he can know. He freely admits Providence is Lovecraft's town; everyone else just lurks there. He is the author of five collections of weird tales as well as the Lovecraftian novel *The Color over Occam* (2012).

Donald Tyson has been writing fiction and nonfiction for four decades. He was drawn to horror stories at an early age and discovered the writings of H. P. Lovecraft at thirteen, when he bought *The Colour out of Space,* a Lancer paperback anthology of Lovecraft stories with a lurid flaming skull on the cover. Since then, it has been his ambition to write the perfect horror story, and although he has not yet arrived at perfection, he finds many rewards along the road.

Scott Wiley grew up in Kirkland, Washington, with two loving and encouraging parents and a younger sister. He lives in Mount Vernon, Washington, with his wife and editor Marina Donnelly and their three cats: in descending order of size, Oswin, Jasper, and Lily. He enjoys eating Mexican food and playing both music and Magic the Gathering. His work has appeared in *Weird Fiction Review* and elsewhere.

Stephen Woodworth is the author of the *New York Times* bestselling Violet series of paranormal thrillers, including *Through Violet Eyes, With Red Hands, In Golden Blood,* and *From Black Rooms,* and the Gothic horror novel *Fraulein Frankenstein*. His short fiction has appeared in such publications as *Nightmare's Realm, Best of Black Wings, Weird Tales, Fantasy & Science Fiction,* and *Year's Best Fantasy*. His first collection of horror stories, *A Carnival of Chimeras,* appeared in 2020 from Hippocampus Press.

www.ingramcontent.com/pod-product-compliance
Lightning Source LLC
LaVergne TN
LVHW010550100826
845148LV00013B/2685
9781614983293